WAITING

(THE MAKING OF RILEY PAIGE—BOOK 2)

BLAKE PIERCE

ISBN: 978-1-64029-625-1

BOOKS BY BLAKE PIERCE

CHLOE FINE PSYCHOLOGICAL SUSPENSE MYSTERY
NEXT DOOR (Book #1)
A NEIGHBOR'S LIE (Book #2)

KATE WISE MYSTERY SERIES
IF SHE KNEW (Book #1)

THE MAKING OF RILEY PAIGE SERIES
WATCHING (Book #1)
WAITING (Book #2)
LURING (Book #3)

RILEY PAIGE MYSTERY SERIES
ONCE GONE (Book #1)
ONCE TAKEN (Book #2)
ONCE CRAVED (Book #3)
ONCE LURED (Book #4)
ONCE HUNTED (Book #5)
ONCE PINED (Book #6)
ONCE FORSAKEN (Book #7)
ONCE COLD (Book #8)
ONCE STALKED (Book #9)
ONCE LOST (Book #10)
ONCE BURIED (Book #11)
ONCE BOUND (Book #12)
ONCE TRAPPED (Book #13)
ONCE DORMANT (book #14)

MACKENZIE WHITE MYSTERY SERIES
BEFORE HE KILLS (Book #1)
BEFORE HE SEES (Book #2)
BEFORE HE COVETS (Book #3)
BEFORE HE TAKES (Book #4)
BEFORE HE NEEDS (Book #5)
BEFORE HE FEELS (Book #6)
BEFORE HE SINS (Book #7)
BEFORE HE HUNTS (Book #8)
BEFORE HE PREYS (Book #9)

BEFORE HE LONGS (Book #10)

AVERY BLACK MYSTERY SERIES
CAUSE TO KILL (Book #1)
CAUSE TO RUN (Book #2)
CAUSE TO HIDE (Book #3)
CAUSE TO FEAR (Book #4)
CAUSE TO SAVE (Book #5)
CAUSE TO DREAD (Book #6)

KERI LOCKE MYSTERY SERIES
A TRACE OF DEATH (Book #1)
A TRACE OF MUDER (Book #2)
A TRACE OF VICE (Book #3)
A TRACE OF CRIME (Book #4)
A TRACE OF HOPE (Book #5)

PROLOGUE

At first, Janet Davis was aware of nothing except the terrible pain that rattled through her skull like a thousand castanets playing out of time.

Her eyes were closed. When she tried to open them, she was blinded by glaring white light, and she had to shut them again.

The light felt hot on her face.

Where am I? she wondered.

Where was I before ... before this *happened?*

Then it began to come back to her ...

She'd been out taking pictures in the marshes near Lady Bird Johnson Park. It was too late in the summer for the millions of daffodils there to be blooming, but the dogwood leaves were a beautiful deep green, especially around sunset.

She'd been standing in the marina photographing the shadowy boats and the beautiful play of the sunset on the water when she'd heard footsteps swiftly approaching her from behind. Before she could even turn to look, she'd felt a sharp crack on the back of her head, and the camera had flown out of her hands, and ...

I lost consciousness, I guess.

But where was she now?

She was too dazed to feel really afraid yet. But she knew that fear would kick in soon.

Slowly she became aware that she was lying flat on her back on some hard surface.

She couldn't move her arms or legs. Her hands and feet felt numb from tight restraints around her wrists and ankles.

But the weirdest sensation was of fingers all over her face, smearing something soft and moist on her hot skin.

She managed to croak out a few words.

"Where am I? What are you doing?"

When no reply came, she twisted her head, trying to escape the annoying movement of the gooey fingertips.

She heard a male voice whisper ...

"Hold still."

She had no intention of holding still. She kept twisting until the fingers moved away.

1

She heard a noisy, disapproving sigh. Then the light shifted so it wasn't shining directly on her face anymore.

"Open your eyes," the voice said.

She did so.

Gleaming in front of her was the sharp blade of a butcher knife. The tip of the knife came nearer and nearer to her face, making her eyes cross so that she saw the blade double.

Janet gasped, and the voice whispered again …

"Hold still."

She froze, facing directly upward, but a spasm of terror surged through her body.

The voice hissed a command again.

"Still, I said."

She willed her body to be still. Her eyes were open, but the light was painfully bright and hot, and she couldn't see anything clearly.

The knife went away, and the fingers resumed smearing, this time around her lips. She gritted her teeth, and she could actually hear them grinding together with terrible pressure.

"Almost through," the voice said.

Despite the heat, Janet was starting to shiver all over from fear.

The fingers began pressing around her eyes now, and she had to shut them again to keep whatever the man was smearing from getting into them.

Then the fingers moved away from her face, and she could open her eyes again. Now she could make out the silhouette of a grotesquely shaped head moving around in the blazing light.

She felt a terrified sob burst out of her throat.

"Let me go," she said. "Please let me go."

The man said nothing. She felt him fumbling around her left arm right now, strapping something elastic around her bicep, then tightening it painfully.

Janet's panic rose, and she tried not to imagine what was about to happen.

"No," she said. "Don't."

She felt a finger probing around the crook of her arm, then the piercing pain of a needle entering an artery.

Janet let out a shriek of horror and despair.

Then, as she felt the needle leave, a strange transformation came over her.

Her scream suddenly turned into …

Laughter!

She was laughing riotously, uncontrollably, filled with a crazed euphoria she'd never experienced before.

She felt positively invincible now, and infinitely strong and powerful.

But when she tried again to free herself from the bonds around her wrists and ankles, they wouldn't budge.

Her laughter turned into a surge of wild fury.

"Let me go," she hissed. "Let me go, or I swear to God, I'll kill you!"

The man let out a whispering chuckle.

Then he tilted the metal shade of the lamp so that its light blazed on his face.

It was the face of a clown, painted white with huge, bizarre eyes and lips drawn with black and red.

Janet's breath froze in her lungs.

The man smiled, his teeth a dull yellow in contrast to the rest of his brightly colored face.

He said to her …

"They're going to leave you behind."

Janet wanted to ask …

Who?

Who are you talking about?

And who are you?

Why are you doing this to me?

But she couldn't even breathe now.

The knife flashed in front of her face again. Then the man teased its sharp tip lightly across her cheek, down the side of her face, and then across her throat. Just the slightest bit of pressure, and Janet knew that the knife would draw blood.

Her breath started to come again, first in shallow gasps, then in huge gulps of air.

She knew she was starting to hyperventilate, but she couldn't bring her breathing under control. She could feel her heart pounding inside her chest, could feel and hear its violent pulse between her ears growing faster and louder.

She wondered …

What was in that needle?

Whatever it was, its effects were coming on stronger by the second. She couldn't escape what was going on in her own body.

As he kept stroking her face with the knife tip, he murmured …

"They're going to leave you behind."

She managed to gasp out …

3

"Who? Who's going to leave me behind?"

"You know who," he said.

Janet realized she was losing control of her thoughts. She was flooded with mindless anxiety and panic, mad feelings of persecution and victimhood.

Who does he mean?

Images of friends and family members and coworkers passed through her head.

But their familiar, friendly smiles turned to sneers of contempt and hatred.

Everybody, she thought.

Everybody is doing this to me.

Every person I've ever known.

Again, she felt a burst of anger.

I should have known better than to ever trust a single soul.

Worse, she felt as if her skin was literally starting to move.

No, something was crawling *all over* her skin.

Insects! she thought.

Thousands of them!

She struggled against her restraints.

"Swat them off me!" she begged the man. "Kill them!"

The man chuckled as he kept staring down at her through his grotesque makeup.

He made no offer to help.

He knows something, Janet thought.

He knows something I don't know.

Then as the crawling continued, it dawned on her ...

The insects ...

They're not crawling on *my skin.*

They're crawling under *it!*

Her breathing came harder and faster, and her lungs burned as if she'd been running for a long distance. Her heart pounded even more painfully.

Her head was exploding with a host of violent emotions—fury, fear, disgust, panic, and sheer bafflement.

Had the man injected thousands, perhaps millions, of insects into her bloodstream?

How was that even possible?

In a voice that shook with both anger and self-pity, she asked ...

"Why do you hate me?"

The man chuckled louder this time.

He said, *"Everybody* hates you."

Janet was having trouble seeing now. Her vision wasn't getting blurry. Instead, the scene in front of her seemed to be twitching and bouncing and jumping. She imagined she could *hear* her eyeballs rattling around in their sockets.

So when she saw another clown's face, she thought she was seeing double.

But she quickly realized …

This face is different.

It was painted with the same colors, but with somewhat different shapes.

It isn't him.

Under the paint lay familiar features.

Then it dawned her …

Me. That's me.

The man was holding a mirror up to her face. The hideously garish face she saw was her own.

The sight of that twisted, tearful, yet mocking countenance filled her with a loathing she'd never known before.

He's right, she thought.

Everybody hates me.

And I'm my own worst enemy.

As if sharing her disgust, the creatures under her skin scurried all about like cockroaches suddenly exposed to sunlight but with nowhere to run and hide.

The man set the mirror aside and began to stroke her face with the knife point again.

He said yet again …

"They're going to leave you behind."

As the knife passed over her throat, it occurred to her …

If he cuts me the insects can escape.

Of course the blade would also kill her. But that seemed a small price to pay to be free of the insects and this terror.

She hissed …

"Do it. Do it now."

Suddenly, the air was filled with ugly and distorted laughter, as if a thousand clowns were noisily gloating in her plight.

The laughter propelled her heart to pound still harder and faster. Janet knew her heart couldn't possibly take much more of this.

And she didn't want it to.

She wanted it to stop as soon as possible.

She found herself trying to count the beats ...

One, two ... three, four, five ... six ...

But the beats were coming both faster and less regularly.

She wondered—which was going to explode first, her heart or her brain?

Then finally she heard her very last heartbeat, and the world dissolved.

CHAPTER ONE

Riley laughed when Ryan snatched the box of books away from her.

She said, "Just let me carry something, OK?"

"It's too heavy," Ryan said, carrying the box over to the empty bookshelf. "You shouldn't be lifting it."

"Come on, Ryan. I'm pregnant, not sick."

Ryan put the box down in front of the bookshelf and brushed off his hands.

"You can take out the books and put them on the shelf," he said.

Riley laughed again.

She said, "You mean you're giving me *permission* to help move into *our* apartment?"

Ryan looked embarrassed now.

"That's not what I meant," he said. "It's just that—well, I worry."

"And I keep telling you, there's nothing to worry about," Riley said. "I'm only six weeks along, and I feel great."

She didn't want to mention her occasional bout of morning sickness. So far it hadn't been very severe.

Ryan shook his head. "Just try not to overdo it, OK?"

"I won't," Riley said. "I promise."

Ryan nodded and went back over to the pile of boxes yet to be unpacked.

Riley pried open the cardboard box in front of her and started putting books on the shelves. She was actually happy to be sitting still and doing a simple job. She realized her mind needed the rest more than her body did.

The last few days had been a whirlwind.

In fact, so had the last couple of weeks.

Her graduation with a psychology degree from Lanton University had been a crazy, life-changing day. Right after the ceremony, an FBI agent had recruited her for the bureau's ten-week Honors Internship Summer Program. Right after that, Ryan had asked her to move in with him when he started his new job.

The amazing thing was that both her internship program and Ryan's new job were in Washington, DC. So she hadn't had to make a choice.

At least he wasn't freaked out when I told him I was already pregnant, she thought.

In fact, he'd seemed delighted at the time. He'd gotten a bit more nervous about the idea of a baby in the days since graduation—but then, Riley felt plenty nervous about it herself.

The very thought of it boggled her mind. They were just getting started in their lives together, and they'd soon be sharing the greatest responsibility Riley could imagine—raising their own child.

We'd better be ready, Riley thought.

Meanwhile, she felt strange putting her old psychology textbooks onto the shelves. Ryan had tried to talk her into selling them, and she knew that she probably should …

God knows, we need every cent we can get.

Still, she had a feeling she'd be needing them in the future. She wasn't sure just why or what for.

Anyway, the box also contained a lot of Ryan's law books, and he hadn't even considered selling any of them. Of course, he probably would be using them in his new job as an entry-level attorney in the DC law firm of Parsons and Rittenhouse.

When the box was empty and the books all on the shelves, Riley sat on the floor watching Ryan, who kept restlessly pushing and repositioning pieces of furniture as if trying to find the perfect place for everything.

Riley suppressed a sigh …

Poor Ryan.

She knew he really wasn't happy with this basement apartment. He'd had a nicer apartment back in Lanton, with the same furniture they'd brought here—a pleasantly bohemian collection of secondhand items.

As far as she was concerned, Ryan's stuff still looked quite nice here. And the little apartment didn't bother her at all. She'd gotten used to a dorm room back at Lanton, so this place seemed positively luxurious, despite the covered pipes hanging over the bedroom and the kitchen.

True, the apartments on the floors upstairs were much nicer, but this one had been the only one available. When Ryan had first seen it, he'd almost refused to rent it. But the truth was, this was the best they could afford. They were already seriously overextended financially. Ryan had maxed out his credit card with moving expenses, the deposit on the apartment, and everything else they had needed for this momentous change in their lives.

Ryan finally looked over at Riley and said, "What do you say we take a break?"

"Sure," Riley said.

Riley got up from the floor and sat down at the kitchen table. Ryan grabbed a couple of soft drinks from the refrigerator and sat down with her. The two of them fell silent, and Riley sensed right away that Ryan had something on his mind.

Finally Ryan drummed his fingers on the table and said …

"Uh, Riley, we've got to talk about something."

This really does *sound serious,* she thought.

Ryan fell silent again, and he had a faraway look in his eyes.

"You're not breaking up with me, are you?" she asked.

She was joking, of course.

But Ryan didn't laugh. He seemed to have barely noticed the question.

"Huh? No, it's nothing like that, it's …"

His voice trailed away, and Riley felt really uneasy now.

What's going on? she wondered. Had Ryan's job fallen through or something?

Ryan looked into Riley's eyes and said …

"Don't laugh at me, OK?"

"Why would I laugh?" Riley asked.

A bit shakily, Ryan got up from his chair and kneeled beside her.

And then Riley realized …

Oh, my God! He's going to propose!

And sure enough, she laughed. It was nervous laughter, of course.

Ryan blushed deeply.

"I told you not to laugh," he said.

"I'm not laughing *at* you," Riley said. "Go ahead, say what you want to say. I'm pretty sure … well, just go ahead."

Ryan fumbled around in his pants pocket and took out a little black jewelry box. He opened it to reveal a modest but lovely diamond ring. Riley couldn't help but gasp.

Ryan stammered …

"Uh, Riley Sweeney, would—will you marry me?"

Trying unsuccessfully to hold back her nervous giggles, Riley managed to say …

"Oh, yes. Absolutely."

Ryan plucked the ring out of the box, and Riley held out her left hand and let him put it on her finger.

"It's beautiful," Riley said. "Now get up and sit down with me."

Ryan smiled sheepishly as he sat down at the table next to her.

"Was the kneeling too much?" he asked.

"The kneeling was perfect," Riley said. "Everything is just … perfect."

She stared at the little diamond on her ring finger raptly for a moment. Her spell of nervous laughter had passed, and now she felt a knot of emotion form in her throat.

She really hadn't seen this coming. She hadn't even dared to hope for it—at least not this soon.

But here she and Ryan were, taking yet another enormous step in their lives.

As she watched the light play on the diamond, Ryan said …

"I'll get you a nicer ring someday."

Riley gasped a little.

"Don't you dare!" she said. "This is always going to be my only engagement ring!"

But as she kept staring at the ring, she couldn't help but worry …

How much did this cost?

As if reading her thoughts, Ryan said …

"Don't worry about the ring."

Ryan's reassuring smile made her worry dissolve in an instant. She knew he was no fool when it came to money. He'd probably gotten a good bargain on this ring—although she'd never ask him about it.

Riley then noticed how Ryan's expression saddened as he looked around the apartment.

"Is something wrong?" she asked.

Ryan let out a sigh and said, "I'll make a better life for you. I promise."

Riley felt strangely jolted.

She asked, "What's wrong with the life we've got now? We're young and we're in love and we're going to have a baby and—"

"You know what I mean," Ryan said, interrupting her.

"No, I'm not sure I do," Riley said.

A silence fell between them.

Ryan sighed again and said, "Look, I'm starting work tomorrow on an entry level salary. I'm not exactly feeling like a huge success in the world. But it's a good firm, and if I stay with it,

I'll be moving up and I might even become a partner someday."

Riley gazed at him steadily.

"Someday, sure," she said. "But you're off to a great start already. And I like what we've got right now."

Ryan shrugged. "We don't have much. For one thing, we've only got the one car, and I'll be needing that to go to work, which means …"

Riley interrupted, "Which means I'll be taking the metro to the training program every morning. What's wrong with that?"

Ryan reached across the table and took her hand.

"It's a two-block walk to and from the nearest metro stop," he said. "And this isn't the safest neighborhood in the world. The car got broken into once already. I don't like it that you have to go out there on your own. I'm worried."

A strange, unpleasant feeling was starting to come over Riley. She wasn't yet sure just what that feeling was.

She said, "Hasn't it occurred to you that I actually like this neighborhood? I've spent my whole life in rural Virginia. This is an exciting change, an adventure. Besides, you know I'm tough. My dad was a Marine captain. He taught me how to take care of myself."

She almost added …

And I survived an attack by a serial killer a couple of months ago, remember?

Not only had she survived that attack, she'd helped the FBI track the killer down and bring him to justice. That was why she'd been offered the chance to join the training program.

But she knew that Ryan didn't want to hear about any of that right now. His masculine pride was feeling delicate at the moment.

And Riley realized something …

I really resent that.

Riley chose her words carefully, trying not to say the wrong thing …

"Ryan, you know, making a better life for us isn't just up to you. It's up to both of us. I'm going to have something to do with it. I'm going to have a career of my own."

Ryan looked away with a frown.

Riley fought down a sigh as she realized …

I said the wrong thing after all.

She'd almost forgotten that Ryan didn't really approve of her summer internship. She'd reminded him that it was only ten weeks and it wasn't physical training. She was just going to be watching agents at work, mostly indoors. Besides, she thought it might even lead to an office job right there in the FBI headquarters.

He'd become more agreeable about it, but he certainly wasn't enthusiastic.

But then, Riley really didn't know what he might prefer for her.

Did he maybe want her to be a stay-at-home mother? If so, he was going to be disappointed sooner or later.

But now was no time to get into all this.

Don't spoil this moment, Riley told herself.

She looked at her ring again and then at Ryan.

"This is beautiful," she said. "I'm really happy. Thank you."

Ryan smiled and squeezed her hand.

Then Riley said, "So who are we going to share the news with?"

Ryan shrugged. "I don't know. We don't really have any friends yet here in DC. I guess I could get in touch with some of my old friends from law school. Maybe you could call your dad."

Riley frowned at the idea. Her last visit to her father hadn't been pleasant. Their relationship had always been deeply troubled.

And besides …

"He doesn't have a phone, remember?" Riley said. "He lives all alone up in the mountains."

"Oh, yeah," Ryan said.

"What about *your* parents?" Riley asked.

Ryan's smile faded a little.

"I'll write to them about it," he said.

Riley had to stop herself from asking …

Why not give them a call?

Maybe then I could actually talk to them.

She'd never met Ryan's parents, who lived in the small town of Munny, Virginia.

Riley knew that Ryan had grown up among working-class people, and he was very anxious to put that kind of life behind him.

She wondered if he was embarrassed by them or …

Is he embarrassed by me?

Do they even know we're living together?

Would they approve?

But before Riley could think of how to broach the subject to him, the phone rang.

"Maybe we could just let the machine take that," Ryan said.

Riley thought about it for a moment as the phone kept ringing.

"It might be something important," she said. She went to the phone and took the call.

A cheerful, professional-sounding male voice said, "May I speak with Riley Sweeney?"

"This is she," Riley said.

"This is Hoke Gilmer, your supervisor for the FBI training program. I just wanted to remind you—"

Riley said excitedly, "Yes, I know! I'll be there bright and early at seven o'clock tomorrow morning!"

"Great!" Hoke replied. "I look forward to meeting you."

Riley hung up the phone and looked at Ryan. He had a wistful look in his eye.

"Wow," he said. "Everything's getting real, isn't it?"

Riley understood how he felt. Ever since the move from Lanton, they'd seldom been away from one another.

And now, tomorrow, they were both off to their new jobs.

Riley said, "Maybe we need to do something special together."

"Good idea," Ryan said. "Maybe go to a movie and find a nice restaurant and …"

Riley laughed as she grabbed him by the hand and pulled him to his feet.

"I've got a better idea," she said.

She pulled him into the bedroom, where they both fell laughing onto the bed.

CHAPTER TWO

Riley felt her breath and heartbeat quicken as she walked from the metro stop toward the massive white J. Edgar Hoover Building.

Why am I so nervous? she asked herself. After all, she had managed her first solo trip on a metro through a larger city than she had even visited before moving here.

She tried to convince herself that this wasn't such a big change—that she was just going to school again, the same as she'd done in Lanton.

But she couldn't help feeling awed and daunted. For one thing, the building was on Pennsylvania Avenue, right between the White House and the Capitol. She and Ryan had driven past the building earlier this week, but the reality was only now hitting her that she was going to be coming here to learn and work for the next ten weeks.

It seemed almost like a dream.

She walked through the front entrance and passed on through the lobby to the security gate. The guard on duty found her name on a list of visitors and gave her a clip-on identification card. He told her to take an elevator three floors down to a small auditorium.

When Riley found the auditorium and went inside, she was handed a packet of rules, regulations, and information that she was supposed to read later. She sat down among about twenty other interns who appeared to be in her general age range. She knew that some, like her, were recent college graduates; others were undergraduates who would be returning to college in the fall.

Most of the other interns were male, and all of them were well dressed. She felt a little insecure about her own pantsuit, which she'd bought at a thrift shop in Lanton. It was the best business-type outfit she had, and she hoped she looked sufficiently respectable.

Soon a clean-cut, middle-aged man stepped in front of the seated interns.

He said, "I'm Assistant Director Marion Connor, and I'm in charge of the FBI Honors Internship Summer Program. You should all be very proud to be here today. You are a very select and exceptional group, chosen from thousands of applicants ..."

Riley gulped hard as he continued congratulating the group.

Thousands of applicants!

How strange it seemed. The truth was, she hadn't put in an application at all. She'd simply been chosen for the program straight out of college.

Do I really belong here? she wondered.

Assistant Director Connor introduced the group to a younger agent—Hoke Gilmer, the training supervisor who had called Riley yesterday. Gilmer instructed the interns to stand and raise their right hands to take the FBI oath of office.

Riley felt herself choke up as she began to speak the words …

"I, Riley Sweeney, do solemnly swear that I will support and defend the Constitution of the United States against all enemies, foreign and domestic …"

She had to blink back a tear as she continued.

This is real, she told herself. *This is really happening.*

She had no idea what awaited her from this moment on.

But she felt sure that her life would never be the same.

*

After the ceremony, Hoke Gilmer took the students on a long tour of the J. Edgar Hoover Building. Riley grew more and more amazed at the size and complexity of the building, and at all the different activities that took place here. There were various exercise rooms, a basketball court, a medical clinic, a printing shop, many kinds of labs and computer rooms, a firing range, and even a morgue and a car repair shop.

It all boggled her mind.

When the tour was over, the group was taken to the cafeteria on the eighth floor. Riley felt exhausted as she put food on her tray—not so much from the miles of walking she'd done, but at everything she'd seen and tried to absorb.

How much of this wonderful facility could she hope to experience in the ten weeks she was to spend here? She wanted to learn everything she could, as fast as she possibly could.

And she wanted to get started right this very minute.

As she carried her tray looking for a place to eat, she felt strangely out of place. The other interns already seemed to be forming friendships and sitting in groups, chattering away excitedly about the day they were having. She told herself she ought to sit down among some of her young colleagues, introduce herself and get to know a few of them.

But she knew it wasn't going to be easy.

Riley had always felt like something of an outsider, and making friends and fitting in had never come naturally for her.

And right now, she felt shyer than she could remember ever feeling.

And was it just her imagination, or were some of the interns glancing at her and whispering about her?

She had just decided to sit alone when she heard a voice next to her.

"You're Riley Sweeney, aren't you?"

She turned to see a young man who had caught her eye back in the auditorium and during the tour. She hadn't been able to help noticing that he was remarkably good-looking—a bit taller than she was, rugged and athletic, with short curly hair and a pleasant smile. His suit looked expensive.

"Um, yes," Riley said, suddenly feeling even more shy than before. "And you … ?"

"John Welch. I'm pleased to meet you. I'd offer to shake hands, but …"

He nodded at the trays they were both carrying and laughed a little.

"Would you care to sit with me?" he asked.

Riley hoped she wasn't blushing.

"Sure," she said.

They sat down across a table from each other and started eating.

Riley asked, "How did you know my name?"

John smiled impishly and said, "You're kidding right?"

Riley was startled. She managed to stop herself from saying …

No, I'm not kidding.

John shrugged and said, "Pretty much everybody here knows who you are. I guess you could say that your reputation precedes you."

Riley looked over at some of the other students. Sure enough, a few of them were still glancing at her and exchanging whispers.

Riley began to realize …

They must know about what happened back at Lanton.

But how much did they know?

And was this a good thing or a bad thing?

She certainly hadn't counted on having a "reputation" among the interns. The idea made her feel extremely self-conscious.

"Where are you from?" she asked.

"Right here in DC," John said. "I graduated with a BA in

criminology this spring."

"What school?" Riley asked.

John blushed a little.

"Um—George Washington University," he said.

Riley felt her eyes widen at the mention of such an expensive college.

He must be rich, she thought.

She also sensed that he felt a little awkward about that.

"Wow, a criminology degree," she said. "I've just got a psych degree. You've really got a head start on me."

John laughed.

"On *you*? I don't think so. I mean, you're probably the only intern in the program with actual field experience."

Riley felt truly taken aback now.

Field experience?

She hadn't thought of what had happened back at Lanton as "field experience."

John continued, "I mean, you actually helped track down and apprehend an actual serial killer. I can't imagine what that must have been like. I really envy you."

Riley frowned and fell silent. She didn't want to say so, but envy seemed like a terribly inappropriate emotion to feel about what she'd been through.

What did John think had gone on during those terrible weeks in Lanton? Did he have any idea what it was like to find the bodies of two of her best friends, their throats brutally slashed?

Did he know how horrified and grief-stricken she'd felt—and also how guilty?

She was still haunted by the thought that her roommate, Trudy, would still be alive if Riley had just done a better job of watching out for her.

And did he have any idea how terrified she'd been when she'd fallen into the killer's clutches herself?

Riley took a sip of her soft drink and poked at her food with her fork.

Then she said, "It was … well, it wasn't like you must think. It's just something that happened."

John looked at her with real concern now.

"I'm sorry," he said. "I guess you don't want to talk about it."

"Maybe some other time," Riley said.

An awkward silence fell. Not wanting to be rude, Riley started asking John questions about himself. He seemed reluctant to talk

17

about his life and family, but Riley was able to draw him out a little.

John's parents were both prominent lawyers who were heavily involved in DC politics. Riley was impressed—not so much by John's affluent background, but by how he'd chosen a different path from anyone else in his family. Instead of pursuing a prestigious career in law and politics, John had dedicated himself to a humbler life of service in law enforcement.

A real idealist, Riley thought.

She found herself contrasting him to Ryan, who was trying to put his humble background behind him by becoming a successful lawyer.

Of course, she admired Ryan's ambition. It was one of the things she loved about him. But she couldn't help also admiring John for the choices he was making.

As they continued talking, Riley sensed that John was putting on the charm for her.

He's flirting with me, she realized.

She was a bit taken aback by that. Her left hand was in full view right there on the table, so surely he could see her new engagement ring.

Should she mention that she was engaged?

She felt as though that would be awkward somehow—especially if she was wrong.

Maybe he's not flirting with me at all.

Soon John started asking questions about Riley, carefully staying away from the topic of the murders at Lanton. As usual, Riley avoided certain issues—her troubled relationship with her father, her rebellious teenage years, and especially how she'd watched her own mother get shot to death when she was a little girl.

Also, it occurred to Riley that, unlike Ryan or John, she really didn't have much to say about her hopes for the future.

What does that say about me? she wondered.

She finally did talk about her budding relationship with Ryan, and how they'd gotten engaged just yesterday—although she didn't mention that she was pregnant. She didn't notice any particular change in John's behavior.

I guess he's just naturally charming that way, she thought.

She found herself relieved at the thought that she'd jumped to conclusions, and he'd never been flirting with her after all.

He was a nice guy, and she looked forward to getting to know him better. In fact, she felt pretty sure that John and Ryan would like each other. Maybe they could all get together sometime soon.

When the interns finished their meals, Hoke Gilmer rounded them up and took them down a few floors to a large locker room that was to be their headquarters for the ten-week term. A younger agent who was assisting Gilmer assigned each of the interns a locker. Then all the interns sat down at the tables and chairs in the middle of the room, and the younger agent started handing out cell phones.

Gilmer explained, "It'll soon be the twenty-first century, and the FBI doesn't like to be behind the latest technology. We won't be passing out pagers this year. Some of you may have cell phones already, but we want you to have a separate one for FBI use. You'll find instructions in your orientation packet."

Then Gilmer laughed as he added, "I hope you'll have an easier time learning to use these than I did."

Some of the interns laughed as well as they claimed their new toys.

Riley's phone felt oddly small in her hand. She was used to larger house phones and had never used a cell phone before. Although she'd used computers at Lanton, and some of her friends there had cell phones, she still didn't own one. Ryan already had both a computer and a cell phone, and he sometimes teased Riley about her old-fashioned ways.

She hadn't liked that very much. The truth was, the only reason she didn't already have a computer or a cell phone yet was because she couldn't afford it.

This one looked almost exactly like Ryan's—very simple, with a small screen for text messages, a number pad, and just three or four other buttons. Still, it felt strange to realize she didn't yet know how to even make an ordinary phone call with it. She knew that it was also going to feel strange to be reachable by phone all the time, no matter where she happened to be.

She reminded herself …

I'm starting a whole new life.

Riley noticed that a group of official-looking people, most of them men, had just filed into the locker room.

Gilmer said, "Each of you will be shadowing an experienced special agent during your weeks here. They'll start off by teaching you their own specialties—analyzing crime data, forensics work, computer lab work, and what have you. We'll introduce you to them now, and they'll take things from here."

As the younger agent matched up each of the interns with their supervising agent, Riley soon realized …

There's one less agent than interns.

Sure enough, after the interns went away with their mentors, Riley found herself without a mentor of her own. She looked at Gilmer with perplexity.

Gilmer smiled slightly and said, "You'll find the agent you'll be shadowing down the hall in room nineteen."

Feeling a little unsettled, Riley left the locker room and walked down the hall until she found the right room. She opened the door and saw that a short, barrel-chested, middle-aged man was sitting on a table.

Riley gasped aloud as she recognized him.

It was Special Agent Jake Crivaro—the agent she'd worked with back in Lanton, and who had saved her life.

CHAPTER THREE

Riley smiled when she recognized Special Agent Jake Crivaro. She had spent her morning among strangers and she was especially glad to see this familiar face.

I guess I shouldn't be surprised, she thought.

After all, she remembered what he'd told her back in Lanton, when he'd handed her papers for the Honors Program …

"I'm eligible for retirement, but I might stay on for a while to help someone like you get started."

He must have specifically requested to be Riley's mentor for her internship.

But Riley's smile quickly faded when she realized …

He isn't smiling back.

In fact, Agent Crivaro didn't look the least bit happy to see her.

Still sitting on the table, he crossed his arms and nodded toward a nondescript but amiable-looking man in his twenties who was standing nearby. Crivaro said …

"Riley Sweeney, I want you to meet Special Agent Mark McCune, from right here in DC. He's my partner on a case I'm working on today."

"Pleased to meet you," Agent McCune said with a smile.

"Likewise," Riley said.

McCune seemed markedly more friendly than Crivaro did.

Crivaro stood up from the table. "Consider yourself lucky, Sweeney. While the other interns are stuck indoors learning how to use filing cabinets and paper clips, you'll be heading right out into the field. I just came up here from Quantico to work on a drug case. You'll be joining Agent McCune and me—we're headed to the scene right now."

Agent Crivaro strode out of the room.

As Riley and Agent McCune followed him, Riley thought …

He called me "Sweeney."

Back in Lanton, she'd gotten used to him calling her "Riley."

Riley whispered to McCune, "Is Agent Crivaro upset about something?"

McCune shrugged and whispered back, "I was hoping you could tell me. This is my first day working with him, but I hear you already got to work on a case with him. They say he was pretty impressed by you. He's got a reputation for being kind of brusque. His last partner got fired, you know."

Riley almost said …

Actually, I didn't know.

She'd never heard Crivaro mention a partner back in Lanton.

Although Crivaro had been tough, she'd never thought of him as "brusque." In fact, she'd come to think of him as a kindly father figure—quite unlike her actual father.

Riley and McCune followed Crivaro to a car in the FBI building's parking level. Nobody spoke as Crivaro drove them out of the building and continued north through the streets of DC.

Riley began to wonder whether Crivaro was ever going to explain what they were supposed to do whenever they got wherever they were going.

They eventually reached a seedy-looking neighborhood. The streets were lined with row houses that looked to Riley like they must have once been pleasant homes but had become awfully rundown.

Still driving, Agent Crivaro finally spoke to her.

"A couple of brothers, Jaden and Malik Madison, have been running a drug operation in this neighborhood for a couple of years now. They and their gang have been brazen about it—selling right on the street, like it was some kind of outdoor market. The local cops couldn't do anything to stop them."

"Why not?" Riley asked.

Crivaro said, "The gang kept careful watch for cops. Also, they had the whole neighborhood scared stiff—drive-by shootings, that kind of thing. A couple of kids got shot for just standing around where they weren't supposed to be. Nobody dared talk to the cops about what was going on."

Looking along the rows of houses, Crivaro continued.

"The FBI got called in to help a few days ago. Just this morning, one of our undercover guys managed to arrest Jaden. His brother, Malik, is still at large, and the gang has scattered. They won't be easy to catch. But because of the arrest, we were able to get a warrant to search the house they've been working out of."

Riley asked, "If the gang is still out there, won't they just start all over again?"

McCune said, "That's where the local cops can really get something done. They'll set up a 'mini station' right out on the sidewalk—just a picnic table and chairs manned by a couple of uniformed officers. They'll work with the locals to make sure the same thing doesn't happen here again."

Riley almost asked …

Won't they just start up in another neighborhood?

But she knew it was a stupid question. Of course the gang would start up somewhere else—at least if they weren't caught. And then the cops and the FBI would have to get to work all over again wherever that happened. That was just the nature of this kind of work.

Crivaro stopped the car and pointed to the nearest house.

"The search is already underway in that one," he said. "And we're here to help."

As they got out of the car, Crivaro wagged his finger at Riley sternly.

"By 'we,' I mean Agent McCune and myself. You're here to watch and learn. So stay the hell out of the way. And don't touch anything."

Riley felt a chill at his words. But she nodded obediently.

A uniformed cop standing in the open doorway led them inside. Riley immediately saw that a big operation was already in progress. The narrow hallway was bustling with local cops and agents wearing FBI jackets. They were piling up weapons and bags of drugs in the middle of the floor.

Crivaro looked pleased. He said to one of the FBI men, "Looks like you folks have hit a real gold mine here."

The FBI man laughed and said, "We're pretty sure this is only the start of it. There's got to be a lot of cash around here someplace, but we haven't found it yet. There are plenty of places to hide stuff in a house like this. Our guys are going over every square inch."

Riley followed Crivaro and McCune up a flight of stairs to the second floor.

She could now see that the house, and apparently the others surrounding it, was larger than it looked outside. Although it was narrow, it was also deep, with a good many rooms along the hallways. In addition to the two floors in ready view, Riley guessed that the house also had an attic and a basement.

At the top of the stairs, four agents almost collided with Crivaro as they came out of one of the rooms.

"Nothing in there," one of the agents said.

"Are you sure?" Crivaro asked.

"We searched it top to bottom," the other agent said.

Then a voice called out from inside the room directly across the hall …

"Hey, I think we've really got something here!"

Riley trailed Crivaro and McCune across the hall. Before she could follow them into the room, Crivaro held out his hand and stopped her.

"Huh-uh," he told her. "You can watch from right here in the hallway."

Riley stood just outside the door and saw five men searching the room. The one who had called out to Jake was standing beside a rectangular shape on the wall.

He said, "This looks like it used to be a dumbwaiter. What do you want to bet we'll find something inside?"

"Bust it open," Crivaro said.

Riley took a step forward to see what they were doing.

Jake looked up at her and yelled …

"Hey, Sweeney. What did I just tell you?"

Riley was about to explain that she didn't actually intend to come inside when Jake ordered a cop …

"Shut that goddamn door."

The door slammed shut in Riley's face. Riley stood in the hallway feeling shocked and embarrassed.

Why is Agent Crivaro so angry with me? she wondered.

A lot of noise was coming from inside the room now. It sounded like somebody was taking a crowbar to the place in the wall where the dumbwaiter had once been. Riley wished she could see what was going on, but opening the door again was out of the question.

She walked across the hallway and into the room on the other side, the one the agents had said was already searched. Chairs and furniture were overturned, and a rug was crumpled from having been pulled up and thrown back down again.

Alone there, Riley walked over to the window that overlooked the street.

Outside she saw a few scattered people moving briskly as if in a hurry to get wherever they were going.

They don't feel safe outside, she realized. It struck her as incredibly sad.

She wondered how long it had been since this neighborhood had been a pleasant place to live.

She also wondered …

Are we really making a difference?

Riley tried to imagine what life might be like here after the "mini station" Agent McCune mentioned was in place. Would

24

neighbors really feel safer because of a couple of cops posted at a picnic table?

Riley sighed as the handful of people on the street continued hurrying to their separate destinations.

She realized she was asking herself the wrong question.

There's no "we"—at least not yet.

She wasn't involved in this operation at all. And Agent Crivaro certainly wasn't showing any confidence in her.

She turned away from the window and headed back toward the door. As she crossed the rumpled rug, she noticed an odd sound under her feet. She stopped in her tracks and stood there for a moment. Then she tapped her heel against the floor.

It sounded oddly hollow where she was standing.

She walked over to the edge of the rug and pulled it off that patch of the floor.

She didn't see anything unusual, just an ordinary hardwood floor.

I guess I was just imagining things, she thought.

She remembered what one of the agents had said coming out of this room.

"We searched it top to bottom."

Surely she wasn't going to find something that four FBI agents had missed.

And yet, she was sure she had heard something odd. She wouldn't have noticed it if anybody else had been moving around the room. She'd only noticed it because it was quiet in here.

She took a couple of steps to the side and tapped her heel against the floor. The floor sound solid again. Then she stooped down and rapped on the spot she'd noticed before with her knuckles.

Sure enough, it *did* sound hollow there. She still didn't see any sign of an opening but …

I wonder.

She could see that one length of board was shorter than the others. It had a dark spot on one end that looked like an ordinary knot.

Riley pressed the knot with her finger.

She almost jumped out of her skin as the board sprang up a little at that end.

I've found something! she thought.

I've really found something!

CHAPTER FOUR

Riley tugged at the end of the board that had popped up a little.

The whole board came loose. She set it to one side.

And sure enough, there was an opening to a space under the floor.

Riley peered closer. Tucked under the floorboards just out of ready sight were bundles of paper money.

She yelled loudly, "Agent Crivaro! I've found something!"

As she waited for a reply, Riley glimpsed something else alongside those bundles. It was the edge of a plastic object.

Riley reached for the object and picked it up.

It was a cell phone—a simpler model than the one she'd been given a little while ago. She realized that this must be one of those prepaid types that couldn't be traced to an owner.

A burner phone, she thought. *That must be very useful for a drug operation.*

Suddenly she heard a voice shout from the doorway …

"Sweeney! What the hell do you think you're doing?"

Riley turned and saw Agent Crivaro, his face red with rage. Agent McCune had entered right behind him.

She held the phone out and said, "I found something, Agent Crivaro."

"I see that," Crivaro said. "And your fingers are all over it. Give me that thing."

Riley handed the phone to Crivaro, who took it gingerly with a thumb and forefinger and dropped it into an evidence bag. She saw that both he and Agent McCune were wearing gloves.

She felt her face flush with shame and embarrassment.

I really screwed up.

McCune knelt down and looked into the space under the floor.

He said, "Hey, Agent Crivaro! Get a look at this!"

Crivaro knelt down beside McCune, who said, "It's the cash we've been looking all over the house for."

"So it is," Crivaro said.

Turning toward Riley again, Crivaro snapped …

"Did you touch any of this money?"

Riley shook her head.

"Are you sure?" Crivaro said.

"I'm sure," Riley said timidly.

"How did you find this?" Crivaro said, pointing to the opening.

Riley shrugged and said, "I was just walking through here and I heard a hollow sound under the floor, so I pulled back the rug and—"

Crivaro interrupted, "And you yanked this board loose."

"Well, I didn't exactly *yank* anything. It just sort of popped up when I touched it in a certain spot."

Crivaro growled, "You touched it. And the phone too. I can't believe it. You got your prints all over everything."

Riley stammered, "I—I'm sorry, sir."

"You damn well should be," Crivaro said. "I'm getting you out of here before you screw anything else up."

He got up from the floor and brushed off his hands.

He said, "McCune, keep the search team working. When you finish the rooms on this floor, keep searching up in the attic. I don't guess we're likely to find much of anything else, but we've got to be thorough."

"I'll do that, sir," McCune said.

Crivaro led Riley back downstairs and out to his car.

As they drove away, Riley asked, "Are we going back to headquarters?"

"Not today," Crivaro said. "Maybe not ever. Where do you live? I'm taking you home."

Her voice choked with emotion, Riley told him her address.

As they drove on in silence, Riley found herself remembering how impressed by her Crivaro had been back in Lanton, and how he'd told her …

"The FBI needs young people like you—especially women. You'd make a very fine BAU agent."

How things had changed!

And she knew it wasn't just because of the mistake she'd made. Crivaro had been cold to her from the start today.

Right now, Riley just wished he'd say something—anything.

She shyly asked, "Did you find anything in that other room across the hall? I mean, where the dumbwaiter used to be?"

"Not a thing," Crivaro said.

Another silence fell. Riley was starting to feel confused now.

She knew she'd made a terrible mistake, but …

What was I supposed to do?

She'd had a gut feeling back in that room that there was something under the floor.

Was she just supposed to have ignored that feeling?

She summoned up her courage and said ...

"Sir, I know I screwed up, but didn't I find something important back there? Four agents searched that room and missed that space. You were looking for the cash, and I found it. Would anybody else have found it if I didn't?"

"That's not the point," Crivaro said.

Riley fought down the urge to ask ...

Then what is *the point?*

Crivaro drove on in sullen silence for several minutes. Then he said in a quiet, bitter voice, "I pulled a lot of strings to get you into this program."

Another silence fell. But Riley detected a world of meaning in those words. She began to realize that Crivaro had really gone out on a limb on her behalf, not only to get her into the program but also to serve as her mentor. And he'd probably made some of his colleagues angry, perhaps by excluding intern candidates they might have deemed to be more promising than Riley.

Now that she thought of things that way, Crivaro's cold behavior started to make sense. He hadn't wanted to show even the slightest bit of preferential treatment toward her. In fact, he'd gone to the opposite extreme. He'd been counting on her to prove herself worthy without any encouragement from himself, and despite his colleagues' doubts and resentments.

And judging from the looks and whispers she'd noticed among other interns during the day, Crivaro's colleagues weren't the only people who harbored those resentments. She'd faced an uphill climb just to achieve even modest success.

And she'd blown it all in a single afternoon, with one stupid mistake. Crivaro had good reason to be disappointed and angry.

She took a long, slow breath and said ...

"I'm sorry. It won't happen again."

Crivaro didn't reply for a few moments.

Finally he said, "I guess you want a second chance. Well, let me tell you, the FBI isn't big on second chances. My last partner got fired for making the same kind of mistake—and he definitely deserved it. A mistake like that has consequences. Sometimes it just means spoiling a case so that a bad guy gets off free. Sometimes it costs someone their life. It can cost your *own* life."

Crivaro glanced over at her with a scowl.

"So what do you think I should do?" he said.

"I don't know," Riley said.

Crivaro shook his head. "I sure don't know either. I guess maybe both of us should sleep on it. I've got to decide whether I misjudged your abilities. You've got to decide whether you've really got what it takes to stay in this program."

Riley felt a lump in her throat, and her eyes stung and she blinked hard.

Don't cry, she told herself.

Crying was the only thing she could think of that would make things worse than they were already.

CHAPTER FIVE

Still stinging from Crivaro's rebuke, Riley arrived at home a full two hours before Ryan did. When Ryan got there, he seemed surprised to see that she'd gotten back so early, but he was too excited about his own day to notice how upset she was.

Ryan sat down at the kitchen table with a beer while Riley heated up macaroni and cheese TV dinners. She could tell that he was really buzzed about everything he was doing at the law firm and eager to tell her all about it. She tried to pay close attention.

He'd been given more duties than he'd expected—a lot of complex research and analysis, writing briefs, preparing for litigation, and other tasks that Riley barely understood. He was even going to appear in a courtroom tomorrow for the very first time. He was only going to be assisting the lead attorneys, of course, but it was a real milestone for him.

Ryan appeared nervous, daunted, maybe a little scared, but above all else exhilarated.

Riley tried to keep smiling as they sat down and ate dinner. She wanted to be happy for him.

Finally Ryan asked …

"Wow, listen to me talk. What about you? How was your day?"

Riley gulped hard.

"It could have been better," she said. "Actually, it was pretty bad."

Ryan reached across the table and took her hand with an expression of sincere concern.

"I'm sorry," he said. "Do you want to talk about it?"

Riley wondered whether talking about it would make her feel better.

No, I'll only start crying.

Besides, Ryan might not be happy that she'd actually gone out into the field today. They'd both been sure that she'd be doing her training safely indoors. Not that she'd been in any actual danger …

"I'd rather not get into any details," Riley said. "But do you remember Special Agent Crivaro, the FBI man who saved my life back in Lanton?"

Ryan nodded.

Riley continued, "Well, he's supposed to be mentoring me. But

he's got doubts now as to whether I belong in the program. And …
I guess I've got doubts too. Maybe this whole thing was a mistake."

Ryan squeezed her hand and didn't speak.

Riley wished he'd say something. But what did she want him to
say?

What did she *expect* him to say?

After all, Ryan hadn't been enthusiastic about Riley being in
the program from the very start. He'd probably be just as happy if
she dropped out—or even got kicked out.

Finally Ryan said, "Look, maybe it's just not the right time for
you to do this. I mean, you're pregnant, we're just getting moved
into this new place, and I'm just getting started Parsons and
Rittenhouse. Maybe you should just wait until—"

"Wait until when?" Riley said. "Until I'm a mom raising a kid?
How is that going to work?"

Ryan's eyes widened at Riley's bitter tone. Even Riley was
startled at the sound of her own voice.

"I'm sorry," she said. "I didn't mean it to come out like that."

Ryan said quietly, "Riley, you *are* going to be a mom raising a
kid. We're going to be parents. It's a reality we both have to deal
with, whether you keep training this summer or not."

Riley was really struggling not to cry now. The future seemed
so murky and mysterious.

She asked, "What am I going to do if I'm not in the program? I
can't just sit around this apartment all day."

Ryan shrugged slightly.

"Well, you can always find a job, help with the expenses.
Maybe some kind of temp work—something you can just walk
away from whenever you get tired of doing it. You've got your
whole life ahead of you. There's plenty of time to figure out what
you really want to do. But before long, I could be successful enough
that you wouldn't have to work at all if you don't want to."

They both fell quiet for a moment.

Then Riley said, "So do you think I should quit?"

"What I think doesn't matter," Ryan said. "It's your decision.
And whatever you decide, I'll do my best to back you up."

They didn't say much for the rest of the meal. After they
finished eating, they watched TV for a while. Riley couldn't really
focus on what they were watching. She kept thinking about what
Agent Crivaro had said …

*"You've got to decide whether you've really got what it takes
to stay in this program."*

31

The more Riley thought about it, the more doubt and uncertainty she felt.

After all, she had more than just herself to think about. There was Ryan, the baby, and even Agent Crivaro.

She remembered something else her would-be mentor had said …

"I pulled a lot of strings to get you into this program."

And keeping her in the program wasn't going to make Crivaro's life any easier. He was likely to keep catching flak from colleagues who didn't think Riley belonged there, especially if she didn't live up to his expectations.

And she sure hadn't lived up to his expectations today.

Ryan eventually took a shower and went to bed. Riley sat on the couch, continuing to mull over her choices.

Finally, she picked up a legal pad and started to draft a letter of resignation to Hoke Gilmer, the training supervisor. She was surprised at how much better she felt as she kept writing the letter. When she came to the end, she felt as if a load had been lifted from her mind.

This is the right choice, she thought.

She figured she would get up early tomorrow morning, tell Ryan about her decision, type her letter into his computer, then print it and send it out with the morning mail. She'd also make a phone call to Agent Crivaro, who would surely be relieved.

Finally, she went to bed, feeling much better about things. She found it easy to go to sleep.

Riley found herself walking into the J. Edgar Hoover Building.

What am I doing here? *she wondered.*

Then she noticed the legal pad in her hand, with her letter written on it.

Oh, yes, *she realized.*

I came to deliver this to Agent Gilmer personally.

She took the elevator down three floors, then went into the auditorium where the interns had met yesterday.

To her alarm, all the interns were seated in the auditorium watching her every move. Agent Gilmer was standing at the front of the auditorium, looking at her with his arms crossed.

"What do you want, Sweeney?" Gilmer asked, sounding a lot more stern than he had yesterday when he'd addressed the group.

Riley glanced at the interns, who gazed at her silently with accusing expressions.

Then she said to Gilmer, *"I won't take any of your time. I just need to give you this."*

She handed him the yellow legal pad.

Gilmer raised his reading glasses to look at the pad.

"What's this?" he asked.

Riley opened her mouth to say ...

"It's my letter of resignation from the program."

But instead, different words came out of her mouth ...

"I, Riley Sweeney, do solemnly swear that I will support and defend the Constitution of the United States ..."

To her alarm, she realized ...

I'm reciting the FBI oath of office.

And she couldn't seem to stop herself.

"...that I will bear true faith and allegiance to the same ..."

Gilmer pointed to the legal pad and asked again ...

"What's this?"

Riley still wanted to explain what it really was, but the words of the oath continued to pour out ...

"... I take this obligation freely, without any mental reservation or purpose of evasion ..."

Gilmer's face was morphing into another face.

It was Jake Crivaro, and he was looking angry. He waved the pad in front of her face.

"What's this?" he snarled.

Riley was surprised to see that nothing was written there at all.

She heard all the other interns murmuring aloud, speaking the same oath but in a confused jumble of voices.

Meanwhile, she was nearing the end of the oath ...

"... I will well and faithfully discharge the duties of the office on which I am about to enter. So help me God."

Crivaro seemed to be seething now.

"What the hell's this?" he said, pointing to the blank yellow paper.

Riley tried to tell him, but no words came out.

Riley's eyes snapped open when she heard an unfamiliar buzzing sound.

She was lying in bed next to Ryan.

It was a dream, she realized.

But the dream definitely meant something. In fact, it meant everything. She'd taken an oath, and she couldn't take it back. Which meant she couldn't resign from the program. It wasn't a legal problem. It was personal. It was a matter of principle.

But what if I get kicked out?

What do I do then?

Meanwhile, she wondered—what was that buzzing sound that kept repeating over and over again?

Still half-asleep, Ryan groaned and muttered …

"Answer your damn phone, Riley."

Then Riley remembered the cell phone she'd been given yesterday at the FBI building. She fumbled around on the side table until she found it, then scrambled out of bed and carried it out of the room and shut the door behind her.

It took her a moment to figure out which button to push to take the call. When she finally succeeded, she heard a familiar voice.

"Sweeney? Did I wake you?"

It was Agent Crivaro, sounding none too friendly.

"No, of course not," Riley said.

"Liar. It's five o'clock in the morning."

Riley sighed deeply. She realized she felt sick to her stomach.

Crivaro said, "How long will it take you to get awake and dressed?"

Riley thought for a moment, then said, "Um, fifteen minutes, I guess."

"I'll be there in ten. Meet me outside your building."

Crivaro ended the call without another word.

What does he want? Riley wondered.

Is he coming here to personally fire me?

Suddenly she felt a rising wave of nausea. She knew it was morning sickness—the worst she'd experienced so far during her pregnancy.

She let out a groan and thought …

Just what I need right now.

Then she rushed to the bathroom.

CHAPTER SIX

When Jake Crivaro pulled up to the apartment building, Riley Sweeney was already waiting outside. Jake noticed that she looked more than a little pale as she got into the car.

"Not feeling well?" he asked.

"I'm fine," Riley said.

She doesn't look fine, Jake thought. *She doesn't sound fine, either.*

Jake wondered if maybe she'd partied too hard last night. These young interns did that sometimes. Or maybe she'd just had too much to drink right at home. She'd certainly seemed discouraged when he'd dropped her off yesterday—and small wonder, after the chewing out he'd given her. Maybe she'd tried to drown her sorrows.

Jake hoped his protégé wasn't too hung over to function.

As he pulled away from the building, Riley asked …

"Where are we going?"

Jake hesitated for a moment.

Then he said, "Look, we're going to start from scratch today."

Riley looked at him with a vaguely surprised expression.

He continued, "The truth is, what you did yesterday—well, it wasn't entirely a screw-up. You found the Madison brothers' drug money. And that burner phone turned out to be plenty useful. It had some important phone numbers in it, which made it possible for the cops to round up a few gang members—including Malik Madison, the brother who was still at large. It was stupid of them to buy a prepaid phone and not dump it after using it. But I guess they just didn't think anybody was going to find it."

He glanced her way and added, "They were wrong."

Riley just kept staring back at him, as if she was having trouble understanding what he was saying.

Jake resisted the impulse to say …

"I'm really sorry I gave you such a hard time."

Instead he said, "But you've got to follow instructions. And you've got to respect procedure."

"I understand," Riley said tiredly. "Thanks for giving me another chance."

Jake growled under his breath. He reminded himself that he

didn't want to give the kid too much encouragement.

But he did feel bad about how he'd treated her yesterday.

I'm overreacting to things, he thought.

He'd pissed off some colleagues at Quantico by pushing for Riley to get into the program. One agent in particular, Toby Wolsky, had wanted his nephew Jordan to be an intern this summer, but Jake had gotten Riley in instead of him. He'd thrown his considerable credentials into that effort and called in a couple of favors owed him.

Jake didn't think much of Wolsky as an agent, and he had no reason to think his nephew had any potential to speak of. But Wolsky had friends in Quantico who were now unhappy with Jake.

In a way, Jake could understand why.

For all they knew, Riley was just some ordinary college psych graduate who'd never even thought about getting into law enforcement.

And the truth was, Jake didn't know much more about her either—except that he'd seen her instincts at work, up close and personal. He remembered vividly how readily she'd understood the killer's thoughts back in Lanton, with just a little coaching from him. Aside from himself, Jake had seldom met anyone with those kinds of instincts—gut-level insights that very few other agents could even understand.

Of course, he couldn't discount the possibility that what she'd done in Lanton had been little more than a fluke.

Maybe today he'd get a better idea of what she could do.

Riley asked again …

"Where are we going?"

"To a murder scene," Jake said.

He didn't want to tell her anything more until they got there.

He wanted to observe how she reacted to a really bizarre situation.

And from what he'd heard, this murder scene was about as bizarre as a murder scene could get. He'd gotten called about it just a little while ago himself, and he was still having trouble believing what he'd been told.

We'll see what we see, I guess.

*

Riley thought maybe she was feeling a bit better as she rode along with Agent Crivaro.

Still, she wished he'd tell her what this was all about.

A murder scene, he said.

That was more than she'd bargained for in the summer program—let alone on her second day. Yesterday had been unexpected enough.

She wasn't sure how she felt about it.

But she *was* pretty sure that Ryan wouldn't like the idea at all.

She realized she hadn't yet told Ryan that she was shadowing Jake Crivaro. Ryan wouldn't approve of that either. Ryan had mistrusted Crivaro from the start, especially for the way he had helped Riley get a glimpse into a killer's mind.

She remembered what Ryan had said about one of those episodes ...

"Are you telling me that FBI guy—Crivaro—played mind games with you? Why? Just for fun?"

Of course Riley knew that Crivaro hadn't put her through all that "just for fun."

He'd been dead serious about it. Those experiences had been absolutely necessary.

They had helped make it possible to eventually catch the killer.

But what am I in for now? Riley wondered.

Crivaro seemed to be being deliberately cryptic.

When he parked the car along a street with houses on one side and an open field on the other, she saw that a couple of police cars and an official van were pulled up nearby.

Before they left the car, Crivaro wagged his finger and said to her ...

"Now remember the goddamn rules. Don't *touch anything.* And don't speak unless you're spoken to. You're only here to observe the rest of us at work."

Riley nodded. But something in Crivaro's voice made her suspect that he expected something a little more from her than just watching quietly.

She wished she knew what that something might be.

Riley and Crivaro got out of the car and walked into the field. It was scattered with lots of debris, as if some kind of big public event had taken place here recently.

Other people, some wearing police uniforms, were standing near a stand of trees and bushes. A wide area around them was cordoned off with yellow police tape.

As Riley and Crivaro approached the group, she realized that the bushes had concealed something on the ground.

Riley gasped at what she saw.

Nausea swelled up in her throat again.

Lying on the ground was a dead circus clown.

CHAPTER SEVEN

Riley felt so dizzy that she thought she might faint.

She managed to stay on her feet, but then she worried that she was going to throw up, like she had back at the apartment.

This can't be real, she thought.

This has to be a nightmare.

The cops and other people were standing around a body that was in a full clown outfit. The suit was puffy and brightly colored with huge pompoms as buttons. A pair of outsized shoes completed the attire.

The stark white face had a bizarre painted smile, a bright red nose, and exaggerated eyes and eyebrows. A huge red wig framed the face. A canvas tarp was bunched up next to the body.

It dawned on Riley that the body was actually a woman.

Now that her head was clearing, she noticed a distinct and unpleasant odor in the air. As she looked around the area, she doubted that the smell was from the body—or at least not much of it. Trash was strewn everywhere. The morning sun was bringing out the odor of various kinds of human residue.

A man wearing a white jacket was kneeling beside the body, studying it carefully. Crivaro introduced him as Victor Dahl, the DC medical examiner.

Crivaro shook his head and said to Dahl, "This is even weirder than I'd expected."

Rising to his feet, Dahl said, "Yeah, weird. And it's just like the last victim."

Riley thought …

The last victim?

Had another clown been killed before this one?

"I just got briefed a little while ago," Crivaro said to Dahl and the cops. "Maybe you folks can fill in my trainee here on what this is all about. I'm maybe not fully up to speed on this case myself."

Dahl looked at Riley and hesitated for a moment. Riley wondered if she looked as sick as she felt. But then the medical examiner began to explain.

"Saturday morning, a body was found in the alley behind a movie theater. The victim was a young woman named Margo Birch—and she was dressed and made up pretty much like this

39

victim. The cops figured it was a weird murder, but one of a kind. Then this corpse turned up last night. Another young woman all painted up and dressed this way."

It hit Riley then. This wasn't an actual clown. This was an ordinary young woman dressed up as a clown. Two such women had been bizarrely dressed and made up and murdered.

Crivaro added, "And that's when it became an FBI case, and we got called in."

"That's right," Dahl said, looking around the debris-strewn field. "There was a carnival here for a few days. It moved out on Saturday. That's where all this junk came from—the field hasn't been cleaned up yet. Late last night some neighborhood guy came out here with a metal detector, looking for coins that might have gotten dropped during the carnival. He found the body, which was covered by that tarp at the time."

Riley turned to see that Crivaro was watching her closely.

Was he just making sure she was minding her own business?

Or was he monitoring her reactions?

She asked, "Has this woman been identified?"

One of the cops said, "Not yet."

Crivaro added, "We're focused on one particular missing person's report. Yesterday morning a professional photographer named Janet Davis was reported missing. She'd been taking pictures at Lady Bird Johnson Park the night before. The cops are wondering if this might be her. Agent McCune is paying her husband a visit right now. Maybe he can help us make an ID."

Riley heard sounds of vehicles stopping nearby in the street. She looked and saw that a couple of TV news vans had pulled up.

"Damn," one of the cops said. "We'd managed to keep the clown angle about the other murder quiet until now. Should we cover her back up?"

Crivaro let out a growl of annoyance as a news crew poured out of one of the vans with a camera and a boom mic. The crew hurried out onto the field.

"It's too late for that," he said. "They've already seen the victim."

As other media vehicles approached, Crivaro and the ME mobilized the cops to try to keep the reporters as far back from the police tape as they could.

Meanwhile, Riley looked at the victim and wondered …

How did she die?

There was no one to ask at the moment. Everybody was busy

dealing with the reporters, who were noisily asking questions.

Riley carefully stooped over the body, telling herself ...

Don't touch anything.

Riley saw that the victim's eyes and mouth were open. She'd seen that same terrified expression before.

She remembered all too well how her two friends had looked after their throats were cut back in Lanton. Most of all, she remembered the staggering amounts of blood on the dorm room floors when she'd found their bodies.

But there was no blood here.

She saw what appeared to be some small cuts on the woman's face and neck showing through the white makeup.

What did those cuts mean? They surely weren't large enough to have been fatal.

She also noticed that the makeup was painted on clumsily and awkwardly.

She didn't put it on herself, she thought.

No, someone else had done that, perhaps against the victim's will.

Then Riley felt a strange shift in her consciousness—something she hadn't felt since those terrible days in Lanton.

Her skin crawled as she realized what that feeling was.

She was getting a sense of the mind of the killer.

He dressed her like this, she thought.

He'd probably put on the costume after she was dead, but she had still been conscious when he smeared her face with makeup. Judging from her dead, open eyes, she'd been all too aware of what was happening to her.

And he enjoyed it, she thought. *He enjoyed her terror as he painted her.*

Riley also understood the small cuts now.

He teased her with a knife.

He taunted her—made her wonder how he was going to kill her.

Riley gasped and rose to her feet. She felt another wave of nausea and dizziness and almost fell down again, but someone caught her by the arm.

She turned and saw that Jake Crivaro had stopped her from falling.

He was looking straight into her eyes. Riley knew that he understood exactly what she'd just experienced.

In a hoarse, horrified voice she told him ...

"He frightened her to death. She died of fear."

Riley heard Dahl let out a yelp of surprise.

"Who told you that?" Dahl said, walking toward Riley.

Crivaro said to him, "Nobody told her. Is it true?"

Dahl shrugged a little.

"Maybe. Or something like it, anyway, if she's like the other victim. Margo Birch's bloodstream was pumped full of amphetamines, a fatal dose that made her heart stop beating. That poor woman must have felt scared out of her mind right until the moment she died. We'll have to do toxicology on this new victim, but …"

His voice trailed off, and then he asked Riley, "How did you know?"

Riley had no idea what to say.

Crivaro said, "It's what she does. It's why she's here."

Riley shivered deeply at those words.

Is this something I really want to be good at? she asked herself.

She wondered if maybe she should have submitted that resignation letter after all.

Maybe she shouldn't be here.

Maybe she should have no part in this.

She was sure of one thing—Ryan would be horrified if he knew where she was right now and what she was doing.

Crivaro asked Dahl, "How hard would it be for the killer to get hold of this particular amphetamine?"

"Unfortunately," the medical examiner replied, "it would be easy to buy on the street."

Crivaro's phone buzzed. He looked at it. "It's Agent McCune. I've got to take this."

Crivaro stepped away and talked on his cell phone. Dahl continued to stare at Riley as if she were some kind of freak.

Maybe he's right, she thought.

Meanwhile, she could hear some of the questions the reporters were asking.

"Is it true Margo Birch's murder was just like this?"

"Was Margo Birch dressed and made up the same way?"

"Why is this killer dressing his victims up like clowns?"

"Is this the work of a serial killer?"

"Are there going to be more clown murders?"

Riley remembered what one of the cops had just said …

"We'd managed to keep the clown angle about the other murder quiet until now."

Obviously, rumors had already been circulating even so. And now there was no keeping the truth quiet.

The cops were trying to say as little as possible in reply to the questions. But Riley remembered how aggressive reporters had been back in Lanton. She understood all too well why Jake and the cops weren't happy that these reporters had shown up. The publicity wasn't going to make their work any easier.

Crivaro walked back toward Riley and Dahl, tucking his phone in his pocket.

"McCune just talked to the missing woman's husband. The poor guy's worried sick, but he told McCune something that might be helpful. He said she has a mole just behind her right ear."

Dahl stooped down and peeked behind the victim's ear.

"It's her," he said. "What did you say her name was again?"

"Janet Davis," Crivaro said.

Dahl shook his head. "Well, at least we've ID'd the victim. We might as well get her out of here. I wish we didn't have to deal with rigor mortis, though."

Riley watched as Dahl's team loaded the corpse onto a gurney. It was a clumsy effort. The body was stiff like a statue, and the puffily clad limbs extended in all directions, protruding from underneath the white sheet that covered it.

Finally dumbstruck themselves, the reporters gawked and stared as the gurney rattled across the field toward the ME's van carrying its grotesque burden.

As the body vanished into the van, Riley and Crivaro pushed past the reporters and headed back to their own vehicle.

As Crivaro drove them away, Riley asked where they were going next.

"To headquarters," Crivaro said. "McCune told me that some cops have been searching around Lady Bird Johnson Park where Janet Davis went missing. They found her camera. She must have dropped it when she was abducted. The camera is now at FBI headquarters. Let's go see what the tech people can find out about it. Maybe we'll get lucky and it'll give us some evidence."

That word jarred Riley …

"Lucky."

It seemed like a strange word to use when talking about something so singularly unlucky as a woman's murder.

But Crivaro had obviously meant what he said. She wondered at how hardened he must have become, doing this work for as many years as he had.

Was he completely immune to horror?

She couldn't tell from his tone of voice as he continued …

"Also, Janet Davis's husband let McCune look through photos she'd taken during the last few months. McCune found a few photos that she had taken in a costume store."

Riley felt a tingle of interest.

She asked, "You mean the kind of store that might sell clown costumes?"

Crivaro nodded. "Sounds interesting, doesn't it?"

"But what does it mean?" Riley said.

Crivaro said, "It's hard to say just yet—except Janet Davis was interested enough in costumes to want to take pictures of them. Her husband remembers her talking about doing that, but she didn't happen to tell him where. McCune is now trying to figure out what store the pictures were taken in. He'll call me then. It shouldn't take him very long."

Crivaro fell silent for a moment.

Then he glanced over at Riley and asked, "How are you holding up?"

"Fine," Riley said.

"Are you sure?" Crivaro asked. "You look kind of pale, like you're not feeling well."

It was true, of course. A combination of morning sickness and the shock of what she'd just seen had definitely gotten to her. But the last thing in the world she wanted to tell Crivaro was that she was pregnant.

"I'm fine," Riley insisted.

Crivaro said, "I take it you got some gut feelings about the killer back there."

Riley nodded silently.

"Anything more I should know—aside from the possibility that he'd scared the victim to death?"

"Not much," Riley said. "Except that he's …"

She hesitated, then found the word she was looking for. "Sadistic."

As they drove on in silence, Riley found herself remembering the spectacle of the body splayed atop the gurney. She felt a resurgence of horror that the victim had to suffer such humiliation and indignity even in death.

She wondered what kind of monster would wish this on anybody.

As close as she'd momentarily felt to the killer, she knew that she couldn't begin to understand the sick workings of his mind.

And she was sure she didn't want to.

But was that what was in store for her before this case was over?

And what about afterward?

Is this what my life is going to be like?

CHAPTER EIGHT

As Riley and Crivaro walked into the clean, air-conditioned J. Edgar Hoover Building, she still felt the ugliness of the murder scene clinging to her. It was as if the horror had gotten into her very pores. How was she ever going to shake it off—especially the smell?

During the drive here, Crivaro had assured Riley that the smell she'd noticed in the field hadn't been from the body. As Riley had guessed, it was just from the trash left scattered from the carnival. Janet Davis's body hadn't been dead long enough to produce much of a smell—and neither had the bodies of Riley's murdered friends when she'd found them back in Lanton.

Riley still hadn't experienced the stench of a decomposing corpse.

Crivaro had said as they drove …

"You'll know it when you smell it."

It wasn't something Riley looked forward to.

Again, she wondered …

What do I think I'm doing here?

She and Crivaro took an elevator to a floor occupied by dozens of forensic labs. She followed Crivaro down a hall until they came to a room with a sign that said "DARKROOM." A lanky, longhaired young man stood leaning next to the door.

Crivaro introduced himself and Riley to the man, who nodded and said, "I'm Charlie Barrett, forensic tech. You got here just in time. I'm taking a break after processing the negatives out of that camera they found at Lady Bird Johnson Park. I was just going back in to make some prints. Come on in."

Charlie led Riley and Crivaro into a short hallway bathed in amber-colored light. Then they passed through a second door into a room awash with the same weird light.

The first thing that really struck Riley was the pungent, acrid smell of chemicals.

Curiously, she didn't find the smell to be at all unpleasant.

Instead, it seemed almost …

Cleansing, Riley realized.

For the first time since she'd left the field where they'd found the body, that clinging, sour stench of trash was gone.

46

Even the horror lifted somewhat, and Riley's nausea disappeared.

It was a true relief.

Riley peered around through the dim, alien light, fascinated by all the elaborate equipment.

Charlie held up a sheet of paper with rows of images and examined it in the dim light.

"Here are the proofs," he said. "It looks like she was one hell of a photographer. A shame what happened to her."

As Charlie laid out strips of film on a table, Riley realized that she'd never been in a darkroom before. She'd always taken her own rolls of exposed film to a drugstore to be processed. Ryan and some of her friends had recently bought digital cameras, which didn't use film at all.

Janet Davis's husband had told McCune that his photographer wife had used both kinds of cameras. She tended to use a digital camera for her professional work. But she considered the shots she was taking in the park artwork, and she preferred the film cameras for that.

Riley thought that Charlie also seemed to be an artist, a true master at what he was doing. That made her wonder ...

Is this a dying art?

Would all this skilled work with film, paper, instruments, thermometers, timers, valves, and chemicals someday go the way of blacksmithing?

If so, it seemed rather sad.

Charlie began to make the prints one by one—first enlarging the negative onto a piece of photographic paper, then slowly soaking the paper in a basin of developing liquid, followed by further soakings in what Charlie called a "stop bath" and a "fix bath." Then came a long rinse over a steel sink under tap water. Finally Charlie hung the pictures by clips to a rotating stand.

It was a slow process, and a quiet one. The silence was only broken by the trickling sounds of liquid, the shuffling of feet, and a few words spoken from time to time in what seemed almost like reverential whispers. It just didn't feel right to talk loudly here.

Riley found the stillness and the slowness to be almost eerily soothing after the noisy disorder at the murder scene, when cops had been struggling to keep reporters at bay.

Riley watched raptly as the images revealed themselves over several long minutes—ghostly and indistinct at first, then finally with sharp clarity and contrast when they hung dripping from the stand.

The black and white photographs captured a quiet, peaceful evening at the park. One showed a wooden footbridge extending over a narrow passage of water. Another seemed at first to be of a flock of seagulls taking flight, but when the image came into clearer focus Riley realized that the birds were part of a large statue.

Another photo showed a rough-hewn stone obelisk with the Washington Monument towering far in the distance. Other images were of paths for biking and walking that passed through wooded areas.

The pictures had clearly been taken as sunset approached, creating soft gray shadows, glowing halos, and silhouettes. Riley could see that Charlie had been correct in his opinion that Janet Davis had been "one hell of a photographer."

Riley also sensed that Janet knew the park well and had chosen her locations long in advance—and also the time of day, when visitors were few. Riley didn't see a single person in any of the photos. It was as if Janet had had the park all to herself.

Finally came some shots of a marina, its docks and boats and water fairly shimmering as the sun finally set. The gentle calmness of the scene was truly tangible. Riley could almost hear the gentle lapping of water and the cries of birds, could almost feel the caress of cool air on her cheek.

Then finally came a much more jarring image.

It, too, was of the marina—or at least Riley thought she could make out the shapes of boats and docks. But everything was blurred and chaotic and jumbled.

Riley realized what must have happened at the very moment she'd snapped that picture …

The camera got knocked out of her hands.

Riley's heart jumped in her throat.

She knew the image had captured the very instant when Janet Davis's world had changed forever.

In a fraction of a second, tranquility and beauty had turned into ugliness and terror.

CHAPTER NINE

As Riley stared at the blurred image, she wondered …

What happened next?

After the camera was knocked from the woman's hands, what happened to her?

What did she experience?

Did she struggle against her assailant until he somehow subdued and bound her?

Did she remain conscious throughout her ordeal? Or was she knocked unconscious right there and then, when the picture was taken?

Did she then awaken to the horror of her final moments?

Maybe it doesn't matter, Riley thought.

She remembered what the ME had said about the likelihood that Janet had died from an overdose of amphetamines.

If that was true, she had actually been frightened to death.

And now Riley was looking at the frozen moment when that fatal terror had really begun.

She shuddered deeply at the thought.

Crivaro pointed to the photo and said to Charlie, "Magnify everything. Not just this one, all the photographs, every square centimeter."

Charlie scratched his head and asked, "Looking for what?"

"People," Crivaro said. "Any people you can find. Janet Davis seems to have thought she was alone, but she was wrong. Someone was lying in wait for her. Maybe—just maybe—she caught him on film without realizing it. If you find anybody at all, get as clear a blow-up as you can."

Although she didn't say so aloud, Riley felt skeptical.

Will Charlie find anybody?

She had a feeling about the killer—that he was far too stealthy to let himself be accidentally photographed. She doubted that even a microscopic search of the photos would reveal any trace of him.

At that moment, Crivaro's phone buzzed in his pocket. He said, "That's got to be McCune."

Riley and Crivaro left the darkroom, and Crivaro stepped away to take the call. He seemed to be excited by whatever McCune was saying to him. When he ended the call, he said to Riley …

"McCune has located the costume store where Janet Davis took some pictures. He's on his way there, and says he'll meet us there. Let's get going."

*

When Crivaro pulled up to the store called Costume Romp, Agent McCune was already there waiting in his own vehicle. He got out and joined Riley and Crivaro as they approached the store. It looked to Riley at first like a modest storefront establishment. The front windows were filled with costumes, of course—ranging from a vampire and a mummy to fancy dress outfits suggestive of earlier centuries. There was also an Uncle Sam costume for the upcoming Fourth of July.

When she followed Crivaro and McCune inside, Riley was startled by the vastness of the long brick interior, filled with racks loaded with what appeared to be hundreds of costumes, masks, and wigs.

The sight of so much make-believe took Riley's breath away. The costumes included pirates, monsters, soldiers, princes and princesses, wild and domestic animals, space aliens, and every other kind of character she could imagine.

It boggled Riley's mind. After all, Halloween only came once a year. Was there really a year-round market for all these costumes? If so, what did people want with them?

A lot of costume parties, I guess.

It occurred to her that she shouldn't be surprised, considering the horrors she was starting to learn about. In a world where such awful things happened, it was small wonder that people wanted to escape into fantasy worlds.

It also wasn't surprising that a talented photographer like Janet Davis would enjoy taking photographs here, in the midst of such a rich array of images. No doubt she used real film here, not a digital camera.

The monster masks and costumes reminded Riley of a TV show she'd enjoyed during the last couple of years—the story of a teenage girl who fought and slew vampires and other kinds of demons.

Lately, though, Riley had found that show less appealing.

After learning about her own ability to enter a killer's mind, the saga of a girl with superpowers and super-obligations now seemed to cut a little too close to home for comfort.

50

Riley, Crivaro, and McCune looked all around but didn't see anybody.

McCune called out, "Hello—is anybody here?"

A man stepped out from behind one of the costume racks.

"May I help you?" he asked.

The man cut a startling figure. He was tall and extremely thin, wearing a long-sleeved T-shirt that was printed to resemble a tuxedo. He was also wearing familiar "Groucho" glasses—the kind with an enormous white nose, black-rimmed glasses, and bushy eyebrows and a mustache.

Obviously taken somewhat aback, Crivaro and McCune took out their badges and told the man who they and Riley were.

Seeming utterly unsurprised to be visited by the FBI, the man introduced himself as Danny Casal, the owner of the business.

"Just call me Danny," he said.

Riley found herself waiting for him to take off the nose glasses. But as she looked at him more closely, she realized …

Those are prescription glasses.

They also had remarkably thick lenses. Danny Casal apparently wore these glasses all the time, and he surely would be quite myopic without them.

McCune opened a manila folder.

"We have photos of two women," he said. "We need to know if you've ever seen either of them."

The eyebrows and fake nose and mustache all bobbed up and down as Danny nodded. He struck Riley as a peculiarly serious and dour man to be wearing such a getup.

McCune pulled out one photo and held it for the shop owner to see.

Danny peered at the photo through his glasses.

He said, "She's not one of our regular customers. I can't guarantee that she's never been in the shop, but I don't recognize her."

"You're sure?" McCune asked.

"Quite positive."

"Does the name Margo Birch mean anything to you?"

"Uh, maybe something in the news. I'm not sure."

McCune pulled out another photo. "What about this woman? We believe she came to your establishment to take pictures."

Riley, too, looked closely at the photograph. This must be Janet Davis. It was the first time she'd seen her living, unpainted face— smiling and happy and unaware of the terrible fate that awaited her.

"Oh, yes," Casal said. "She was in here not long ago. Janet something."

"Davis," Crivaro said.

"That's right," Casal said with a nod. "A nice lady. A nice camera too—I'm something of a photography buff myself. She offered to pay me to let her take pictures here, but I wouldn't accept. I was flattered that she found my establishment worthy of her efforts."

Casal tilted his head and looked at his visitors.

"But I don't suppose you're here with good news about her," he said. "Is she in some kind of trouble?"

Crivaro said, "I'm afraid she was murdered. Both of these women were."

"Really?" Casal said. "When?"

"Margo Birch was found dead five days ago. Janet Davis was murdered the night before last."

"Oh," Casal said. "I'm sorry to hear that."

Riley barely noticed any change in his tone of voice or facial expression

McCune changed tactics. He asked, "Do you sell clown costumes here?"

"Of course," Casal said. "Why do you ask?"

McCune abruptly took another photo out of his folder. Riley almost gasped when she got a look at it.

It showed another dead woman dressed in a clown costume. She was splayed on concrete next to an alley dumpster. The costume was similar to the one that Janet Davis, the victim found in the park this morning, had worn—puffy fabric with huge pompom buttons. But the colors and patterns were somewhat different, and so was the makeup.

Margo Birch, Riley realized. *The way she was found.*

McCune asked Casal, "Do you sell costumes like this one?"

Riley noticed that Crivaro was scowling at McCune. McCune was obviously testing Casal's response to the photo, but Crivaro seemed to disapprove of his blunt approach.

But like McCune, Riley was curious as to how the man was going to react.

Casal turned to look at Riley. She simply couldn't read his expression. In addition to the bushy eyebrows and mustache, she could now see how really thick the lenses were. Although he was surely making eye contact with her, it didn't look like it. Refracted through the lenses, his eyes appeared to be directed slightly elsewhere.

It's like he's wearing a mask, Riley thought.

"Is this Ms. Davis?" Casal asked Riley.

Riley shook her head and said, "No. But Janet Davis's body was found in a similar condition this morning."

Still with no change in his tone of voice, Casal said to McCune

…

"In answer to your question—yes, we do sell this sort of costume."

He led his visitors over to a long rack full of clown costumes. Riley was startled at how varied they were.

As Casal browsed among some tattered jackets and baggy, patched up pants, he said, "As you can see, there are several different types of clowns. For example, there's the 'tramp' here, often personified as a hobo or a vagabond, with a worn-out hat and shoes, sooty sunburned makeup, a sad frown, and a painted stubble of beard. The female equivalent is often a bag lady."

He moved on to group of more motley costumes.

"Somewhat related to the tramp is the 'Auguste,' a traditional European type, more of a trickster than a vagabond, an underling and a flunky. He wears a red nose and mismatched clothes and alternates between inept clumsiness and agile cunning."

Then he shuffled through some costumes that seemed to be mostly white, some of them spangled and with colored trim.

He said, "And here we have the traditional European whiteface, the 'Pierrot'—composed, poised, graceful, intelligent, always in control. His makeup is simple—completely white, with regular features painted in red or black, like a mime, and he often wears a conical hat. He's an authority figure, often Auguste's boss—and not a very nice boss. Small wonder, though, since many of Auguste's jokes are at his expense."

He moved through dozens of wildly different costumes, saying

…

"Now here we've got lots of different 'character' clowns, based on types familiar from everyday life—cops, maids, butlers, doctors, firemen, that kind of thing. But here's the type you're looking for."

He showed his visitors a row of brightly colored costumes that definitely reminded Riley of the victims in the picture and the field.

"This is the 'grotesque whiteface,'" he said.

That word caught Riley's attention.

Grotesque.

Yes, that certainly described what had been done to Janet

Davis's body.

Fingering one of the outfits, Casal continued, "This is the most common type of clown, I suppose, at least here in America. It doesn't reflect any particular type or profession or status. The grotesque whiteface is just generally clownish-looking, ridiculous and silly. Think Bozo the Clown, or Ronald McDonald—or Stephen King's 'It,' to cite a scarier example. The grotesque typically wears a baggy colorful costume, outsized shoes, and white makeup with exaggerated features, including a huge wig and a bright red nose."

Crivaro seemed to be genuinely interested in what Casal was now saying.

He asked, "Have you sold any of these grotesque-type costumes lately?"

Casal thought for a moment.

"Not that I remember—not at least during the last few months," he said. "I could look through our receipts, but that might take a while."

Crivaro handed him his FBI card and said, "I'd appreciate if you'd do that and get back to me."

"I'll do that," Casal said. "But remember, the grotesque costume is extremely common. It might have been bought at any costume shop anywhere in the city."

McCune smirked a little and said, "Yeah, but this isn't just *any* costume store. One of the victims was here pretty recently taking pictures."

His expression still inscrutable, Casal put his hands in his pockets and said, "Yes, I can understand why that might concern you."

Casal looked off into space for a moment, as if deep in thought.

Then his whole body seemed to jerk to attention.

"Oh, my," he said, finally sounding unsettled. "I just thought of something I think you'd better know."

CHAPTER TEN

Riley felt a surge of excitement as she and the two FBI agents followed Casal away from the costume rack.

Are we about to get a break? she wondered.

Without revealing what he'd just remembered, the store manager had whirled around and headed back to the front of the store.

When he reached the front desk, Casal stopped and began to explain.

"Janet Davis came back here a second day to take more pictures. But she left rather abruptly—and she wasn't at all happy."

Riley, Crivaro, and McCune exchanged interested glances.

"Why not?" Crivaro asked.

Casal opened a filing cabinet and thumbed through its contents.

"Well, she complained about a young man who was working here at the time—Gregory Wertz is his name. Apparently he'd said something improper to her. She wasn't specific, but she was quite upset about it, and it wasn't the first time a female customer complained about him. I'd also suspected him of stealing for some time, so I fired him on the spot."

Crivaro asked, "Can you give us his address?"

"Certainly," Casal said, taking a sheet of paper out of the drawer and handing it to Crivaro. "Here you go—his name, Social Security number, phone number, and address. Also, the last day he worked here—exactly two weeks ago today."

Crivaro thanked him for his cooperation, and Riley followed the two agents out of the store.

She was startled when, as soon as they were outside, Crivaro grabbed McCune by the shoulder.

"What do you think you were doing back there?" he asked angrily.

McCune looked surprised.

"You mean showing him that photo? I wanted to see his reaction, of course."

"It was a stunt," Crivaro said. "I don't like stunts."

McCune's face reddened with anger.

"A stunt, huh?" he said. "Are you telling me you trust that Casal guy? He seemed as suspicious as hell to me. Actually, he

55

gave me the creeps, the way he talked and all. He didn't even give us a good look at his face."

That's true, Riley thought.

But it really hadn't occurred to her to suspect Casal of anything.

Crivaro paced back and forth, barking at McCune.

"So you just thought you'd put the screws to him, huh? You decided to go for some kind of instant confession. Figured you'd get a lot of glory if you succeeded. Well, let me put your mind at ease about something. Casal's not our killer."

"How do you know?" McCune asked.

Crivaro rolled his eyes and said, "Didn't you get a good look at him? He's blind as a bat without those glasses, and he's as skinny as a rail. Our killer abducted two women—at least one of them probably forcibly. Then he managed to subdue them. Can you imagine Casal pulling that off?"

Looking as embarrassed as angry now, McCune began, "Maybe with an accomplice—"

Crivaro interrupted, "There wasn't any accomplice. My every instinct tells me our killer acts alone. And he's sure as hell not Danny Casal. Casal's maybe an important witness, though. We're all just lucky you didn't spook him into not cooperating."

McCune hung his head and shuffled his feet.

Crivaro jabbed his finger at him.

"Now listen to me. No more stunts, not when you're working with me. If you get any ideas, talk to me about them first. This is not the Boy Scouts. Initiative is *not* a virtue right now. Either I call all the shots, or you can get off the case."

In a whisper, McCune said, "I hear you. It won't happen again."

"It sure as hell had better not," Crivaro growled.

A silence fell among the three of them.

Riley felt distinctly uncomfortable—and a little bit sorry for McCune.

She remembered what McCune had told her about Crivaro when they'd first met …

"He's got a reputation for being kind of brusque."

Brusque is a good word for it, Riley thought.

She'd gotten a good taste of his brusqueness yesterday when she'd screwed up at the drug house. When they'd met in Lanton, she hadn't found him to be quite that prickly. Of course, she'd also come to realize that now Crivaro had some reason to be like that

56

with her …

"I pulled a lot of strings to get you into this program," he'd said.

But she really hadn't expected him to lash out at a full-fledged FBI agent like McCune.

She wondered again what it was going to be like shadowing Crivaro. Was she going to feel like she was walking on eggshells the whole time?

Meanwhile, Crivaro had fallen silent and was looking over the sheet of paper that Casal had handed him.

Finally he said …

"This Gregory Wertz sounds interesting—especially the fact that something disagreeable happened between him and Janet Davis, not long before both of the murders. We don't have enough on him to get a warrant for his arrest. But I think we'd better pay him a visit."

Then he looked at both McCune and Riley and added …

"But I don't want any shenanigans from either one of you. Follow my orders—nothing more, nothing less. Do both of you hear me?"

Riley nodded, and so did McCune.

Crivaro then shared Gregory Wertz's address with McCune. McCune got into his own vehicle, and Riley and Crivaro returned to their car.

Crivaro drove them to another neighborhood much like the one they'd been in yesterday, rundown and with graffiti everywhere. But there were more people outdoors, including kids on skateboards. Gangs and drugs were likely a problem here too, but they hadn't completely terrorized everyone off the streets—at least not yet.

Riley wondered if maybe the kind of "mini station" that McCune had said was coming to the other neighborhood might be a good idea here also. It seemed a shame that nobody was likely to consider the possibility until things got much worse.

Crivaro parked the car, and McCune pulled into a space right behind them.

Crivaro turned to Riley. "You wait right here."

When the agents got out of their cars, the two of them stood talking about what to do next.

Riley could hardly believe what Crivaro had just said and done …

He's leaving me out completely.

How was she supposed to learn from the sidelines like this?

And why had Crivaro made this decision?

Just this morning things had seemed fine between them. Crivaro had even assured her that what she'd done yesterday hadn't been a total disaster. In fact, he told her she'd made it possible to round up more gang members.

So what had changed?

Maybe nothing, she thought.

Maybe he was simply concerned about her safety. If so, maybe she should feel grateful to him for keeping her out of danger.

At the same time, she couldn't help but wonder …

Is he still mad at me about yesterday?

*

As he walked with Crivaro toward the apartment building, Special Agent Mark McCune was still stinging from the scolding he'd gotten a little while ago. He still didn't get why Crivaro had reacted that way. And he still didn't think he'd been out of line putting some pressure on that Danny Casal character.

What harm did it do? he wondered. Casal had still come through with some information—if he wasn't flat-out lying. McCune still didn't trust the guy.

And he really didn't like being humiliated like that—especially in front of an intern like Riley Sweeney.

Like many others in the agency, McCune wondered …

What's Crivaro's thing with her, anyway?

He'd heard all the stories about how she'd helped stop that serial killer in Lanton. Word had it that Crivaro thought she was some sort of prodigy. He had certainly thrown his weight around to get her into the program, and he'd pissed some people off in the process.

There were also some rumors that maybe Crivaro had the hots for her.

McCune smirked at the idea. He didn't sense anything like that between Riley and Crivaro. For one thing, Crivaro had shown the good sense to leave her in the car while they checked out a possible suspect. Besides, Crivaro had a reputation for utmost integrity, and he didn't seem to McCune as the type to let himself get professionally distracted by an attractive young woman.

Not that I'd blame him.

McCune had noticed the first time he'd seen her that she was decidedly good-looking. He'd have been interested in her himself if he hadn't noticed she was wearing an engagement ring.

Of course, it could be that she was wearing it just to keep guys away.

In any case, he reminded himself …

Riley Sweeney is definitely off limits.

As they walked up the steps to the glass door of the apartment building, McCune reminded himself to get his head in the game. The suspect they hoped to interview might or might not be dangerous.

Crivaro looked over the list of buzzers until he found the right name and apartment, then pushed the button.

When someone answered over the intercom, Crivaro asked, "Is this Gregory Wertz?"

"Who's asking?" the man asked.

Crivaro exchanged a meaningful glance with McCune.

Then he said into the intercom, "We're Special Agents McCune and Crivaro, FBI. We'd just like to ask you a few questions."

A silence fell.

"What's this about?" the voice asked.

Crivaro said, "We'd like to discuss it face to face."

McCune heard a low growl over the intercom, and then …

"OK, come on up."

The door buzzed, and McCune and Crivaro entered the building. The front hallway was seedy, and a sour odor of mildew and mold hung in the air. They made their way up the stairs to the first floor, where they found Wertz's apartment.

Crivaro rapped sharply on the door.

A voice called out, "Come on in."

McCune looked at Crivaro and nodded down inquisitively to his holstered weapon.

Crivaro shook his head and whispered, "Just be ready."

Crivaro turned the doorknob, and a filthy and chaotic apartment came into view. Standing facing them just a few feet away was a muscular African-American man with his hair in dreadlocks. He was wearing a T-shirt and jeans and sneakers, and he had his hands in his pockets.

Nothing in his body language suggested any danger to McCune. The guy just seemed to be trying to make his visitors feel unwelcome.

He's succeeding at that, McCune thought.

59

But McCune sensed that Crivaro had abruptly tensed up, as if on high alert.

McCune wondered …

Does Crivaro know something I don't?

Gregory Wertz said, "What do you want?"

Crivaro said, "We'd like to know what you were doing on Sunday night and all during Monday."

A smirk crossed Wertz's face.

"I don't exactly recall," he said.

Crivaro added, "What about Friday and Saturday?"

Wertz let out a low chuckle and glanced around the apartment.

He said in a sarcastic tone, "As you see, I'm kind of a busy guy, so I couldn't tell you for sure. You'll have to ask my personal assistant. She's off today. Maybe you should come back when she's here. Not sure when that'll be, though."

McCune could think of a half-dozen questions he wanted to ask, but he remembered what Crivaro had said.

"Follow my orders—nothing more, nothing less."

McCune figured he'd better let Crivaro take the lead.

Crivaro said, "We understand you recently worked for Danny Casal at a store called Costume Romp."

Wertz's smirk broadened.

"Yeah. It didn't exactly work out."

"What happened?" Crivaro asked.

"I quit. Danny was a paranoid asshole. He kept accusing me of a lot of things I didn't do."

McCune wondered if maybe the man was telling the simple truth.

If so, had Danny Casal deliberately sent them up a blind alley?

Wertz said, "I take it you talked to Danny about me. What the hell did he say, the lying bastard?"

McCune could see that Crivaro had locked eyes with Wertz.

Instead of answering his question, Crivaro said …

"Does the name Margo Birch mean anything to you?"

Wertz shrugged a little.

"I can't say it does."

"What about Janet Davis?" Crivaro asked.

"I don't believe I've made the lady's acquaintance. Why do you ask?"

McCune noticed that a change was coming over Wertz. He seemed to be growing more anxious and nervous under Crivaro's steady gaze.

Crivaro took a small step toward him.

"Nice little place you've got here. Maybe you'd like us to sit down, make ourselves at home."

"I don't think so," Wertz said, frowning.

"Why not?"

"Do you have a warrant?" Wertz asked.

Crivaro let out a little grunt of mock incomprehension.

"Why would we? This is just a friendly visit."

Wertz stood and stared at him, his teeth clenched. His hands were still in his pockets.

Crivaro said, "Why are you asking about a warrant? I don't remember saying we were here to search for anything. Do you remember saying anything like that, McCune?"

McCune silently shook his head, wondering where this was going.

Crivaro took another small step toward him.

"Are you hiding something, Mr. Wertz?" he asked. "Should we get a warrant?"

Wertz took a step back.

"Don't come any closer," he said.

"Why not?" Crivaro said, taking another step. "I'm not looking for trouble."

Wertz took his hands out of his pockets and held them at his sides. Then he made a gesture with his right hand.

In what seemed like a split-second, Crivaro had drawn his pistol and was pointing it straight at Wertz.

Without any change in his tone of voice, Crivaro said …

"We can do this the easy way or the hard way, Mr. Wertz."

CHAPTER ELEVEN

McCune stared with his mouth hanging open, unsure what to do.

What the hell does Crivaro think he's doing? he wondered.

Crivaro was holding his pistol perfectly steady. It was pointed at Wertz, who seemed to waver indecisively for a moment.

The man hadn't posed any threat that McCune could see. He sure hoped Crivaro wasn't going to open fire for no reason at all.

Then Wertz raised his hands slowly.

Crivaro grunted. "You heard what I said. Easy or hard. Just turn around. That's all I want."

With a growl of dismay, Wertz turned slowly around.

Now McCune could see the revolver tucked under the man's belt in back. Just a few moments ago, Wertz had taken his hands out of his pockets, then gestured with his right hand.

Now McCune understood …

He was going to draw his weapon.

Crivaro had sensed this and reacted with lightning speed, drawing his own gun first.

And it was a good thing, too. If Crivaro's reflexes hadn't been so sharp, one or both of them might be dead now.

Crivaro nodded toward McCune and said, "Perhaps you'd be so kind as to relieve him of that gun."

McCune walked toward Wertz and took the gun out of the belt. He set it down on the floor.

"On your knees, hands behind you," Crivaro said to Wertz.

As Wertz obeyed, Crivaro asked him …

"Is there anybody else in the apartment?"

Wertz shook his head silently.

"I didn't hear you," Crivaro barked.

"No," Wertz said.

Crivaro got out his handcuffs and said to McCune …

"He's probably telling the truth. But you'd better have a look around."

McCune heard Crivaro reading Wertz his rights as he walked on into the small apartment. He looked into a messy bedroom with a closet door standing wide open, and saw no one. He found no one in the bathroom either, nor in a hallway closet.

Then McCune stepped into the kitchen, the only room he hadn't checked yet. Right there on the Formica table, he saw five rubber masks, the kind that pulled all the way over the head. McCune recognized the faces from Universal monster movies—the Mummy, the Creature from the Black Lagoon, Karloff's Frankenstein monster, Lugosi's Dracula, and the Wolf Man.

Casal had definitely been telling the truth about Wertz stealing.

And now McCune had no reason to doubt that Casal was also telling the truth about Wertz's confrontation with one of the murder victims.

We've caught our guy, he thought with satisfaction.

Meanwhile, he knew better than to even touch the masks.

He walked back into the living room, where Wertz was now safely cuffed and kneeling.

McCune said to Crivaro, "You'd better have a look in the kitchen." He drew his own weapon.

Crivaro nodded and went to check that out.

McCune stood guard over Wertz until Crivaro came back and said, "We'd better get a forensics team over here to conduct a proper search. We won't have any trouble getting a warrant at this point."

As McCune holstered his weapon, he noticed the prisoner's dark scowl.

"Let's get this guy to headquarters," he said.

*

Riley was still waiting impatiently in the car when she saw Crivaro and McCune emerge from the apartment building. They were escorting a handcuffed man wearing dreadlocks.

That must be Wertz, she realized.

The man looked muscular and dangerous and angry.

Surprised, Riley got out of the car. She remembered Crivaro saying they didn't have enough evidence to arrest this man. But they were obviously doing exactly that.

Crivaro glanced over at her with a scowl and snapped …

"Get back in the car."

At that moment, the prisoner slammed to one side, knocking McCune off balance. He reached both hands toward Crivaro's holstered gun.

But Crivaro was too fast. He grabbed the attacker's hands and threw him to the ground.

63

Then both agents had their guns out. Their prisoner got slowly to his feet, looking like the fight had been knocked out of him.

Riley was glad it was all over so quickly.

She realized that her own impulse had been to rush forward to stop the man, and she knew that had been a bad idea.

Her father had given her a single lesson in the ultra-aggressive Israeli fighting system Krav Maga during recent months, and she'd used it to fend off a male attacker. Otherwise, she'd had very little self-defense training. Besides, she was pregnant. Again she wondered ...

Maybe I shouldn't be doing fieldwork at all.

She got back into Jake's car and waited while the two agents put Wertz into McCune's vehicle, which she could see was equipped with a prisoner partition. They cuffed him in place.

Riley wondered if Crivaro would have allowed her anywhere near this situation if he knew she was pregnant. She felt a little guilty for never telling him about that.

But she remembered what Crivaro had said to her just yesterday about what the other interns would be doing ...

"... learning how to use filing cabinets and paper clips ..."

Of course Crivaro had been making the usual intern activities sound a lot more boring than they really were. Surely there were plenty of exciting things to learn about crime data, lab work, forensics, and such. But just this morning, Riley had gotten a taste of what it might be like to work on a murder case.

When the suspect was secured in McCune's vehicle, Crivaro came over and got into the driver's seat beside Riley, giving her a stern and silent look.

As he started driving away, Crivaro tersely described what had just happened—that Gregory Wertz had greeted them with a weapon, and they had found a stash of masks apparently stolen from Costume Romp.

"Masks?" Riley asked.

"Yep. Five monster masks, like for Halloween."

"What do you suppose he wanted them for?" Riley asked.

"Beats me," Crivaro said. "But we've got him on possession of stolen goods, threatening two law enforcement officers with a deadly weapon, and resisting arrest. That's plenty to bring him in on. I've already called in a request for a warrant to search his apartment, and we'll get a forensics team there in just a little while. Meanwhile, we'll have to see what he has to say for himself under questioning. Maybe we'll get lucky and he'll give us a confession."

Riley was excited by the thought of an interrogation.

She said, "Agent Crivaro, can I—"

Crivaro interrupted, "Participate in questioning the guy? Not a chance. But you can stand outside the interrogation room and watch and listen. Maybe you'll learn something."

Riley was pleased. She really hadn't intended to ask for more than that.

They said little else during the rest of the drive to the J. Edgar Hoover Building. Just as Crivaro was pulling into a space in the parking garage, his phone rang.

He answered the phone as he and Riley got out of the car and walked toward McCune, who was leading the now docile handcuffed suspect toward an entrance into the building.

Crivaro stopped in his tracks as he talked, and so did Riley. Crivaro sounded annoyed with whoever he was talking to.

"You're kidding," he said. "Forget about it. I don't have time for it. Neither does McCune. And he interviewed the guy already. Can't you just tell him to go away? Uh, nicely?"

Crivaro scratched his head and listened for a moment.

Finally he said, "OK. I guess we'll manage it somehow."

He stared after McCune and the suspect, who were already passing through the door into the building.

Crivaro turned back to Riley.

"I've got a little job for you." he said.

"Me?" Riley said with surprise.

"Yes, I need you to take care of something."

Riley felt her excitement building.

Crivaro continued, "Janet Davis's husband just showed up here. He wants answers about what happened to his wife. McCune already visited him this morning, but neither of us can talk to him right now—we need to get right to work questioning this suspect. I need for you to take care of the husband."

"The husband of the … the victim? The victim we just saw this morning?"

"Yeah. He's down at the security gate in the front lobby. You can meet him there."

Riley's head buzzed with confusion.

"But what do I tell him? Who do I say *I* am?"

Crivaro shrugged.

"Tell him the truth, that you're an intern shadowing two agents who are working on the case. Otherwise, tell him as little as you can. You can tell him we've got a suspect in custody, but don't go into any details—and I mean no details at all. Whatever you do, don't get his hopes up. Tell him …"

Crivaro paused, then said, "Just tell him we'll get back to him as soon as we know more. Tell him … well, just try to get him go home and wait."

Crivaro let out a growl and added …

"I hate it when this happens. Such a goddamn distraction, a real waste of time. We've got to focus on catching the killer. On keeping anybody else from getting killed. Just take care of it with as little fuss as possible, OK? Show some compassion, but don't get carried away. It's really pretty simple. Do you think you can handle it?"

Riley nodded slowly.

"Great," Crivaro said. "His name's Gary, by the way. Gary Davis."

Crivaro walked away without another word.

Riley stood there for a moment, trying to process what had just happened.

She thought about what Crivaro had said …

"Such a goddamn distraction, a real waste of time."

Riley felt a twinge of resentment as she understood …

He just stuck me with a job he didn't want to do.

Meanwhile, Crivaro and McCune were going to be interrogating the suspect, and Riley would miss all of it.

But she swallowed down her irritation as she walked into the building and headed toward an elevator.

After all, what did she expect? As an intern, she was going to get stuck with unenviable tasks a lot of the time.

She took the elevator to the vast lobby and headed toward the security gate. She briefly wondered who she should ask to help her find Gary Davis.

But she quickly saw a young man with an unmistakably anguished expression, anxiously pacing back and forth.

Her heart jumped up in her throat as she realized …

That's him.

And the task she'd been given was going to be a lot harder than she'd expected.

CHAPTER TWELVE

Riley's anxiety mounted as she walked toward the husband of the murdered woman.

She stepped out through the security gate to join him, reminding herself of Crivaro's instruction …

"Show some compassion, but don't get carried away."

How was she going to manage that?

She asked him, "Are you Gary Davis?"

The man turned toward her and nodded.

She began, "I'm Riley Sweeney, and I'm …"

She gulped as she realized …

The last thing he wants to hear is that I'm a summer intern.

Instead she said, "I'm sorry for your loss."

The man looked confused now.

"What's going on?" he asked. "It's been driving me crazy, not knowing what's going on. Please tell me *something*."

Riley took a deep breath, trying to settle her own nerves.

Then she said, "The lead detective told me to come here and tell you—that they've got a suspect in custody."

Gary Davis's eyes widened.

"Who is he?" he said with a gasp. "How did they find him?"

Riley's heart jumped up in her throat.

She thought something else Crivaro had said …

"Don't go into any details—and I mean no details at all."

But how could she help it?

How could she *not* tell this grieving, desperate man what little she knew?

She sternly told herself …

Orders are orders.

She took a slow breath and said …

"I can't tell you that."

Davis looked completely aghast now.

"Why on earth not?" he asked.

Riley stammered, "I'm just … I'm not at liberty right now. But I promise …"

She stopped short in mid-sentence, wondering …

Promise him what?

She said the only thing she could think of saying …

"We're doing everything we can."

"Who is 'we'?"

Riley said, "Special Agent Mark McCune—the agent who came to see you earlier. And Special Agent Jake Crivaro. He's in charge of the investigation."

"And you?" Davis asked.

Riley gulped hard.

"I'm Riley Sweeney. I'm a summer intern and I'm working on this case."

Davis's look of frustration gave way to one of pure disbelief.

"An intern? I can't believe this. This isn't right. I demand to talk to one of the real agents. Right now. Right this minute."

"That's not possible," Riley said, surprised by the sudden stern firmness in her voice. "Agents McCune and Crivaro are both interrogating the suspect. Please believe me when I say we're all doing everything we can. And we'll let you know when we know anything—anything at all."

Riley hoped she was telling him the truth. But she really had no idea what to tell him to expect.

The anger and frustration faded from Davis's face, replaced by a look of terrible sadness.

"It's no use," he said, choking back a sob. "None of this matters. None of it is going to bring Janet back."

He turned slowly and started to walk away.

Riley knew she ought to feel relieved that her awful little task was done. Instead, questions swelled her mind.

She said, "Mr. Davis, wait a minute."

Davis turned and looked at her.

Riley said, "We understand that your wife took some pictures at a costume shop. She went there for a couple of days. But the owner says she was upset the last time she left. Did she happen to mention to you why?"

Davis squinted with thought.

"I think maybe so," he said. "Yes, a clerk there was rude to her. Actually, I think he kind of came on to her. She said she wasn't going back there again. But …"

Riley held her breath.

But what?

Davis shook his head.

"I wouldn't say she was especially upset about it—at least not by the time she got home. Really, she pretty much laughed it off. She was a very attractive woman. Things like that happened to her a lot, I'm sorry to say. She learned not to let it get to her. Why do you ask?"

Riley hesitated.

Should she tell him that the man who had offended her was the same man they now had in custody?

No details, she reminded herself. She'd probably said and asked too much already.

"Just trying to be thorough," she said, immediately realizing what a lame thing it was to say.

Without another word, Davis turned and walked out of the building.

Riley felt a surge of relief that the conversation was over. But she stood there for a moment, filled with vague uncertainties as she replayed his words about the incident between Janet and Gregory Wertz …

"I wouldn't say she was especially upset about it."

"Really, she pretty much laughed it off."

Riley wondered why those words were nagging at her.

Was it odd that Janet had "laughed off" a crude advance like that?

Maybe not, Riley thought.

After all, how could she have known that the man was going to kill her?

Still, something about what Davis had just said somehow troubled Riley.

But she couldn't figure out why. And anyway, it hardly seemed to matter right now. She remembered Crivaro telling her she could watch and listen to the interrogation. It must still be going on, but where?

She had no idea where in this vast building the interrogation might be taking place.

Riley sighed aloud with irritation. Again, she had the feeling that Crivaro had dumped her just to keep her away from really important matters.

But she wasn't going to let that happen—not if she could help it. She took out her cell phone and called Crivaro's number. She sighed again when she got his outgoing answering machine. At the sound of the beep, she said …

"Agent Crivaro, this is Riley. I'm done talking with the husband."

She paused for a moment, then said, "Where are you? What should I do now?"

She ended the call and paced nervously, wondering how long it would be before Crivaro called her back.

Long after the interrogation was over, maybe?

Or maybe even not at all?

Riley certainly felt unimportant and left out at the moment. Maybe it had completely slipped Crivaro's mind that there even was a summer intern who was supposed to be shadowing him right now.

Maybe the whole case would be solved while she was standing around waiting.

If so, why should she even bother waiting?

Maybe I should just catch the metro and go home, she thought, feeling thoroughly indecisive.

Then Riley realized that she was really hungry. She hadn't had anything to eat since she'd left her apartment that morning. Still grumbling to herself, she bought a package of crackers from a vending machine there in the lobby.

As soon as she started to open them, her phone buzzed. When she answered, she heard Crivaro's gruff voice.

"Third floor. Room 17B."

The call ended with an abrupt click. Riley stared at the phone for a moment. Crivaro certainly hadn't sounded the least bit welcoming, but at least he had told her where to go. She tucked the crackers in her purse, then went through the security gate again and took the elevator up to the third floor. She found the door she was looking for and knocked.

Crivaro opened the door, looking momentarily surprised to see her.

Then he said, "Oh, yeah. Riley. Come on in."

Riley joined Crivaro in a small room with a large pane of glass on one wall. Riley quickly realized the glass was a two-way mirror …

An interrogation room.

She'd stood looking through a mirror like this once before, back in Lanton.

Inside she saw Gregory Wertz, who was sitting handcuffed to a heavy gray table. Agent McCune was pacing silently back and forth in front of him.

Riley asked Crivaro quietly, "What's going on?"

"Not much," Crivaro growled, crossing his arms. "Wertz wants to lawyer up, of course. A public defender is on his way here right now. Meanwhile, Wertz isn't saying a whole lot. We're not likely to get a damn thing out of him."

Riley heard McCune's voice crackle over a speaker.

"What did you say to upset the woman?"

Wertz rolled his whole head and said, "What woman?"

McCune leaned across the table impatiently.

"The woman I keep asking about. Janet Davis. The woman who came into Costume Romp to take pictures. The woman who left because of something you said to her. The woman who showed up dead yesterday morning. Just like Margo Birch wound up dead on Saturday."

Wertz said, "I don't remember either of those names."

McCune stood staring at the suspect for a long moment. Finally he said, "What about the masks?"

"What masks?" Wertz said.

"The masks in your kitchen."

"I don't remember any masks."

McCune leaned closer and said, "I'm talking about the masks you stole from Costume Romp."

"I didn't steal any masks from anybody."

It was a lie, of course. Riley could see it in the man's face.

But something else was tugging at her consciousness—something about the masks.

She remembered Crivaro mentioning them during the drive here ...

"Five monster masks, like for Halloween."

What did those masks have to do with the murders of two women?

McCune said to Wertz, "Mr. Casal said you were stealing from his store."

"Casal's a lying bastard," Wertz said. "I didn't steal anything. I bought the masks from him at an employee discount."

"OK, then," McCune said. "Why did you want those masks, anyway?"

Wertz only shrugged.

Riley felt a strange, unexpected tingle all over.

She wasn't sure what that feeling meant, but she turned to Crivaro and said ...

"That's the wrong question."

Crivaro looked at her. "Huh?"

"Agent McCune asked why Wertz wanted the masks. It's the wrong question."

Crivaro held Riley's gaze.

"What do you mean, it's the wrong question?" he asked.

Riley felt briefly intimidated by Crivaro sharp tone of voice.

And the truth was, she really wasn't at all sure what she meant. Still, that tingling persisted.

She said, "He's not going to answer that. McCune should ask him—*who* the masks are for."

Crivaro squinted hard at her.

Does he think I'm crazy?

She wasn't sure she could blame him if he did. She couldn't think of a single rational reason for what she'd just said—just an irresistible gut feeling.

Then Crivaro spoke into an intercom connected with the interrogation room.

"McCune, I want a word with you."

McCune turned toward the mirror, looking a little displeased by the interruption. Then he exited the room and came out into the booth.

"What?" he asked Crivaro.

Crivaro stared through the window at Wertz for a moment. Wertz was leaning back in his chair, looking unfazed and sure of himself.

Finally Crivaro said to McCune …

"Go in there and ask him *who* the masks were for."

"Why?" McCune asked.

Crivaro grunted slightly, then said …

"Just humor me."

McCune glanced at Riley suspiciously, as if he'd guessed that this was her idea. Then he shrugged and went back into the interrogation room. He stood square in front of the table and asked Wertz …

"Who did you steal the masks for?"

Wertz's eyes widened and he sat bolt upright, looking very anxious.

CHAPTER THIRTEEN

Riley felt a slight thrill as she watched Wertz closely.

I've stumbled onto something, she thought.

She wished she had some idea of what it might be.

"Huh?" Wertz asked.

"You heard me," McCune said. "Who were the masks for?"

Just moments ago, Wertz had seemed calm and self-confident. Now he suddenly looked very anxious.

"When's my lawyer going to get here?" he said.

"Soon," McCune said. "Meanwhile, what's the harm of talking to me? I mean, if you've got nothing to hide?"

Wertz shook his head nervously.

"No way," he said. "I don't have anything else to say to you. Not one word."

Wertz turned his head away from McCune, keeping completely silent as McCune repeated the question over and over again. The suspect was obviously upset and defensive.

Riley studied Crivaro's reactions as he watched and listened. His mouth hung slightly open, and he seemed fascinated by what was happening—or perhaps by what wasn't happening.

Suddenly, the door to the small room opened, and a short, hunched-over man carrying a briefcase charged in from the hall.

"What's going on here?" he asked.

Before Crivaro could say a word, the man looked through the two-way mirror and saw what was happening in the interrogation room.

He shook his head and grumbled, "Jesus, you scavengers don't waste any time, do you? Get your man out of there right now. My client isn't going to say another word."

Looking thoroughly annoyed, Crivaro said into the intercom, "That's all for now, McCune. Come on out."

McCune looked toward the window with surprise, then came out into the smaller room.

His eyes darting back and forth from Riley to McCune to Crivaro, the small man asked, "OK, who are you people? I know that you're FBI. But I want names."

Crivaro introduced himself and McCune, and also Riley.

The man said, "I'm Lewis Gelb, Wertz's public defender.

73

Forgive me for not shaking hands. I'm sure you understand that ours is an adversarial relationship."

Crivaro nodded and said, "We were expecting you."

Gelb let out a snort of disgust.

"Yeah, I'll bet you were. And you worked fast violating my client's rights as much as you could before I could get here."

McCune snapped, "Relax, he knows his rights. He demanded a lawyer, didn't he? You can't blame us for asking questions while he was waiting. It's our job. Anyway, he hasn't said anything useful."

Gelb said, "I'll make sure of that. Well, your tomfooleries are over. Get out of here right now. I've got to confer with my client."

Gelb reached over and turned off the switch to the intercom, then went on into the interrogation room. Riley could see him open his briefcase and start talking to Wertz, but she couldn't hear a word of what either of them was saying.

Crivaro growled, "You heard what he said. We're through here."

Crivaro, McCune, and Riley went out into the hall, where they stood looking at each other uncertainly.

"Damn lawyers," McCune said. "If I'd just had a few more minutes—"

Crivaro interrupted him, "He wasn't going to tell you anything. At least nothing we wanted to know."

"What makes you think that?" McCune asked.

Crivaro didn't reply, just looked thoughtfully back at the door to the interrogation room. Riley sensed that there were wheels turning in his mind—and it had something to do with the question she'd suggested ...

"Who are the masks for?"

The question had seemed to catch the suspect off guard.

But why? Riley wondered.

Crivaro finally said ...

"The day isn't over and we've still got work to do."

Then he turned directly toward Riley and asked ...

"Any suggestions as to what we do next, Sweeney?"

Riley gulped and her eyes widened.

He's asking me?

She could see that McCune looked surprised too—and not at all pleased.

She thought hard for a few seconds, then asked ...

"What about the family of the first victim? I take it the local police have already talked to them. Shouldn't we talk to them too?"

Crivaro half-smiled at her, as if he'd been thinking the same thing.

"Sounds like a plan," Crivaro said. "Let's get going."

As she followed Crivaro and McCune toward the parking garage, Riley felt puzzled by Crivaro's sudden display of confidence in her judgment.

Meanwhile, McCune kept glancing back at her with a frown.

He's not very happy with me, she thought.

Riley felt sure that he'd realized the question about the masks was her idea. And now Crivaro had just asked her—and not him—for ideas on what to do next. She wasn't surprised at his annoyance.

But she worried …

How bad are things going to get between us?

Now was no time for petty rivalries—especially if they hadn't yet caught the killer.

She didn't know why, but her instincts were telling her that Wertz wasn't that man.

She also sensed that Crivaro felt the same way.

*

As Crivaro drove north through Washington, McCune sat in the front passenger seat and Riley in back. McCune got on his cell phone and called the first victim's family to let them know they were on the way.

When McCune ended the call, he said …

"They're expecting us. But I've got a feeling we're not in for a warm welcome. They sounded pretty upset."

Riley could well understand why, especially after her troubling encounter with Gary Davis, the second victim's husband, and how he'd said …

"It's been driving me crazy, not knowing what's going on."

Riley didn't see any reason why Margo Birch's family should feel any differently.

McCune opened his manila file and flipped through some papers. He filled both Riley and Crivaro in about the people they were about to meet. Margo Birch had lived with her parents in Witmer Grove, Maryland, while taking a bus into DC daily to go to college. Margo's parents, Lewis and Roberta, hadn't even known that anything had happened to their daughter—not until the horrifying moment when DC police arrived at their door with a picture ID that they'd found on Margo's body.

The police had interviewed the couple then and there. Then the officers had taken the parents to the DC morgue to identify the body. No law enforcement officers had talked to them since. Now that the FBI was on the case, interviewing them was definitely a priority.

During the rest of the drive, Riley listened to the two agents trying to brainstorm about the case. Both of the victims' bodies had been found in DC's Northwest quadrant. Janet Davis had lived in that area, and Margo's home was just across the DC line in Maryland.

Were there any other connections between the two victims? So far, no one had found any. Crivaro and McCune couldn't think of any, either. The two women didn't even look alike. So why had the murderer singled them out as victims?

Crivaro grumbled, "There's so damn much we don't know. We don't even know when or how Margo was abducted."

Riley's mind drifted as the conversation between Crivaro and McCune meandered vainly on. She remembered again how Gary Davis had said that his wife had "laughed off" Gregory Wertz's crude advances.

It didn't sound as though Janet Davis had sensed any danger from Wertz.

And what were Riley's own impressions of the man she had seen on the other side of that two-way mirror?

Riley pictured again that dark face framed by dreadlocks. And his voice as well—so smug and self-confident at first, then alarmed and defensive when asked *who* the masks were for.

She hadn't trusted that face and voice, and sensed that he was definitely a criminal.

But were those the face and voice of a murderer?

Deep down inside, she didn't think so.

Meanwhile, she remembered the crackers in her purse. She knew that Crivaro hadn't had anything to eat all day either, and the same was probably true of McCune. Neither of the agents seemed in the mood to stop anywhere for food, so Riley offered to share her crackers with them, and they accepted right away. She kept a couple crackers for herself and handed over the rest, wishing she'd bought more than one package.

Evening was setting in by the time they pulled into the sleepy working-class neighborhood where the Birches lived.

Crivaro parked in front of a little brick house with a small yard and immaculate hedges.

As soon as they got out of the car, a stout, middle-aged woman rushed out the front door and down the sidewalk toward them, weeping and screaming with rage.

"How dare you not tell us the truth!" she cried. "How dare you!"

Riley's heart jumped up into her throat as she wondered ...

What have we just walked into?

CHAPTER FOURTEEN

Exchanging perplexed looks, Crivaro and McCune took out their badges and tried their best to introduce themselves as the woman ranted on.

"Was this some kind of a joke, letting us find out like that? How dare you!"

Riley realized that the woman must be Roberta Birch, Margo's mother.

She remembered what McCune said after talking to the Margo's parents on the phone ...

"I've got a feeling we're not in for a warm welcome. They sound pretty upset."

Riley had expected grief and even anger, but not this kind of raging, incomprehensible hysteria.

After all, the police had already informed the couple of their daughter's death. They'd even gone to the morgue to identify her body.

But Roberta Birch was acting almost like she'd just now learned the truth.

A heavyset, balding man had also come out of the house— Margo's father, Lewis, Riley was sure. He took hold of his wife and tried to calm her down.

"Darling, don't be like this. They're here to help."

"Like hell!" Roberta screamed at him. "What kind of sick game are they playing with us?"

Lewis put his arms around his wife, whose screaming subsided into bitter sobbing.

"She was our only child," she whimpered. "She was all we had."

Riley's heart sank at the sadness of those words.

Lewis led his wife into the house, turning around toward the three visitors and saying ...

"Please. Come on in."

Riley, Crivaro, and McCune followed the couple into the cozy little living room. Lewis took his wife into a bedroom and came out and shut the door. Riley could still hear the woman crying.

Crivaro was now able to properly introduce himself and McCune and Riley.

Lewis nodded and suggested that they all sit down. He was visibly upset himself. His hands were shaking and his face was red.

In a trembling voice he said to the three visitors …

"I want you to know, I'm angry too. I don't understand why we weren't told."

In a gentle voice Crivaro said, "I'm sorry, sir. I'm not sure I understand."

Lewis said, "We had no idea that our daughter's death had anything to do with a serial killer."

Crivaro said, "I understand how you feel. But the other victim hadn't yet been found. When the local police came to talk to you, they didn't know—"

Lewis interrupted, "And we weren't told—the other thing either."

Crivaro fell silent. Riley sensed that he didn't know what to say. She hoped that Lewis would explain.

Lewis took a long, slow breath, then said …

"When we went to the morgue, Margo was … she was naked lying under a sheet and her face … well, she looked pale and unnatural but Roberta and I thought that was just because …"

Lewis choked back a sob and fell silent.

Riley could hear Crivaro let out a sigh of realization. She, too, now understood what this was all about.

The ME had already removed the clown makeup from Margo's face when Lewis and Roberta identified her body. They'd had no idea that their daughter had been found wearing a clown costume and makeup. Not until …

How had they found out? she wondered.

Finally Lewis said …

"We had to find out about it on the TV news. The 'Clown Killer,' they're calling him. Why weren't we at least told about how she'd been … ?"

Lewis fell silent again.

Riley could see Crivaro hunch down in his chair uncomfortably. She could guess the answer to Lewis's unfinished question.

She also understood why Crivaro didn't want to say it.

She remembered this morning at the murder scene, how annoyed one of cops had been when reporters showed up and saw the woman's body …

"We'd managed to keep the clown angle about the other murder quiet until now."

The cops who had interviewed the Birches earlier hadn't wanted them to know about that. They'd still been trying to keep it a secret because they knew the media would go crazy with a thing like that. So they'd said nothing about it. But the secret had been out since this morning—and the Birches had found out the truth in the worst possible way.

Crivaro said slowly, "I'm sorry. It wasn't our call. It wasn't our case then."

For a moment, Lewis said nothing in reply, just stared at Crivaro with a stricken expression. Then he spoke quietly. "She never liked clowns. She was afraid of them. That just made it …"

Riley almost gasped aloud. What would it be like to know you were made to look like a thing you feared? Because the reports said that the victims had been alive when the makeup and costumes were put on them.

Lewis fell silent again, staring down at his clenched hands.

Riley found herself wondering what kind of a "call" Crivaro would have made if he'd been the first to talk to the couple instead of the local cops.

Would he have told them the truth about the makeup and the costume?

Would that have made this any easier for them, or even more of a nightmare?

Would he have trusted them to keep quiet about it?

And for that matter …

What would have been my own "call" if it had been up to me?

She really had no idea. But she knew it could be one of the countless dilemmas she would surely face if she went into law enforcement. It was a daunting thought.

As Crivaro continued to talk to Lewis Birch, Riley heard gentleness in his voice she hadn't noticed from him before.

"Mr. Birch, I hope you'll understand that I've got to ask you some questions that you've been asked already. Your daughter's murder case has entered a new and very unexpected phase. We've got to look at everything in a new light."

Lewis nodded.

Crivaro said, "When did you first notice that your daughter was missing?"

Lewis shrugged slightly.

"Margo was at home Thursday night, we all had dinner together. My wife and I went to bed and Margo stayed up to study. The next morning we just guessed she'd left earlier than usual for school. We started to worry when she didn't she come home that afternoon, and she didn't call to tell us why. She wasn't home by suppertime, and we got really worried, so we called the police. They told us it was too soon to file a missing person report. We couldn't sleep all night."

His face twisted with anguish as he added …

"Then the police came to our door the next morning—with her photo ID …"

He fell silent.

Indicating Riley, Crivaro said to him, "Would it be all right for our young intern here to have a look around your place?"

Lewis nodded.

For a moment, Riley wondered …

What does Crivaro want me to do?

Did he expect her to look for something specific? Or was he just trying to get her out of the way?

She wished she had some idea.

Riley got up from her chair and walked on into the little house. She looked inside a spotless, charmingly decorated kitchen. Then she stopped in the hallway outside the door to the parents' bedroom. She could still hear Roberta Birch sobbing in there.

Should I go in and talk to her?

She shuddered as she remembered her painful encounter with Janet Davis's husband.

She didn't think she could do anything like that right now.

And besides, it surely wasn't what Crivaro had in mind for her to do.

But what *did* he want her to do?

As she stood indecisively in the hall, she could hear Crivaro asking Lewis whether he knew of any connection between his daughter and the other victim. Riley turned toward a door on the opposite side of the hall and opened it.

It led into what was obviously Margo's bedroom. It was small and cozy, like everything else in the house. Riley felt a tightness in her throat as she remembered what Roberta had said through her tears …

"She was our only child. She was all we had."

This was definitely the bedroom of an only child—not spoiled, but deeply treasured by her parents, and well-liked by everyone she knew. Most of all, Riley could tell that Margo had been happy here.

The walls were hung with countless framed pictures of her at every age since she'd been a toddler—photos taken with friends, relatives, and most of all, with her parents.

The shelves were filled with a young lifetime of books, ranging from picture books and early readers to grown-up novels. It didn't look like Margo had ever thrown away a book in her life.

Every piece of furniture was piled high with memorabilia— figurines, diplomas, awards, and souvenirs from all kinds of family vacations. And there must have been dozens of plush animals— bunnies, sheep, giraffes, tigers, and more teddy bears than Riley could count. Crowded among the animals on a chest of drawers was a yellow rubber duck, the kind of toy a toddler might play with in a bathtub.

Riley felt a strange new emotion as she moved through the room, taking everything in. She couldn't put her finger on what the feeling was.

Envy? she wondered.

How could she possibly envy a young woman who had been brutally murdered?

And yet Riley couldn't help but realize—she'd never had a bedroom like this in her own difficult life. Wouldn't it have been wonderful to have a refuge like this, a place to escape life's troubles and anxieties?

And wouldn't it have been wonderful to have such unconditionally loving parents, so many close friends, so many joys and comforts?

But Riley shuddered deeply as she thought of Margo's fate— forcibly abducted, grotesquely dressed and made up, her mind and heart racing uncontrollably on amphetamines, and finally literally frightened to death.

All the love and protection Margo had received during her life had made no difference in the end.

It seemed heartbreakingly, cruelly unfair, and Riley found herself wondering …

Is no one really safe?

Riley tried to shake off her sickening horror. She reminded herself that she had work to do—although she still didn't understand exactly what it was.

She looked around and noticed that the blind was drawn over the room's one window.

She walked over to the window and raised the blind.

She found herself looking out over a small, perfectly kept backyard. Twilight was falling, but she could still see everything clearly. In the middle of the yard stood a sturdy old tree. A swing hung from one of its branches.

The swing had surely been there for many years, for as long as Margo had been big enough to enjoy it.

Riley felt strangely drawn to that swing. She decided to go out and look at it more closely.

She went back into the hallway and overheard Crivaro asking Lewis Birch whether Margo had mentioned any unpleasant or alarming encounters recently. Riley could tell from Crivaro's slightly tired, discouraged tone of voice that the interview wasn't proving to be very helpful.

Riley also noticed that the sobbing in the other bedroom had stopped. Perhaps Roberta Birch had cried herself to sleep.

Riley walked through the kitchen and found the back door.

As she reached for the doorknob, she briefly wondered …

Should I ask if it's OK for me to go out there?

She remembered Crivaro clearly asking Lewis Birch …

"Would it be all right for our young intern here to have a look around your place?"

Surely "your place" included the backyard.

Riley turned the doorknob and went outside.

The backyard was startlingly pleasant—the air fresh and cool, the entire neighborhood quiet.

It looked like a perfect place for a child to play with neighbor friends. Riley wondered—how often had Margo continued to come out here, even after she'd grown to be a young woman?

She walked across the lawn to the swing and looked down at the ground under it.

Sure enough, the soil was bare and grassless, and she could see fresh heel marks.

Margo had never stopped sitting on this swing. She had doubtless spent many happy hours here, reminiscing about wonderful times.

Riley was feeling an impulse to sit down on the swing herself when her eye was drawn between some bushes in back of the yard. Beyond them, Riley could see between two houses all the way to the next street.

And for a moment, Riley thought she saw somebody standing between those houses—a shadowy man who seemed to be looking directly at her.

She quickly realized it was just her imagination.

But still the presence lingered, and Riley felt her skin tingling all over.

It's happening again, she thought.
She was getting a sense of the killer's mind.

CHAPTER FIFTEEN

Riley shivered deeply even after the shadowy image had faded away. She couldn't stop staring at the space between the two houses where she'd imagined the man to be.

She remembered when she'd felt connected to the murderer early that morning while looking at Janet Davis's body—the surge of cruelty and sadism she'd sensed as she'd imagined how he'd felt while killing her.

And now it was happening again.

No, she thought. *I can't handle it.*

She wanted to turn around and run back into the house.

Then she remembered something Crivaro had said during the drive here …

"There's so damn much we don't know. We don't even know when or how Margo was abducted."

Riley gulped hard as she realized …

Maybe I'm about to find out.

She walked between a pair of bushes in a row that separated the Birches' yard from the property behind it. Then she turned and took in the view the man might have had of the family's home and backyard.

It was all too easy to imagine.

It had been late at night, after Margo's parents had gone to bed.

After she'd finished studying, Margo had come out here to do what she often did—sit alone on this swing and listen to the crickets and enjoy the cool night air, all the while reminiscing about her happy childhood, and also dreaming of possibilities to come.

She'd been facing the house, of course …

And he was standing near here, looking at her from behind, unnoticed.

He hadn't just happened to be standing there by chance.

Riley sensed that he'd already targeted this young woman to be his first victim—although she had no clue to why he'd chosen her.

He'd been stalking her for a while.

Had she ever noticed him hovering nearby, studying her habits and movements?

Had she been frightened of him?

No, Riley thought.

She'd never even known he was around.

He's too stealthy for that.

He'd been stealthy enough to approach Margo right here, unawares, in her own backyard. He'd sneaked up directly behind her …

What then?

Riley remembered the blurred images of boats and docks from the last photo in Janet Davis's camera, which had obviously been knocked out of her hand at that very second.

He knocked Janet out, Riley thought.

Maybe he did the same with Margo.

She walked over to the swing and looked down again at the bare patch of ground under it. The soil was scraped a bit. But with her untrained eye, Riley couldn't tell whether that indicated any sign of a struggle.

Her sense of the killer's presence was fading now, becoming blurred like the last photograph Janet Davis had ever taken.

All she knew for sure was that she needed to talk to Crivaro—right now.

She hurried back into the house and straight to the living room. Crivaro, McCune, and Lewis Birch were all seated exactly as she had left them.

A bit breathlessly, Riley said …

"Agent Crivaro, I—I think I've got something to show you."

Crivaro and McCune got up from their chairs and followed her out of the house. Darkness was deepening now.

Riley pointed to the back yard swing. "I think Margo was abducted there—by a man who came between those houses."

McCune let out a grunt of skepticism.

"Have you got any solid reason for thinking that?" he asked.

Riley didn't reply. How would McCune react if she told him the truth—that she was simply following her gut?

Meanwhile, Crivaro crouched down beside the swing. He took a penlight out of his pocket and pointed it at the ground. After scanning the ground for a few moments, he said …

"McCune, Sweeney—come here and have a look."

Riley and McCune walked over and crouched beside him.

Crivaro shined the penlight to show them something Riley hadn't noticed before. A stretch of grass had been dug into, as if someone had dragged something away from the swing.

Not something, she thought. *Somebody. Margo Birch.*

Crivaro looked at McCune and said, "Sweeney's right. The girl was snatched right here."

Crivaro pointed toward the darkening space between the two houses.

"He must have carried her through there to a waiting vehicle."

McCune's mouth dropped open in amazement.

Crivaro got to his feet, and so did Riley and McCune.

Crivaro said, "McCune, I need for you to call forensics, tell them to get a team here right away to tape this place off. They'll need to check the area and then go over it again with a fine-toothed comb in the morning."

McCune immediately took out his cell phone to make the call. Crivaro went inside to inform Lewis Birch that a forensics team would be arriving in a few minutes.

McCune was still talking on the phone when Crivaro came back outside.

He said to Riley …

"Now I want you to talk me through exactly what you experienced just now."

Riley told him everything, starting with when she'd been in the bedroom and had noticed the swing through the bedroom window, then her growing sense of the killer's presence as she came outside.

Crivaro seemed to be deep in thought by the time she finished. He didn't say a word to her. Riley wished he'd say something …

"Good work" might be nice.

Meanwhile, McCune ended his phone call and walked toward them.

"The forensics guys will be here shortly. I've got some news about their search of Gregory Wertz's apartment. They found something tucked under the refrigerator—a blueprint of a bank and some hand-scrawled notes. The man was planning an armed robbery."

"Holy smoke," Crivaro said.

"It gets better," McCune said. "There was also a list of names and phone numbers—four names in all."

"Accomplices," Crivaro said, stroking his chin. "So that's what the five stolen monster masks were for. Wertz and his gang were going to use them for disguises for the robbery."

Suddenly, things started becoming clearer to Riley—things that had been puzzling her since her talk with Janet Davis's husband and the interrogation of Gregory Wertz.

She remembered how confident Wertz had been until that very moment when McCune had asked the question Riley herself had suggested.

"Who did you steal the masks for?"

Right then Wertz had become agitated and anxious.

And for good reason.

Until that moment, McCune had been questioning the suspect about two murders he'd known nothing about. But as soon as McCune asked that question, Wertz was afraid McCune had figured out his plans for a robbery.

Riley also understood why Janet Davis had "laughed off" Wertz's coarse advances.

She hadn't been afraid of him.

She'd had no reason to be afraid of him.

Or at least that was things now seemed to Riley.

She was surprised when McCune said …

"So Wertz is guilty after all."

"Maybe," Crivaro said.

Riley hesitated for a moment, worrying about whether she was about to ask a stupid question.

Then she said, "I'm not sure I get it. We know that Wertz is guilty of planning a robbery. How does that make him guilty of the two murders as well?"

McCune scowled at her and said, "We know he's a *criminal.* That seriously increases the likelihood that he committed the murders. Actually, it pretty well cinches it in my book. I'm sure we didn't stumble across him just by accident."

Riley was really startled now. Her instincts were telling her just the opposite of what McCune was saying.

Was she just jumping to rookie conclusions?

Crivaro didn't say anything, just kept looking around the backyard.

Riley wondered …

Does Crivaro agree with McCune?

She wished he'd say something.

The forensics team soon arrived and started work as Crivaro gave them instructions. They were going to tape off the area and record anything they could see with their night-lights. A couple of team members would wait there all night until morning, making sure the area wasn't disturbed. Tomorrow morning they could do a more thorough search.

While the team kept working, Crivaro asked McCune and Riley …

"Any suggestions as to what we do next?"

McCune said, "I say we call it quits. The forensics guys can take it from here."

Riley tried to hold her tongue, but couldn't help blurting …

"Wait a minute. We haven't been to where the first victim was found—behind the movie theater. Maybe we should check it out."

McCune scoffed and said, "Right now? When it's getting dark?"

Riley didn't know what to say in reply.

I guess it does sound like kind of a dumb idea, she thought.

McCune patted the manila folder he'd been carrying and added, "Besides, I've got photos and information right here, taken by the local cops who examined the scene. Everything we need to know, especially now that we've got a surefire suspect in custody. I think we can consider the case pretty much closed as far as we're concerned. We can move on to other things."

Crivaro glared at McCune and said, "Your surefire suspect isn't talking. That means we've still got to find evidence to make a murder case against him. Our job isn't done yet."

Crivaro paused for a moment, then said, "Let's go to the movie theater."

Riley and the two agents went back into the house. Lewis Birch was just staring down at his hands in his lap. Roberta Birch had come back out of the bedroom and was sitting beside her husband. She gazed up at the agents with an anguished expression.

"From the yard?" she asked in a whisper. "He took her right from our own yard?"

"We're going to find out," Crivaro said. "That's why I have the team here."

He thanked the two bereaved parents for their cooperation, and the agents left.

As Crivaro drove them back into Northwest DC, McCune flipped through the information in his folder.

He said, "The Capri Theater is a little art house movie theater that specializes in classic movies."

Crivaro asked, "Does the report say what movie was playing when the body was found?"

"Yeah," McCune said. "Some really old flick called *Freaks*."

Crivaro let out a growl. "Jesus. I saw that when I was a kid. It gave me nightmares for weeks. It's a 1932 horror film that was considered so horrifying it barely got released and was actually banned in some places, like in England. It's still considered to be one of the most shocking movies ever made."

"What's it about?" Riley asked from the back seat.

Crivaro said, "Carnival freaks—you know, people with grotesque deformities and such. The freaks were played by real, authentic sideshow performers—people without limbs, bearded ladies, conjoined twins, little people, and the like. The freaks are actually the sympathetic characters—kind and honest and trusting. The 'normal' characters are the real villains. In the end, the freaks get their revenge on a really evil female trapeze artist and ..."

Crivaro shuddered.

"Let me put it this way. They mutilate her, turn her into a freak herself. And it's not pretty."

Riley thought for a moment. "So the second victim was found in a field where a carnival had just left. And the first victim was found behind a theater where a movie was playing about carnival performers."

Crivaro said, "Yeah, our killer has definitely got a theme going, with carnivals and clowns and all."

During the rest of the drive, Riley found herself thinking about Gregory Wertz and what had been found in his house aside from plans for a bank robbery.

Monster masks.

She tried to think of how those masks might connect with carnivals and clowns.

Nothing came to mind.

When Crivaro parked in front of the theater, Riley saw that the movie currently playing was *The Philadelphia Story,* an old Katharine Hepburn romantic comedy. She suspected the management had switched to a more pleasant movie right after the murdered woman was found nearby.

Crivaro, McCune, and Riley got out of the car and walked around the corner into the alley. Night had fully set in, but there was plenty of light spilling into the dank alleyway from the street lamps.

Beside a dumpster was the taped outline of the woman's corpse.

Riley crouched down for a closer look.

With a shudder, Riley flashed back to the photo she'd seen of the victim alongside this very dumpster—made up just like Janet Davis and wearing the same kind of puffy colorful suit. It was easy to imagine the victim splayed in front of her right now.

And it was easy to imagine what the killer had felt like crouching over her, savoring his handiwork.

A sharp tingle passed through her body.

Again, she felt a sense of unspeakable cruelty and sadism.

Her stomach turned at this renewed sense of connection with the killer. She was afraid she was going to be violently sick.

She thought back to when she'd looked through the two-way mirror at Gregory Wertz. She tried to match Wertz's face with that of the man whose presence she sensed right now—a vicious killer who had gloated over Margo Birch's body right here where she was crouching.

She couldn't do it.

Instead, her connection with the killer's mind vanished like a popped soap bubble.

She heard Crivaro say ...

"I don't see anything interesting here. You're right, McCune. It's time to call it quits for tonight. Let's all go home. We'll start again tomorrow."

Riley rose shakily to her feet, lagging behind Crivaro and McCune as they walked back toward the car.

She hurried to catch up with Crivaro and whispered in his ear ...

"Wertz isn't the killer. I'm sure of it now."

Crivaro simply grunted. Riley had no idea what that grunt might mean.

Did Crivaro agree with her hunch, or was he dismissing her input altogether?

She felt a surge of deepening horror about that mind she'd sensed ...

He's still out there.

And he's going to kill again.

CHAPTER SIXTEEN

Very early the next morning, Riley's cell phone rang while she was in the kitchen eating cereal. When she saw that the call was from Agent Crivaro, she almost dropped the phone in her eagerness to answer. Maybe something exciting was already in the works today.

"Sweeney, I've got something I want you to do," Crivaro said.

Riley's excitement rose. He must be going to assign her a new task.

"What is it?" she asked, trying to sound calm.

"There's going to be a lecture in the Hoover Building auditorium this morning. I want you to be there."

A lecture, Riley thought, feeling deflated. But she didn't comment.

Crivaro continued, "An old colleague of mine, Elliot Flack, is going to be talking to interns about the Behavioral Analysis Unit. I want you to hear it."

Riley's hopes sank. She'd already known about that lecture, but hadn't planned on attending. After all, she was working a real case. She'd expected to spend today with Crivaro and McCune.

When she didn't reply, Crivaro said, "Hello? Are you still there?"

"Yeah, I'm still here," Riley said.

She didn't know what else to say. Crivaro certainly wouldn't like it if she told him she wasn't interested in the lecture.

After a pause, Crivaro said, "Look, if you get through this program and keep on going, it's as likely as not that you'll wind up going into the BAU. I want you to know more about it."

"OK," Riley said. She realized she sounded unenthusiastic, but Crivaro didn't seem to notice.

"Great. I'll talk to you later."

Before he could hang up, Riley said, "Wait a minute, Agent Crivaro. Is there any news about the case?"

She could hear him scoff.

"Nothing new this early in the morning. What were you expecting? Look, don't worry about the case. McCune and I are on it."

Crivaro ended the call without another word.

Riley sat staring at the phone in disappointment.

Of course, she told herself, *he's right.*

What Crivaro was saying made sense. She really ought to attend a lecture that focused on the BAU. She really didn't know much about it, and it sounded like an interesting branch of the FBI. It might even be her future career.

She remembered Crivaro's words when he'd talked her into joining the summer intern program …

"You'd make a very fine BAU agent."

That made Riley feel a little better. But she still couldn't help wondering yet again whether Crivaro was brushing her off.

Did this have anything to do with what she'd said to him when they'd left the alley behind the theater last night?

"Wertz isn't the killer. I'm sure of it now."

Had she put him off by being so presumptuous?

Maybe I should have just kept my mouth shut.

But how could she, when her gut feeling had been so powerful? Weren't her intuitions the main reason Crivaro had gotten interested in her in the first place?

But was he having second thoughts now?

Had he decided to leave her out of the case from now on?

She had no way of knowing.

Riley tried to push such thoughts out of her mind as she finished her cereal and coffee. Then she crept quietly into the bedroom so as not to wake up Ryan. She silently collected her clothes and ducked into the bathroom.

After a quick shower, she put on a makeshift pantsuit—a clean pair of slacks and a jacket. She didn't have a lot of the sort of professional clothes expected of an FBI intern, so she made a mental note that she had to do laundry soon. Fortunately, the building's laundry room was right here in the basement, down the hall from their apartment.

When she came out of the bathroom, Ryan was sitting up in bed. He looked barely awake.

"Off so soon?" he said, rubbing his eyes.

"Yeah, sorry to rush," Riley said, kissing him on the cheek.

"You got in kind of late," Ryan complained. "You didn't have a lot to say."

"I know. It had been a long day. I was really tired."

Riley hesitated. She didn't want to talk about the clown-painted dead woman and the bereaved family. At least not until she had more time to explain everything.

Ryan yawned and stretched, and Riley remembered that she'd found him hunched over books and papers when she'd gotten home.

"You were kind of preoccupied yourself," she said.

"I guess I was," Ryan said with a yawn. "I got sent home with a lot of work. It was a big day."

He looked up at her. "Are you having problems with your classes?"

Riley was startled by the word ...

Classes!

Ryan still had no idea how she'd spent yesterday, or for that matter the day before yesterday. What would he think if he knew all that she'd really been doing? How could she tell him?

For the time being, Riley could think of nothing to do except evade the question.

"We'll talk when I get home," she said.

She gave him another quick kiss and started to walk away.

"Hey," he said, his voice stopping her.

She turned toward him and saw a worried look on his face.

He said, "You've got to take care of yourself, you know."

"I know," Riley said, "I am."

He was frowning now and she didn't want to give him a chance to ask for details about her work.

"I'll be home early tonight," she said cheerfully. "I'll fix dinner. Don't worry. Bye."

Riley hurried on out of the apartment, feeling confused and a little guilty.

She and Ryan hadn't had time to talk seriously for a couple of days. She'd told him about some of her problems with Crivaro and about some of her own doubts.

But so much had happened since then!

She would make sure they had time to talk tonight.

During the two-block walk to the metro stop, she started feeling better.

It seemed a shame that Ryan felt bad about them living here. True, the neighborhood was a little seedy, but it was visibly upgrading. And even at this early morning hour, people were bustling around the sidewalks and the streets were heavy with traffic.

When she got onto the subway train, it was crowded with other people on their way to their daily routines.

Her early years in rural and small-town Virginia seemed so far away. And she found that she really liked the change. She felt like she was really starting to get in step with the rhythms of a big, exciting city.

Riley also felt a renewed sense of determination to succeed in the intern program.

I've really got to make the most of this great opportunity, she thought.

*

As Riley walked into the auditorium, she noticed that many of the interns who were already seated were staring at her. She felt their gaze even more intensely than she had during her first day here. Although she'd had no contact with them while she was working with Crivaro and McCune, it was as if their curiosity about her had grown.

What's going on? she wondered.

She took her seat just as the lecturer was stepping up to the podium. At that moment, someone sat down in the seat beside her. She turned and saw that it was John Welch, the good-looking guy she'd suspected of hitting on her the day before yesterday.

He whispered to her, "We've got to talk when this is over. You've got to tell me all about it."

All about what? Riley wondered.

Then she realized …

Oh my God!

Word had gotten around among the interns about her involvement with the "Clown Killer" case. That's why some of them seemed to be especially interested in her today. But what exactly had they heard?

And what was she going to tell John about it?

She was relieved when the man at the podium shuffled some notecards and started talking.

"Good morning, folks," he said in a gruff but cheerful voice. "I'm Special Agent Elliot Flack, and I'm here to talk to you about the Behavioral Analysis Unit."

Then with a self-effacing chuckled he added, "I'm not much of a public speaker. Getting into the brains of bad guys is more my thing. I hope I don't bore you."

His remark stirred up a bit of laughter in his audience. Obviously nobody expected his talk to be boring.

And it certainly wasn't.

Flack had a hard-as-nails demeanor that reminded Riley of

Agent Crivaro. But he also had a dry and sometimes dark sense of humor.

He began by talking about the beginnings of the BAU back in 1972, with the founding of the FBI's Behavioral Sciences Unit. Back then criminal profiling had seemed a radical and even somewhat crazy idea. The early proponents of profiling did what was widely considered to be unthinkable—they spent hundreds of hours talking with the most vicious killers currently incarcerated, trying to understand their minds.

"Ah, the 1970s," Flack said with a certain sly relish. "That was a rich time to study psychopathic killers."

Flack pointed to the screen in front of the room and said, "Consider this guy for example."

Suddenly, an image came up on the screen that made Riley's heart jump up into her throat.

It was the face of a clown, painted stark white with exaggerated, brightly colored features, especially a huge, red, smiling mouth.

Riley remembered the term Danny Casal had used for such a clown …

A "grotesque whiteface."

It was the same sort of makeup she had seen on the two murdered women—the one in the field and the other in a photograph.

Riley wondered …

What on earth is he going to tell us about?

CHAPTER SEVENTEEN

Riley wondered for a moment if she might be dreaming.

But she knew she wasn't.

She really was sitting in a lecture hall looking at a disturbing image, a face that strongly resembled two murder victims.

It was the painted face of a clown.

As she waited for Agent Flack to speak again, her thoughts raced. Was he going to talk about the very murders she'd been helping Crivaro and McCune investigate?

Flack walked to the side of the screen with a pointer.

He said, "The fellow you're looking at was known as 'Pogo the Clown,' or sometimes 'Patches the Clown.' He was a generous soul who performed at children's parties, and also for at charity events and for hospitalized children. He was well-liked by most people who knew him."

Flack paused for a moment, then added …

"He also raped, tortured, and murdered some thirty-three boys and young men between 1972 and 1978. He kept most of their bodies hidden in a crawlspace under the floor of his own home. People called him the 'Killer Clown.'"

The whole audience gasped; so did Riley.

"Killer Clown!"

This was not the face of a victim. It was the face of a killer.

Even so, the name was close—too close—to the nickname that was circulating about the recent murders—the "Clown Killer."

A series of images flashed across the screen—the killer's mug shots, photographs of his youthful victims, and of the crawlspace where the bodies had been discovered.

Flack continued, "His name was John Wayne Gacy. And once he was apprehended, he became a subject of intense study by pioneering profilers. They got to spend a long time talking to him. Although he was convicted in 1980, he wasn't executed until 1994."

Flack turned away from the screen and looked out over his listeners.

"Any questions so far?" he asked.

Riley's hand shot right up, and Flack nodded to her.

She asked, "What did the profilers manage to learn about him?

97

I mean …"

She paused, then added, "Why did he do … the things he did?"

Flack's lips formed into a bitter half-smile.

"That's a good question. I wish I could give you a clear-cut answer. It's no surprise, I guess, that he had a difficult childhood. His father was a brutal alcoholic who beat him and berated him. But how much does that explain? Lots of people have rough childhoods and cruel fathers, and not all of them turn out to be sexual predators and killers."

Flack shrugged and added …

"My own dad wasn't the nicest guy in the world."

Nor was mine, Riley thought.

And she'd never felt any desire to inflict pain on anybody, much less kill people.

And yet …

She shuddered at the thought of how easy it was getting to be for her to get inside a killer's mind.

Did her own childhood have anything to do with that?

Flack brought up another slide with a crude oil painting of a clown.

He said, "While in prison, he painted this picture of himself as 'Pogo.' He gave it to one of the profilers who spent many hours interviewing him, with this written on the back …"

Another photo showed Gacy's handwritten message …

"Dear Bob Ressler, you cannot hope to enjoy the harvest without first laboring in the fields. Best wishes and good luck. Sincerely, John Wayne Gacy, June 1988."

After reading the message aloud, Flack continued …

"When Bob asked Gacy what the message meant, Gacy said to him, 'You're the criminal profiler. You figure it out.'"

Flack shrugged and said, "And I guess you could say that's exactly what the BAU has been trying to do all along—figure out what makes monsters tick. We've learned a lot over the years, and we've gotten a lot better at tracking and apprehending those monsters. What we still can't usually do is stop them before they act."

He fell silent for a moment, then said, "And our work comes at a personal risk. The trick is to understand monsters without becoming a monster yourself. It isn't always easy."

Riley listened to the rest of his lecture with rapt fascination.

She was surprised to learn that the very term "serial killer" wasn't very old. It was coined sometime during the 1970s by Robert Ressler, the profiler Gacy had signed that picture for. Ressler had said he'd thought of the term because successive murders reminded him of "serial adventures," short movies that he'd seen as a child on Saturday afternoons.

Each episode of those movies always ended in a cliffhanger, with the hero in extreme danger. Viewers had to wait for next Saturday's episode to find out how the hero escaped death. Ressler had remembered the dissatisfaction he'd felt at the end of each episode—a dissatisfaction that didn't lift when the hero survived, and that seemed to grow sharper with every episode. Maybe, he thought, killers who murdered successive victims were driven by the same sort of dissatisfaction.

When the lecture was over, Riley's head was buzzing with thoughts and ideas. She sat there for a moment trying to absorb all that she'd heard.

She also felt eerily seized by frustration.

Somewhere today, probably right at that very moment, Crivaro and McCune were out searching for clues, either proving or disproving that Gregory Wertz was guilty of two ghastly murders …

And I'm missing it.

The thought worked itself inside her like a gnawing hunger …

Dissatisfaction.

Yes, that was what it was—a palpable dissatisfaction, like waiting for the next episode in a movie serial.

Was it the same kind of dissatisfaction that drove serial killers to commit their awful deeds?

If the same feeling drove murderers, what did that say about her?

What did it say about anybody who felt drawn to this kind of work?

Did solving a murder offer any satisfaction, any closure?

Or was this like some kind of sick addiction?

She touched her cell phone in her pocket and thought …

I wish Crivaro would call.

CHAPTER EIGHTEEN

Still sitting in the front row of the auditorium, Riley was struggling with her own indecision. Agent Flack was gathering his notes and getting ready to leave, so she had to make up her mind right now. Should she ask him the awful question that was lurking in her mind—the question of whether killers and their pursuers shared the same kind of dissatisfaction?

She finally made up her mind. *Yes, I'm going to do it.*

But before she could get out of her chair, she felt a hand on her arm.

It was John Welch. In her fascination with the lecture, she'd forgotten that he was sitting beside her.

"Come on, Riley," he said. "You've got to talk to me. I'm dying to hear what's been going on."

Riley glanced back at Agent Flack and saw that other students were already clustering around him. She'd have to wait in line. Worse, she'd have to discuss her question with other people listening.

She looked back at John. He seemed eager and anxious to talk to her.

"OK, let's go," she said.

As the two of them left the auditorium, Riley felt a pang of regret about what she might be missing. But she'd lost her nerve, and besides, she didn't want to be rude to John.

The truth was, she kind of liked him. Glancing at his athletic figure as they walked, she thought …

Maybe I like him a little more than I should.

When they got out into the hall, John was fairly bouncing around from excitement.

"So tell me all about it!" he said. "Is it true what I've been hearing?"

"I don't know," Riley said. "What have you been hearing?"

"That you've been working on the Clown Killer case with Crivaro and McCune."

Riley nodded shyly.

John gasped.

"Wow!" he said. "How did you score something like that? The rest of us are stuck in workshops and seminars."

Riley didn't know what to say. The truth was, she wasn't sure just why Crivaro had brought her onto the case.

She recalled what Crivaro had said to the medical examiner after Riley sensed that the killer had frightened his victim to death.

"It's what she does. It's why she's here."

But where was Crivaro now?

Had he lost confidence in her?

John said, "I guess I shouldn't be surprised. I mean, you're the only intern who came into the program with actual hands-on experience. Of course you're going to get a head start on the rest of us. But you've got to tell me—what was it like, working in the field? What all did you do?"

Yesterday flashed through Riley's mind—the early morning call from Crivaro, going to see the grotesquely clad and made-up corpse in the field, the smells and eerie light in the darkroom, the visit to the costume shop, the arrest and questioning of Gregory Wertz, and finally the visit to Margo's parents, where she got such a powerful hit on how the young woman was abducted.

Riley could hardly believe it all had happened in one day.

How do I begin? she wondered.

Or maybe the more important question was …

Should I even talk about it?

Crivaro hadn't said anything about what she could or couldn't talk about. Was he counting on her to use good common sense? What would that even mean?

"OK, just tell me one thing," John finally said. "Is it true that there's a surefire suspect in custody? I mean, did you really get the guy? There's nothing in the news media about it yet, but word gets around in this place."

Riley was jolted by the question. She didn't think that Gregory Wertz was really the killer but …

Crivaro?

She had no idea whether Crivaro thought the suspect was guilty of anything more than planning a bank robbery.

Riley said haltingly …

"John, I … I think maybe I just shouldn't get into it."

John just stared at her.

"I'm really sorry," Riley added.

John flashed a delighted grin.

"Hey, don't be sorry," he said. "You're not at liberty to discuss it. That's even cooler!"

Riley was relieved at being let off the hook.

"So where are you headed next?" she asked him.

"I've got a workshop about computers," John said. "What about you?"

Riley shrugged and said, "I guess I don't have anything right now."

"Why don't you come along?" John asked. "I'm sure you'll be welcome."

"That would be nice," she said. But as they headed toward the lab where the workshop was going to be held, Riley found herself wondering …

Is this going to be over my head?

She didn't even own a computer. Back at Lanton, Riley sometimes used the school's computers or Ryan's—but neither of them very much. Old-fashioned textbooks were more her style. She found computers rather intimidating, and the Internet struck her as vast and confusing.

Was she in for a lot of high-tech talk about coding and programming?

She was relieved to see that the lab was full of ordinary desktop computers and modems just like what Ryan used back at the apartment. The instructor's topic of the day was recent developments in Internet search engines, and how they could be used in criminal investigations.

Riley became fascinated as she logged onto the Internet and participated in several exercises. She quickly learned to use search terms to find long lists of information that she then had to winnow down to useful and pertinent items of interest.

What Riley found most amazing was the fact that this technology wasn't really the least bit out of the ordinary—certainly not just for elite experts in computer science.

Anybody can do this, she realized.

The instructor said that this technology was getting faster and more powerful by the day. Riley wondered what that might mean for the future. Was it going to completely transform the nature of investigative work? Were ordinary civilians going to be able to track down bad guys without leaving their homes—like real-life "armchair detectives"?

The possibilities boggled her mind.

When the workshop was over, Riley and John went to the cafeteria for lunch. As he talked a bit about himself—about his privileged childhood and his idealistic dreams for the future—Riley found herself liking him more and more.

As for whether he was flirting with her or not—well, she wasn't altogether sure today. But at least she'd been clear with him that she was engaged, so she felt confident that she wasn't sending him confusing signals. As far as she could tell, he was just being friendly. And it was nice to finally have a friend here in DC.

Riley talked a little about her own life, but there were still some details she didn't discuss. She steered clear of her mother's murder and played down her father's ill temper. And she still didn't mention that she was pregnant. She wasn't sure just why. The truth was, Riley couldn't remember having told anybody about that yet except Ryan, and she didn't think Ryan had talked about it either.

Had he even told his parents?

If he had, he'd never mentioned it. Why were they both being so secretive?

Riley really didn't know.

Interrupting her thoughts, John stood up from the table and said, "My group is scheduled to visit another lab. Come on with me."

Riley thought she might as well since she'd still heard nothing from Crivaro. As she walked down the hallway next to John, she tried to ignore curious glances from other interns in his group. She kept her head down and followed him through a doorway.

Inside the room, a man wearing lab clothes greeted them. He introduced himself as a forensic pathologist and then pulled back the cover on a table in front of him.

There was the actual corpse of a teenage boy, his eyes wide open, his body marred by four gaping bullet wounds.

We're in the morgue, Riley then realized.

The pathologist explained that this was a seventeen-year-old male who had been killed in an episode of gang violence.

Riley felt a pang of sadness at the thought of a life cut so terribly short.

Several of the other interns gasped or gagged, and three of them ran out of the room.

One of those three students was John.

She figured it might be the first time that he and most of the interns had ever seen a dead body, much less someone who had been murdered. As for Riley, this was the fourth body of a murder victim she'd seen in her short life.

The most recent had been Janet Davis, lying in that field just yesterday.

Just a few weeks ago at Lanton she had found two bodies with their throats slashed open. Both girls had been her friends—one had been her best friend and roommate.

And of course, Riley had seen her own mother lying dead at her feet when she'd been just a little girl.

She had to wonder …

Am I getting numb to the horror?

As she listened to the pathologist's lecture, "numb" didn't seem to be the right word for what she was feeling.

Curiosity was more like it.

As the man spoke, she learned things she hadn't known about guns and bullet wounds—for example, that a typical bullet travels at 1,126 feet per second. And few people knew the horrendous damage a bullet caused to the human body.

The pathologist pointed to where one bullet had entered the victim's shoulder.

"You might guess that a bullet wound to the shoulder wouldn't be too severe," he said. "That's not true. When this bullet hit the shoulder blade, it burst into fragments, each fragment ricocheting through his flesh and causing its own share of damage to nerves, muscles, and blood vessels. Each of those fragments felt like a hot coal under the victim's flesh."

Indicating another wound, he added, "The same is true of this one, which looks like it hit his pelvis."

He pointed to another wound in the victim's belly.

"This one was even more painful," he said. "It must have either shredded his intestines or ripped the stomach wide open. This wasn't the wound he died from, though."

He pointed to a wound in the victim's thigh.

"This one was fatal," he said. "It hit the femoral artery, and nobody was around to help him by stopping the bleeding. But it must have seemed like forever before he lost consciousness from blood loss."

The pathologist looked up at the interns and added, "As you can see, getting shot is nothing like what's on television. The pain is beyond imagining. And if you survive, you're likely to carry some physical damage for the rest of your life. And psychological damage as well. People who have been shot often undergo deep and permanent personality changes, becoming depressive, angry, and paranoid."

He paused to look over the body and said, "Of course, if you're lucky, you'll take a bullet to the brain or the heart, and you're likely to die instantly. If not, you'll probably wish you were dead. And that feeling just might never go away for the rest of your life."

As the lecture continued, Riley noticed that two of the interns who had fled the room had come back—but not John. When the workshop ended, Riley went out into the hallway and looked around. She didn't see him anywhere.

She wondered … was he embarrassed at how he'd reacted at the sight of a murder victim?

Riley hoped not. She knew that his reaction had been perfectly natural. And this particular lecturer had been unduly blunt with the interns.

As she remembered her own rapt curiosity, she wondered …

Was my *reaction perfectly natural?*

As she wandered aimlessly down the hallway, she felt her frustration rising again.

When is Crivaro going to call?

Is he ever *going to call?*

CHAPTER NINETEEN

Riley felt stranded. She stood there in the hallway, wondering when or if Crivaro was going to call. After two days of such intense activity, it felt positively unbearable to have no place to go and nothing to do.

She found herself wondering …

Am I getting addicted to this kind of work?

Already, after just two days?

It was a scary thought. This case didn't involve her directly, like the murders when she was in college. But she could feel herself being drawn to it—to trying to solve a deadly mystery.

She had to do something to let off steam.

Maybe a good physical workout would help.

She went to the interns' locker room and used the restroom to change into her gym workout clothes. Then she headed for the FBI's exercise room. She was glad to see that the room was very well-equipped. It even included a hanging punching bag.

After using her one lesson in Krav Maga to fend off a would-be rapist, she'd spent some time in the Lanton gym learning some basic sparring tactics from a graduate assistant in phys ed. So she knew how to work out with a bag like this.

She started slow, keeping her hands in a defensive position and throwing only a few mild punches. She felt her aggression mount as she attacked harder and harder with jabs, uppercuts, body shots, and hooks. But even when she added kicks to her attacks, she didn't feel the release she yearned for.

She pushed the bag so that it swayed and turned about, trying harder to pretend that it was a real opponent. Dodging and moving around the bag, she ducked, shuffled, bobbed, lunged, and pivoted, trying to catch her imaginary nemesis off guard. Her attacks became more and more brutal but …

Something is missing, she realized.

And that something was a real opponent, someone who genuinely wanted to hurt or even kill Riley, someone she had to fight desperately for her very life …

I want that bag to be him.

She wanted the dumb, heavy object to be the killer himself.

But it wasn't.

She didn't even have any idea what the man looked like.

He was strong, apparently—at least strong enough to subdue and abduct two women by force.

He was also deeply sadistic—Riley had gotten that sense of him more than once now.

But what did he look like?

Did he look like a clown himself, made up and costumed?

Or was he just an ordinary person she might pass by on the street without even noticing him?

What would it be like to stare into his very eyes?

Would she see a world of evil there?

What would it be like to be locked in a fight to the death with him?

At last Riley backed away from the bag and stood bent over with hands on her knees, gasping for breath as her heart pounded and sweated coated her body.

It's no good, she thought.

Bashing away at the bag was too much like the old-time movie serials, always promising some gratification that never came through.

Riley felt like she was going crazy with frustration.

But what on earth could she do about it?

As her heartbeat slowed and her breathing settled down, a possibility started to dawn on her—something that would at least give her the feeling of *doing* something. And it was something she could do all alone,

Would Crivaro approve of her idea?

She doubted it very much.

But she really didn't care.

She headed back to the locker room and took a shower and changed into her regular clothes. Then she looked at the metro map on the locker room wall and figured out which train to take to get to Lady Bird Johnson Park. Attached to the metro map were batches of free maps of DC. She found the one that showed the park in the most detail, and she took it with her.

Then she left the building, went to the subway station, and caught the next train. It was a forty-five-minute trip to Lady Bird Johnson Park, so she had plenty of time to consider what she was about to do.

That park was where Janet Davis had been abducted while taking photographs at dusk. The local cops, of course, had gone over the place and found the camera that had been knocked out of

Janet's hands at the moment of her capture. Riley had seen the telling images from that. But according to the reports, the police hadn't found any other clues.

Riley knew there would be no signs left from what had happened there. But she remembered that powerful sense of connection with the killer she'd gotten in Margo Birch's back yard. Could she get a similar connection at the park?

I might even learn something important.

Something nobody else has figured out.

Of course, she knew that her plan might have its flaws.

Riley hadn't been to that crime scene yet, and as of yesterday neither had Crivaro and McCune. Surely the two agents would check out the park sometime today

She didn't want to run into them there. Crivaro might blow a fuse about her not minding her own business. But they'd probably already been there and left.

To her surprise, Riley realized that she didn't much care one way or the other. She didn't like being shut out today, and she wasn't going to put up with it.

When she got off the train and walked the rest of the way to the park, she saw that the sky was overcast and threatening rain. She wasn't dressed for rain and didn't have an umbrella. But the risk of getting caught in a downpour and getting soaked to the skin didn't worry her much.

She soon recognized the footbridge that led across a small channel of water to Columbia Island, where the park was located. She'd seen the bridge in the first of Janet's black-and-white photos. It wasn't yet dusk, but as Riley walked across the bridge, the overcast sky made everything eerily like the photo, with the same soft shadows and muted surfaces.

When she reached the island, she unfolded the map to look for familiar locations. First she walked to the statue she'd seen in one of the photos—a cresting wave forged from aluminum, topped by several seagulls that seemed to be uncannily frozen in flight. According to the map, it was the Navy-Merchant Marine Memorial.

She noticed that several park visitors were hurrying past the statue toward the footbridge, fleeing the park because of the threat of rain.

That's good, Riley thought.

Much like Janet had on that fateful night, Riley would soon have the park seemingly all to herself. She just hoped that the rain would hold off until she managed to do what she wanted to do …

If I can do it.

Her instincts were still pretty untested, after all, and she might fail to feel that connection again.

I didn't come all this way for nothing, she told herself firmly.

She followed a footpath until she got to her next destination— the rough-hewn obelisk she'd seen in one of the photos, which turned out to be the LBJ Memorial Grove Monolith. Just as Riley had in the photograph, she could see the Washington Monument towering in the far distance.

By now, there were no visitors in sight.

Riley looked all around, trying to imagine how Janet had felt standing here snapping her pictures of the moody scene.

Did Janet have any feeling of being watched and followed? No, Riley had already sensed that Janet's abductor was stealthy. Janet had felt safe and content and alone.

Riley felt a deep chill.

Janet was wrong.

He was definitely here somewhere.

She remembered what Crivaro had said to Charlie in the darkroom …

"Magnify everything … all the photographs, every square centimeter."

Charlie must have done that by now. Had he found any telltale figures or faces?

No, the killer had surely stayed out of sight, mostly behind her, or …

Riley looked across the way into a grove of pine and dogwood trees. He might have hidden himself somewhere over there—in fact, Riley felt almost sure of it. She continued on through the grove, taking a path Janet might well have taken to her last location.

She felt the killer's presence, sensed him darting among the trees just behind her as she walked along.

She found herself wondering …

Is he really here?

Right now?

If so, was she in terrible danger herself at this very moment?

No, she realized. In spite of that vivid sensation of menace, what she was feeling wasn't happening now. She was tuning into something that had already taken place.

She could tell that Janet hadn't been a random target, and neither had Margo Birch. The killer was anything but spontaneous or impulsive. He had stalked both of them stealthily and skillfully until he'd known just when and where to strike.

As she walked along, a strange feeling came over her.

She was no longer imagining the episode from her point of view.

Instead, she saw the whole scene as the killer must have seen it.

She envisioned herself darting among these trees, avoiding the sight of the young woman who kept walking blithely and unsuspecting just up ahead.

Riley felt a surge of terror, just as she had during those other times when she'd gotten a sense of the killer's presence.

But she fought down her fear and continued on until she arrived at the marina, its wooden docks jutting out into a peaceful lagoon. Margo had taken most of her pictures from those docks. It must have been her favorite spot, and the killer must have known it.

The dimmed daylight continued to remind Riley of the photos she'd seen. As she heard the gentle lapping of water and the cries of gulls, the black-and-white images flashed through her mind vividly.

She ducked behind among some trees and peered ahead, imagining that she was the killer watching Janet moving along the docks.

Finally, Riley remembered that final blurred photograph, with its chaotic and jumbled shapes of boats and docks. As unclear as those shapes had been, Riley felt as though they lined up with the view she had of the marina right now …

She came back this way to take that picture.

And he was waiting.

He must have had some kind of a hard, blunt object in his hand—a short piece of pipe, maybe.

Riley could now almost feel the weight of that object in her hand.

She stepped out from among the trees, feeling the readiness and excitement he must have felt as he slipped up behind her and cracked her on the skull and watched her drop to his feet …

Riley gasped.

Her point of view snapped back into her own mind.

She felt that the killer was still there in front of her.

For a moment, she thought she could grab him by the throat and demand …

Who are you? Where can we find you right now?

But she couldn't do that. And her perception of him was fading.

She got a fleeting sense of the smirk on his face as he peered down at his stricken prey, looking forward to what came next—the ritual of dressing her and making her up, injecting the fatal drug into her veins, teasing and tormenting her literally to death.

He had to move her. How?

She looked around and saw a small parking lot nearby. It was almost empty right now. It might well have been completely empty when he'd attacked Janet. If so, it wouldn't have been hard to drag her to his parked vehicle, dump her inside, and then drive her …

Where?

She flashed back to when she'd been sitting in Crivaro's car, watching Crivaro and McCune drag Gregory Wertz out of his apartment building. She hadn't seen Wertz's apartment, but judging from the looks of the neighborhood and the building and the man himself, it was surely fairly small and cramped and disorderly.

No, she thought.

It didn't happen there.

That was not the setting for such ritualistic, almost ceremonial sadism.

Had Wertz dragged her somewhere else entirely?

No, the man lacked some characteristic needed to maintain such a place and conduct such a ritual …

Imagination.

Riley closed her eyes, trying to picture the place where the victims' torment had taken place.

She murmured aloud, in an almost pleading voice …

"Where? Where did you do it?"

A few droplets of rain hit her, jarring her out of her dark reverie.

Her connection to the killer was completely undone.

But she knew one thing that she hadn't known before …

He has a lair.

We've got to find the lair.

CHAPTER TWENTY

Alone at last in his secret rooms, Joey shed his "costume"—the clothes he wore out in the world of ordinary people, the clothes that made it possible for him to blend in with them, make them think he was one of them.

If they only knew, he thought.

He wondered—could he ever teach anyone the terrible truth?

The truth about themselves and the world they lived in?

Could any of them ever learn?

It wasn't an easy lesson. He knew that better than maybe anybody else in the world.

When he was fully undressed, he went to the clothes rack where a dozen or so wonderful puffy, gaudy, garish clown costumes hung.

He picked out one and slipped into it, then stood looking at himself in the mirror.

There, that's better, he thought.

Now that he felt more himself again, his thoughts turned to the young women who had died under his hand.

He knew it couldn't be easy for them, having to learn his terrible lesson in so short a time—a lesson he'd spent his whole life having to learn and live with.

It had actually been impossible for the two girls he'd chosen already, feeling fear and loneliness arise in sudden uncontrollable surges, looking in a mirror and finally seeing their faces ...

Not the faces they usually saw in the mirror, but their truer faces, the faces the rest of the world really saw, bright and loud and alien, the rejected faces, the faces of the shunned.

For after all—that's what people really were, all of them.

Shunned.

Oh, those girls hadn't understood. Few people ever did. They thought they were surrounded by people they could trust—parents, relatives, spouses, friends, coworkers. But all that kindness and goodwill and even love were only feigned, an act, a mockery of how people really felt.

He'd tried to explain it to the women ...

"They're going to leave you behind."

He'd said it again and again.

And yet they hadn't understood.

It was so simple, really. How could he have made it clearer?

He remembered what the latest girl had cried out as he'd teased her with a knife …

"Why do you hate me?"

What a strange question!

He'd answered with the truth, of course.

"Everybody *hates you.*"

She'd panicked then.

He knew that her panic was only natural. He'd lived for many years in such a state of perpetual horror. It was normal for him. He couldn't imagine life without that horror.

But it had been all new to her, and he remembered how she'd writhed and cried out …

"Swat them off me! Kill them!"

She'd thought she was swarming with insects.

As her terror had mounted, she'd seem to think that the insects were under her very skin.

The other girl had felt those insects too—an effect of the drug, apparently.

But finally, when he'd shown the girl her face in the mirror, he'd seen a change in her.

She'd really understood, was undeluded, even if just for a moment.

She saw the *self* that everybody saw.

She knew that she was truly outcast, just like he was.

She knew for a fact …

"They're going to leave me behind."

… and that *he* was the only person in the world who would accept her as she was.

But she'd rejected that opportunity.

As he'd held the knife to her throat, she'd hissed out …

"Do it. Do it now."

He'd had no intention of killing her, of course.

It was up to her to choose between a lonely death and the only kind of companionship she could ever hope for …

A life with me.

She hadn't been strong enough to choose that life, and neither had the other girl.

They'd both chosen to die instead.

The next one will be stronger, he told himself.

And he'd already chosen the next girl, although she didn't

know it yet.

He'd been watching her, following her, waiting for his perfect moment.

But that moment hadn't come.

Soon, he told himself. *Soon.*

Meanwhile, he'd tease the world that had tormented him— tease it with a message that people would read tomorrow ...

A riddle.

Because there was no direct way to say what he had to say.

It could only be said in a riddle.

Was there anyone out there who could crack the riddle's secret—especially its one key, paradoxical word?

There must be, he thought.

Just one person.

A young woman, maybe.

Maybe someday soon he'd meet her face to face.

Surely she would understand.

Meanwhile, he was tired to the very bones from spending the day out in the world, pretending to be just one more of its wretched, lonely denizens.

He took down one of the countless clown sketches he had tacked on the wall. He'd sent one of those sketches out with his riddle, and he wondered if the picture would appear along with his words.

Then he went to a shelf and took down a metal box. He set it down on the counter in front of his mirror and opened it. It was full of bottles of latex and spirit gum, colorful prostheses, and tubes of greasepaint.

He'd gone out into the world in disguise, wearing the kind of clothes that other people wore, wearing the mask of his own skin.

He needed to put on his own true face to go to bed.

He smeared the welcome white makeup all over his face. Referring to the sketch as he added more detail, he said aloud the title of the riddle people would be reading tomorrow ...

"Welcome to the Labyrinth."

CHAPTER TWENTY ONE

Riley was soaked to the skin by the time she got back to her apartment building. The rain had hit hard as she was going from Lady Bird Johnson Park to the metro station and it was still raining much later when she arrived at her stop near home. Running that last two blocks had seemed futile.

Ryan was sitting at the kitchen table, but he jumped up when she walked in.

"Oh no," he exclaimed. "I guess you didn't take an umbrella."

Riley shook her head, her hair slinging water about. "At least it's warm outside," she said, laughing.

Ryan hustled her into the bathroom and started rubbing her down with one of their towels.

"You need to take better care of yourself," he scolded her.

"Stop," she protested. "I'll change. I'll be out in a minute."

She undressed, dried herself off, and put on dry clothes.

When she got back to the kitchen, she felt a surge of guilt at what she saw.

Two places were set at the table. Ryan had put out a bowl of tuna and pasta salad—a quick and easy meal that Ryan liked to make. He was sitting there waiting for her.

Riley remembered her words from this morning

"I'll be home early tonight. I'll fix dinner. Don't worry."

"Oh, my God," she said in a choked voice. "Ryan, I'm so sorry."

Ryan shrugged, then said, "It was getting late."

He put some salad on his own plate.

"I'm really, really sorry," Riley said shakily. "I lost track of time."

Ryan started eating silently.

Oh, no, Riley thought.

She knew from Ryan's silence that he was really upset.

As she took some salad for herself, Riley said, "Um. How was your day?"

Without looking up at her, Ryan said, "Good. My second day in a real courtroom."

"Wow," Riley said. "That must be really exciting."

Ryan didn't reply.

His second day, Riley thought with regret.

He hadn't mentioned this yesterday when she'd come in. She'd been tired, and he'd been hunched over a pile of work he'd brought back from home.

They ate in silence for a few moments.

Finally Ryan glanced up at her and said, "So how about you? How was your day?"

Riley gulped hard.

She had promised herself she'd tell him the truth about her involvement with the murder case as soon as they had some time together.

Right now seemed to be that moment.

Riley decided maybe she could ease into the truth with some of her more innocuous activities …

"Well, I went to a couple of workshops today. One was about computers and how to use the Internet. I did some hands-on stuff."

She laughed nervously and added, "You'll be glad to know that I'm finally learning how to use a computer. I mean, you've been bugging me about my backward ways. Maybe I'll even be ready for the new millennium."

Ryan didn't laugh or even smile. He just kept eating.

Then Riley said …

"After that I went to a workshop in the morgue—"

Before she could continue, Ryan looked up at her with a startled expression.

"The morgue? Oh, my God! How bad was it?"

Riley was puzzled.

Why is he so worried?

She shrugged silently.

Ryan put down his fork and looked at her with concern.

"Oh, Riley—please tell me you didn't have to look at a corpse."

Riley nodded.

Ryan was looking really alarmed now.

He said, "That must have been so hard for you—I mean after what happened to your mom when you were little, and then all that happened back in Lanton. How did you handle it? Are you OK?"

Riley stammered, "Sure, I'm … it was no big deal."

Ryan reached across the table and took Riley's hand.

"But it *was* a big deal. They shouldn't have made you do that."

Riley almost protested that nobody had "made" her do it, that she'd gone to the workshop on her own impulse, but …

No, I just can't tell him that.

Still, she just couldn't be completely dishonest with him.

She said, "It wasn't traumatic, Ryan. In fact, it was really interesting. I learned a lot about gunshot wounds that I hadn't known before."

Ryan's eyes widened.

Riley added, "Really, it's nothing to worry about."

Ryan shook his head and said, "I don't like this, Riley. A couple of days ago you were wondering if this program was right for you. Are you still unsure? Because I certainly am. Riley, you've got to remember—"

"I know," Riley said, interrupting gently. "I'm pregnant and I've got to take care of myself. Don't worry. It's nothing I can't handle."

Ryan squeezed her hand.

"Are you sure?" he asked.

"I'm sure," Riley said.

Ryan shrugged a little and said, "Well, as long as you're sure. You should do what you want to do. I'll support you, no matter what decision you make."

Ryan's words stabbed Riley to the heart …

He says he supports me!

What would he say if he knew the truth, that she'd visited a grisly murder scene and was now involved in a real-life murder case—so deeply involved that she had deliberately gotten inside the mind of the murderer?

Oddly, she felt as though she might be able to tell him if only he were still angry with her. Then they might really be able to have things out.

But now when he was being supportive and concerned and respectful of her wishes?

I just can't.

I can't upset him like that.

Anyway, the icy discomfort between them had thawed because of his concern. They chatted more comfortably during the rest of the meal, mostly about Ryan's extremely busy day at Parsons and Rittenhouse, and the work he still had to do at home tonight.

As they talked, though, Riley sensed that something else was on Ryan's mind—something that maybe he felt they needed to talk about, but that he was wary of bringing up. Riley wondered what it might be.

After dinner, they cleared off the table and Ryan sat there to focus on the legal work he'd brought home. Riley cleaned up the dishes and then settled down in the living room to watch TV. But she found it impossible to keep her mind on the programs. She felt terribly guilty about not coming clean with Ryan about what was really happening in her life. She tried to talk herself into telling him right now, but …

I can't bother him when he's working.

She knew that was mostly an excuse, though. She simply didn't have the nerve to tell him the truth.

She also felt restless and uneasy about other things.

Was Crivaro ever going to call?

Was she off the "Clown Killer" case for good?

Was it even a case anymore?

For all she knew, Crivaro and McCune had already proven Gregory Wertz's guilt once and for all. Or maybe they had moved on to an altogether different suspect. She wished she had some idea.

After a while, Ryan came in and sat down on the couch beside her. When a commercial came on, he clicked the mute button on the remote.

Riley looked at him with surprise.

"Riley we've got to talk," Ryan said with a very serious expression.

Riley swallowed hard, wondering what was coming next.

Ryan said, "I called my parents today and told them …"

He paused and Riley thought …

Oh, God.

He told them I was pregnant.

Instead he said …

"I told them we were engaged. I'd planned to write to them about it sometime soon, not right away. But they called me at work today and … well, I just felt that it was time I told them."

He took her hand again and added …

"So we've got to make plans—where the wedding's going to be, and when."

Riley could hardly believe her ears.

"Oh, Ryan, I don't know …"

She fell silent. She really didn't know what to say.

Ryan said, "What's wrong, Riley? Please don't tell me you're having second thoughts. About getting married, I mean."

"Oh, no, it's not that," Riley said. "It's just … well, right now, there's so much going on in our lives. And making plans like this … I don't know even know where to even begin."

Riley could see disappointment in Ryan's eyes. She realized he'd hoped she'd be excited and eager to have this discussion. She wished she actually felt that way. She wasn't quite sure why she didn't.

Ryan said, "Well, let's start by talking about *when*. We need to work it in sometime this summer."

Riley's dropped open.

"This summer?" she said.

Ryan shrugged and said, "Sure, why not?"

"Well, you've got your important new job, for one thing. And I'm in this intern program."

Ryan said, "Aren't interns allowed to take one day of leave per month? You could make one of those days a Friday or a Monday, turn it into a long weekend. I can do the same thing with my job."

Riley stared hard at him.

"But what's the hurry?" she asked. "Why can't we wait till the end of summer?"

Ryan looked as if he were surprised at the question.

He said, "Riley, you're six weeks along in your pregnancy. You've got more than nine weeks to go in the summer program."

Riley was starting to understand his sense of urgency now. He hadn't yet told his parents—or anybody else—that she was pregnant. And nine weeks from now, her pregnancy would definitely be showing.

Riley felt a twinge of resentment.

"You don't want to be embarrassed," she said.

Ryan let out a deep sigh.

"Riley, I wish you wouldn't look at it that way."

"How else am I supposed to look at it?"

Ryan said, "Well, can you blame me? Don't you feel the same way? About your own father, I mean?"

Riley was taken aback. She hadn't really given any thought to how her father might feel about her pregnancy.

In fact, she hadn't given any thought as to whether …

She said slowly, "Ryan, I don't even know if I want to invite him. You know things have never been good between us. You don't know him."

"Maybe I'd like to get to know him," Ryan said.

Riley shook her head.

"No, you wouldn't. Believe me. He's always been impossible for *anybody* to get along with. And living alone up in the mountains all these years has only made him worse. And …"

She swallowed hard and said ...

"And he's never approved of anything I've done in my whole life."

Ryan said, "Then what about your aunt and uncle? Don't you want them to come?"

Riley felt a pang at the mention of her Aunt Ruth and Uncle Deke. They had brought Riley to live with them in Larned, Virginia, after her mother had been killed and Daddy had gotten too abusive. She was grateful to them now, but she'd been rebellious and difficult during her teenage years, and she'd put them through some terrible times. Her drinking and sex and irresponsible behavior had taken a toll in Riley's relationship with them.

She hadn't been in touch with them since she'd started college. She felt bad about that, and she wished she could think of some way to make it up to them.

But the idea of them coming to the wedding was too much for Riley to think about.

She said to Ryan, "They've retired to Florida, and they're really getting along in years. I wouldn't feel right asking them to make the trip."

An uncomfortable silence fell between her and Ryan.

Riley decided not to even mention her estranged older sister, Wendy, who had run away from home as a teenager. Riley didn't even know where Wendy might live anymore. She couldn't remember having ever told Ryan anything about her.

Finally Ryan spoke in a husky, bitter voice ...

"So what do you want to do? Just get our wedding done and over with in a civil ceremony, and not invite any guests at all?"

Riley struggled not to say aloud ...

Actually, that sounds like a wonderful idea right now.

Instead, she said nothing at all.

Finally Ryan got up from the couch. "I guess now isn't a good time to discuss it."

He sounded quietly angry. But Riley couldn't argue with him. He was obviously right.

"I'm sorry," Riley said.

Ryan went back to his work without another word. Riley sat staring at the silent images on the TV for several long minutes, feeling absolutely miserable. She was also deeply exhausted after three long, difficult, and confusing days. She went to the bathroom, took a shower, and then went straight to bed.

She lay there for a little while wondering whether she could really sleep.

She remembered how excited she'd been about moving to DC and living with Ryan and starting a family with him.

But now …

Everything is such a mess.

She had no idea what she was going to wind up doing this summer—could she work with Crivaro and McCune, or would she be just taking classes and workshops like the rest of the interns? She still wondered if things would be best if she simply dropped out and found a job.

She remembered words her father had said to her countless times over the years …

"You can't do anything right, girl."

Daddy had scarcely kept secret that he even blamed her for her mother's murder.

Rationally, she knew better—or at least she thought she did …

I was only six.

But she knew that her father's blame had taken root deep inside her. No matter what she did, no matter what she succeeded at, it was never enough—at least not for herself.

She felt a sob well up in her throat as she wondered …

Are things ever going to be any different?

She started crying freely as she lay there. Her tears came as a relief, and she felt sure that pretty soon she was going to be able to sleep after all.

But as her consciousness faded, she again felt the horrible presence of the killer.

No, it wasn't Gregory Wertz.

She was sure of it.

He's still out there.

And he's going to kill again.

CHAPTER TWENTY TWO

Riley's eyes snapped open at the sound of her cell phone buzzing on the nightstand.

She heard Ryan let out a sleepy growl of annoyance as she reached for the phone. When she saw that the call was from Agent Crivaro, she leapt out of bed and rushed out of the bedroom to keep from waking Ryan.

"Are you awake?" Crivaro asked when she took the call.

"Yeah," Riley said.

And she wasn't lying. She'd been sleeping deeply just a moment ago, but now she felt jolted as fully awake as if she'd already had a cup of coffee.

"I need you here at the Hoover Building ASAP," Crivaro said.

"What's going on?" Riley asked breathlessly.

"Gregory Wertz isn't the killer. We checked and double-checked his alibis yesterday. He's in the clear for both murders. So today we've got to start all over at square one. The worst part is, the media found out that we got the wrong guy, and they're going crazy today. So the pressure's on. I need all hands on deck. How soon can you get here?"

"Twenty or thirty minutes," Riley said. "Or a little more. I have to catch the metro."

"Get going right now," Crivaro said. He told her the room where she should meet him when she got to the building, then abruptly ended the call.

Riley realized she was hyperventilating as she stared at the phone.

She flashed back again to what she'd told Crivaro two nights ago ...

"Wertz isn't the killer. I'm sure of it now."

Now Riley wondered ...

Is that why he's bringing me back?

Because my instincts turned out to be right?

Maybe.

Or maybe the only thing that mattered to him right now was, as he'd just put it ...

"I need all hands on deck."

She had no idea, but she quickly decided that it didn't make any difference. She was back on the case again, and she needed to get to the Hoover Building right now. She gathered up some clothes and got dressed and ready as quietly as she could while Ryan kept on snoring.

She didn't have time for her usual cereal and coffee, so she grabbed an energy bar out of a kitchen cabinet. Then she dashed off a hasty note to Ryan explaining that she'd had to rush off to a meeting. She left it on the kitchen table and hurried on out toward the metro stop.

As she did every morning, Riley bought a newspaper at a vending box on the way to the stop. She looked at the front page as she sat down to wait for her train.

She could see at a glance that Crivaro was right—the media was all over the case. The headline blared …

Clown Killer Still at Large

She skimmed the story. It said that the FBI had had a suspect in custody who turned out not to be guilty—and so, as Crivaro had put it, they were back at "square one." The rest of the story seemed hardly worth reading—just wild rumors and innuendo from all sorts of unreliable sources.

Riley caught her train and on the short trip she leafed through the rest of the newspaper, looking at columns and features that normally interested her. One of those regular items was called "Poetry Place." Every day it featured a poem sent in by one of the newspaper's readers, often signed with just a first name. The poems were usually awful and sometimes unintentionally funny, but they made for entertaining reading.

The title of today's poem immediately caught her attention …

Welcome to the Labyrinth

She felt a prickle all over, although she wasn't sure why. The prickling increased as she continued to read the rest of the poem …

Come, my chosen dear;
Don't falter and don't cringe;
Join me without fear
For one last merry binge.

Let's dance and play amid

The palpable public crush
Of revelers who bid
A wild farewell to flesh.

We'll put on without shame
A flamboyant display
And look and dress the same
In colorful array.

A merry couple we,
Locked in our embrace—
Just wait until you see
The look upon your face!

The poem was signed simply …

Joey

Riley felt a gnawing feeling deep down in her gut.
The killer! He wrote this! she felt sure.
It's a message!

She took a few deep breaths and told herself not to jump to conclusions. After all, did she have any rational reason for thinking the poem had been written by the killer himself? She began to read it more carefully, picking out specific words and phrases.

The title itself piqued her interest. She remembered that feeling she'd gotten at Lady Bird Johnson Park—her near-certainty that the killer carried his victims off to some special place, a lair. Was the poem itself his riddling way of hinting at the location of his lair—his "labyrinth"?

The first line of the poem was plenty suggestive …

Come, my chosen dear …

The killer had definitely "chosen" his victims, studying their movements and stalking them before abducting them.

Then there were words and phrases like "flamboyant display," and "colorful array." Weren't those obvious references to clown makeup and costumes?

The writer of the poem said that he and his "chosen dear" would "look and dress the same." Might that mean that he himself dressed and made himself up as a clown while he tormented his costumed victim?

And there were the last two lines …

Just wait until you see
The look upon your face!

Riley felt all but sure those lines meant that he showed the victim her made-up face in a mirror as she was in her last dying agony.

But perhaps the most chilling line of all was …

A wild farewell to flesh.

What could that mean except death—a "wild" farewell to life brought on by amphetamine-induced fear?

Riley shivered all over.

I feel so close to him right now.

She felt even closer than she'd had at the murder scene, or the Birches' home, or the alley behind the movie theater, or at the marina in Lady Bird Johnson Park.

She also felt cruelly taunted, almost as if the message had been intended for her personally.

Be careful, she told herself.

She couldn't let her imagination run away with her, and she mustn't succumb to paranoia.

It was a public message, after all.

Surely I'm not the only person who noticed it.

And surely it had caught the FBI's attention. She was curious to find out what Crivaro and the other investigators working on the case had to say about it.

*

When Riley walked into the vast lobby of the J. Edgar Hoover Building, she saw more people roaming around than she'd seen on other days, many of them with video cameras.

Reporters, she guessed.

They had come here hoping to catch some news about the Clown Killer as soon as anything broke. Right now they looked discouraged and frustrated, with no one around to pester for information. Riley kept her head low as she made her way to the security gate, hoping none of them would recognize her from the scene where Janet Davis's body had been found.

Riley was relieved that she got into the secure areas without incident. She found the room Crivaro had mentioned on the phone and knocked on the door.

The stranger who opened the door looked at her with surprise.

The man said, "Um—may I help you? Because we're rather busy here."

Riley could see that some eight or nine men were sitting at a conference table. She recognized two or three of the cops from two mornings ago. She figured the others were FBI agents. Of course Agents Crivaro and McCune were here.

Sitting next to Crivaro was Elliot Flack, the special agent who had lectured the interns yesterday. Riley remembered Crivaro referring to Flack as "an old colleague of mine."

Crivaro spoke to the man who had opened the door …

"Let her come in."

The man waved Riley inside, so she found an empty chair and sat down. The conversation resumed right away without any introduction or comment.

Riley felt invisible.

The cops and agents sounded irritable and anxious. At the moment, they seemed to have been talking over a list of possible suspects, none of whom were proving to be plausible.

When they were finished with the list, Flack said …

"If anybody's got any ideas, now's a good time to speak up."

There were grunts of discouragement around the table.

Riley wondered …

Have they talked about the poem already?

If they had, what conclusions had they drawn about it?

Riley shyly held up her hand.

Crivaro said, "What have you got, Sweeney?"

Riley took the newspaper out of her purse and folded it open to the poem.

"I was just wondering … what do all of you think about this?"

The men looked at her and the newspaper curiously.

"What do we think about *what*?" asked one of the cops.

"This poem," Riley said, pointing at the paper. "You've seen it already, right? I mean, it was written by the killer, wasn't it?"

Everybody stared at her like she was out of her mind.

Crivaro growled softly …

"Explain yourself, Sweeney."

Riley gulped hard. Then in a shaky voice she read the title and the poem aloud. By the time she finished, most of the men were fidgeting and grumbling.

Riley stammered as she went on to try to explain her own thoughts about the poem, especially the significance of certain words and phrases like "chosen dear," "farewell to flesh," "flamboyant display," and "colorful array."

But she felt so flustered that she was afraid she wasn't making much sense.

Apparently, most of the men at the table didn't think so either.

One of the cops said to her, "So you think the killer actually *wrote* this poem? Like it's a message or something?"

Riley said, "Well ... yeah. It seems obvious to me."

With a smirk, McCune said, "I've got to hand it to you, Sweeney—you've got a hell of an imagination."

Riley cringed as she heard others chuckle in agreement.

One of the FBI agents shook his head and said, "We can't waste our time on this kind of crap. We need viable theories. What kind of profile can we come up with?"

The FBI agents began brainstorming about the killer himself, throwing out lots of questions ...

Where did he live?

What kinds of relationships did he have?

What did he do for a living?

Riley was sure they were all excellent questions, the kind that skilled profilers would always ask about such a killer. As she listened, she felt embarrassed at her own silly and irrelevant attempt to participate in the discussion.

But questions came coming, and nobody was providing answers.

Were his killings sexually motivated?

If not, what was driving him?

Anger, thrill-seeking, revenge, a desire for fame?

Riley couldn't help feeling that the men sitting around her were just spinning their wheels. And from their testy voices and scowling faces, she guessed that they were feeling the same way.

She found herself staring at the poem, still lying on the table in front of her.

She felt a renewed sense of certainty ...

This really means something.

But how was she, a mere intern, going to convince all these seasoned investigators that she was really onto something?

She was sure that lives depended on it.

But she felt invisible again. In fact, no one seemed to notice as she got up and slipped out the door.

CHAPTER TWENTY THREE

As Riley walked away from the room and down the hallway, she thought wryly ...

Invisibility has its advantages.

After all, nobody had stopped her from leaving. The men must have assumed she had gone to the restroom—if they had assumed anything at all. She found herself wondering why Crivaro had bothered calling to tell her to come here in the first place if he hadn't expected her to contribute anything.

She smiled a little as she thought ...

Maybe I'll surprise them all by making myself useful.

She headed to the nearest elevator, then went straight to the computer room where she'd participated in yesterday's workshop. She showed her intern ID to the room monitor, then went to one of the computers and logged into the Internet.

She placed the poem on the typing stand next to the computer and looked it over, wondering ...

Where do I start?

How do I start?

Well, first there was the title ...

Welcome to the Labyrinth

Riley knew that the word "labyrinth" referred to a maze. She remembered seeing a popular fantasy movie about such a maze when she was little. But she also had vague recollections of reading or hearing about a specific labyrinth in Greek mythology.

She ran a search on the word and quickly found the ancient story of a vast labyrinth on the island of Crete. At its center lived a monstrous creature called the Minotaur, half man and half bull, who devoured any hero who found his way inside.

Riley felt a twinge of encouragement.

Yes, the image of a maze with a monster dwelling deep inside it fit well with her sense that the man tormented and killed his victims inside his personal lair.

But some of the following lines bothered her ...

Let's dance and play amid

The palpable public crush
Of revelers who bid
A wild farewell to flesh.

She'd been sure that "farewell to flesh" meant death. But now that she read the stanza more closely, there also seemed to be a sense of a crowd of people—a "public crush" of them bidding "a wild farewell to flesh."

How did this fit with her image of a private lair?

Did it fit?

Maybe I've got the whole thing wrong, she worried.

No, she still felt sure that the phrase "farewell to flesh" meant death, but …

Maybe it means something else as well.

She ran a search on the phrase and quickly found something.

"Farewell to flesh" was a literal translation of the Latin phrase *carne vale*—from which came the word carnival.

Carnival!

Riley's interest rose as she kept on reading.

Carnival was a festive season coming before the Catholic observance of Lent. Riley had heard Catholic friends explain that Lent was a time of penance, self-denial, and sometimes fasting. *Carne,* Riley saw, could also be translated to mean "meat." So *carne vale* was a time of partying and feasting and "living it up" before one had to say "farewell" to pleasures of the flesh.

But of course, "carnival" had a different significance to a non-Catholic like Riley.

She ran a search on the word and she found it defined as …

a traveling amusement show or circus

Of course, that definition was more familiar to Riley than the religious one. She had been to a few carnivals over the years. They were colorful, noisy, happy events with food vendors, games of chance, circus-style acrobatics, and amusement rides …

And clowns.

Riley was sure she was on the right track now. And she was convinced that the phrase "farewell to flesh" really did have a dual meaning here.

It did, indeed, mean death.

But it also literally referred to an actual place.

Somehow, that's what his "labyrinth" was, his lair—a carnival.

Riley's head buzzed as pieces of the puzzle seemed to come together. Riley was now curious about the supposed name of the poet …

Joey

She typed in "Joey meaning."

At first, the list of results that came up didn't look encouraging.

Joey was, of course, an abbreviation of the name "Joseph." Riley also saw that the word "joey" could refer to "a young kangaroo or other marsupial," which didn't strike her as at all helpful.

She scanned through several search pages, hoping that something useful would jump out at her. Finally she stumbled across an article about Joseph Grimaldi, an English actor of the early nineteenth century. Skimming the article, she saw that he had been a famous comedian and pantomimist.

Then she noticed that Grimaldi's most popular stage character was named "Joey."

Riley felt a surge of excitement as she read further …

Because of his thieving, mischievous, buffoonish white-faced character Joey, Grimaldi is said to be the first true circus clown. In fact, the name "Joey" has been used for countless circus clowns ever since.

Riley gasped aloud.

Joey is a name for a clown!

Pieces of the puzzle seemed to be rapidly fitting together.

She glanced at the poem again and noticed again the lines …

We'll put on without shame
A flamboyant display
And look and dress the same
In colorful array.

Her earlier hunch had been right! The killer not only dressed and made up his victims to look like clowns, he looked like that himself …

He is *a clown!*
And his "labyrinth" is a carnival!

For a moment, Riley just stared at the computer, overwhelmed with the realization of what a fantastic tool this was.

Her hand shook as she jotted down all this information on a notepad. Then she rushed out of the room and headed back to the room where the meeting was being held. She didn't bother to knock this time, just walked right in.

Again, nobody seemed to notice her. Riley sensed that the meeting was coming to an end. She heard the men murmuring to one another about breaking up into teams and who was going to do what today. Crivaro was talking intently with McCune and Special Agent Flack.

Feeling suddenly bold, Riley tapped Crivaro on the shoulder. When he turned to look at her, she said …

"Agent Crivaro, could I have a word with you?"

Crivaro stared at her for a moment. Then he turned toward Agent Flack and gave him a nod. Both Crivaro and Flack got up and followed Riley out into the hall.

Riley wasn't sure how she felt about Crivaro including Flack in their talk. She'd hoped to be able to talk to Crivaro alone, to try to persuade him of her tentative theory one to one, face to face.

She started feeling nervous again, and breathed slowly to try to calm herself down.

She handed the newspaper poem to Crivaro, and Flack stood beside him looking at it. She talked them through the computer search she'd just done, explaining the significance of "labyrinth," "farewell to flesh," and the name "Joey."

When she finished, Crivaro and Flack just looked at each other.

Riley couldn't read their expressions.

Do they think I'm being stupid? she wondered.

Then Crivaro looked at her and said without smiling …

"Good work, Sweeney."

Riley's knees weakened with joy and pride.

I've finally done something right, she thought.

Now it was up to Crivaro to decide what to do about it.

CHAPTER TWENTY FOUR

As he stood in the hallway with Flack and Riley Sweeney, Jake Crivaro tried not to smile at the girl's look of pride.

Don't want her to get too complacent, he thought.

He'd meant it when he said "good work." It wasn't often that a rookie came up with a solid insight like that. He couldn't remember an intern ever doing it. But he wasn't ready to give her too much praise right away. In fact, he couldn't help but wonder whether she might be reading too much into the poem.

He looked at the paper in his hand and scanned the text again.

No, she's not reading too much into it.

Crivaro felt positive that she was right about the significance of all those words and phrases, especially that name ...

Joey.

It wasn't a coincidence that Joey was a clown's name. This was most likely a message from the killer, who was hinting at ...

Well, something.

The message was plenty cryptic even now that Riley had at least partially deciphered it. But Crivaro felt pretty sure that it suggested the killer's whereabouts—his "lair," as Riley called it.

They hadn't nailed down any essential details, but he had a strong feeling that they were on the right track.

Crivaro looked up from the poem at his longtime colleague, Elliot Flack. Crivaro could tell from Flack's fascinated expression that he, too, had been persuaded of the poem's significance.

Flack said, "That column invites readers to submit poems, so they must have some kind of information on whoever sent this one in. My guess is that it'll be a fake name and won't lead us anywhere. But I'll get somebody over to the newspaper office to find out whatever they know."

Crivaro nodded approvingly.

He opened the newspaper and flipped through its pages until he found what he'd hoped would be there.

It was an advertisement for a traveling carnival that had already been playing for a week in DC's Northwest quadrant. It seemed to be the only carnival currently running in the area.

His lair, he thought.

Crivaro showed the ad to Flack and said, "Sweeney and I are

going to check this place out,"

He heard Riley gasp with delight.

Flack nodded. "You two get right on it. And I'll go back in there and bring the guys up to speed on this new info. We've got to rethink our strategy."

Flack went back into the room and shut the door behind him. Crivaro and Riley headed straight to the parking garage and got into his car. As he drove out of the building, Crivaro remembered what the girl had said the night before last behind the theater where Margo Birch's body had been found ...

"Wertz isn't the killer. I'm sure of it now."

He'd thought exactly the same thing at that very moment, although he hadn't said so.

Maybe he should have.

Would a few words of encouragement kill me?

The girl definitely had good instincts. That was why he'd been drawn to her in the first place. But he knew perfectly well that he hadn't been making her feel very good about herself. And he knew why.

He said, "Look, I know I've been cutting you out of the investigation some. There really hasn't been anything much going on, but that's not the whole reason."

Riley just stared at him without reply.

Jake swallowed hard and continued, "You might have heard rumors that I had troubles with my last partner. Gus Bollinger was his name. A real shit-for-brains rookie ..."

The words were out before Crivaro could think ...

This girl's a rookie too.

He didn't want her to think he thought that *all* rookies were idiots.

He added, "He wasn't anything like you, believe me."

He paused for a moment, then went on.

"Bollinger and I were working together in central Virginia on a serial case—the so-called 'Matchbook Killer,' maybe you heard about it. Someone was murdering young women in motel rooms. When he buried them in shallow graves, he left matchbooks with the victims—matchbooks from bars in the area."

Crivaro fell silent again.

Did he really want to go into details how badly Bollinger had screwed up—how he'd handled a drinking glass the killer had touched in one of the bars, hopelessly smearing up any fingerprints that had been on it?

No, Crivaro's anger was too fresh.

If he went into all that, he'd probably lose his temper yet again, and to no purpose at all.

Finally he said, "Suffice it to say Bollinger botched the whole case. The murderer seems to have stopped killing young women— at least for now, maybe for good. It looks like maybe we'll never catch the bastard."

He shook his head and growled ...

"Damn, but I hate cold cases. Anyway, maybe you can understand now why I'm kind of skittish about partners of any sort. In fact ..."

He was about to say that he didn't think all that highly of Agent Mark McCune. So far, McCune seemed to be an improvement on Bollinger. But as far as Crivaro was concerned, McCune didn't have much of anything to offer as an investigator—not a lot of intelligence, and certainly no special instinct.

But he told himself ...

I'd better keep my mouth shut about that. They're liable to have to work together.

But maybe there was one other thing he should tell her.

"Riley, I've got a son about your age. I'll have to admit I was kind of relieved when he decided not to follow in my footsteps. Looks like he's headed for real estate."

She still didn't say anything, but he could see that she was watching him closely.

"You've got real potential," he said. "That's why I got you here this summer. But if you're not interested in an FBI career, I want you to know that's okay too."

"I don't really know yet," Riley muttered.

Crivaro fell silent again. He couldn't remember ever having talked about the thing that was on his mind. Why was he saying it now?

He continued, "I don't see much of my son, these days. I've been divorced for years, and believe me it was really ugly. And it wasn't my wife's fault, none of it. It was all because I was married to my work."

Riley said, "I'm sorry."

"Don't be," Crivaro said. "Just remember what I'm telling you. You've got a boyfriend, right? I mean, with that ring, I guess you're actually engaged. Well, hang onto that as best you can. Because believe me, getting obsessed with the darkest parts of human nature wreaks havoc on relationships. It gets hard to just ... be a human

135

being. Keep that in mind, that's all I'm saying."

When Riley said nothing, Crivaro glanced over and saw that she seemed to be deep in thought.

I guess she's really taking my advice to heart, he guessed.

Either that, or she's just not paying attention.

He sure hoped she was paying attention. Crivaro had done some research about Riley before submitting her application for the program. So he knew something that she probably didn't suspect he knew—that she'd seen her own mother murdered when she was six years old.

He wondered whether he should bring that up now.

After all, it did pertain to the talk he'd been giving her. Pursuing this kind of work was almost certainly going to bring on flashbacks and reawaken her trauma …

If it hasn't happened already.

Maybe he should say something about it.

Maybe later, he decided.

Meanwhile, he had a feeling that Riley wasn't telling him something that was going on in her life right now—something that he probably should know. He'd suspected that since two mornings ago, when she'd looked ill and out of sorts. She looked better today, but his curiosity still nagged at him.

He was trying to think of a way to broach the subject when Riley spoke.

"What about the other carnival?"

"Huh?" Crivaro said.

"The carnival back in the field. You know, the carnival that had left the night before Janet Davis's body was found there. What do we know about it?"

Crivaro said, "I assigned a small FBI team to investigate that outfit. The guys spent all yesterday trying to find any connection between the carnival and the victim or the crime. They came up dry."

They both fell quiet again.

Then Crivaro added …

"That was a good question, by the way."

He glanced over and saw that she grinned a little.

*

As Crivaro kept driving, Riley basked a little in what he'd just said …

"That was a good question, by the way."

She also appreciated that he'd shared such candid and personal thoughts with her. It almost seemed that he liked having her around. Maybe things were really looking up for her today.

Of course, a lot probably depended on what she and Crivaro found out at the carnival.

What if they turned up nothing at all?

The question worried Riley. Back at the meeting, the whole team had changed tactics because of her interpretation of the poem.

What if I was wrong? she wondered.

What if the poem had nothing to do with the murders after all?

Would everybody be mad at her?

Another thing worried her. Crivaro had just been honest with her. Should she be honest with him, tell him about her pregnancy?

Maybe, she thought.

But then, would he just take her off the case—and out of the program?

She frowned at the idea.

That shouldn't be his call, she thought.

She'd had a prenatal checkup recently, and everything was fine. And although the case was strange and troubling, was it any more stressful than anything else in her life—her problems with Ryan, for instance? The case didn't involve any physical stress—far less than the boxing workout she'd given herself yesterday, and her physician had assured her she'd be fine for that sort of thing.

She decided not to bring it up.

They arrived to find that the carnival was located in a mall parking lot. Above the entrance was a sign that read ...

Mercer and Mathers Midway Entertainments

Riley's heart started beating faster.

What were they going to find out here?

Was her theory right, or would she be proven horribly wrong?

CHAPTER TWENTY FIVE

Riley tried to keep her excitement in check as she and Crivaro got out of the car. She wanted to look like an experienced investigator, not a wide-eyed beginner. But after all, they were checking into a theory that she had come up with—that the killer might be found in a carnival.

Could this be the one?

As they walked toward the entrance, Riley saw that it looked and sounded pretty much like any ordinary carnival, with rides and blaring music. It also looked …

Small.

Riley thought about the title of the poem …

Welcome to the Labyrinth

The carnival didn't look like much of a labyrinth. Riley started to have sinking doubts that this was really any kind of lair.

When they reached the main box office, Crivaro said to the man who was selling tickets, "We'd like to talk to carnival owner."

Inside the booth behind the vender, a burly man was reading a newspaper.

He lowered the paper and asked Crivaro in a rough, wheezy voice, "Who's asking?"

Crivaro pulled out his badge and introduced himself and Riley.

The man squinted at Crivaro. "Have you got a subpoena on you?"

Crivaro looked surprised.

"No," he said. "Do I need one?"

The big, balding man grunted with physical effort as he got up from his folding chair.

"Depends on what your business is," he said.

"We're investigating two murders," Crivaro said.

The man let out a raspy laugh of relief.

He said, "Oh, that's OK, then. As long as it's not about my alimony payments. Come on through. I'll be right out to meet you."

Crivaro and Riley walked through the carnival gate, where the heavy man met them, huffing and puffing with every step. He was smoking a cheap-smelling cigar, which didn't strike Riley as a good idea for a man in his condition.

He shook hands with Crivaro and said, "Clyde Mercer is my name. I'm the sole owner of this outfit, Mercer and Mathers Midway Entertainments. Have been since my partner Barrett Mathers croaked twenty years ago, may the crooked bastard rot in hell."

Crivaro asked, "How long have you been at this location?"

"Just a week now. We're in the middle of our summer tour around these parts, playing county fairs and fundraisers and civic celebrations, that kind of thing. We play right here in this parking lot a week or so every year."

"Where were you before you came here?" Jake asked.

"Over north in Rigbury, doing a couple of days' gig for a church bazaar there. We're heading out of here tomorrow for another stop-over in Fleetwood, a fundraiser for a volunteer fire department."

Riley studied Crivaro's expression as he listened to Mercer's answer, and she could imagine his brain clicking away. Surely he'd want to check out whether anything unusual had happened back in Rigbury while the carnival had been there—especially any murders.

Also, she guessed he was mulling over what it might mean that the carnival was leaving here tomorrow.

After all, the last time a carnival had left the DC area, a corpse had been found the next morning in the field where it had played.

Was another corpse going to be found right here in this parking lot?

Not if we can help it, Riley thought.

But if there was a killer traveling with this carnival, was he going to murder more women in other locations during the rest of its summer tour?

Crivaro said to Mercer, "Maybe you could give us a look around."

"Glad to," Mercer grunted. "We've got a nice little outfit here."

As Riley and Crivaro started following Mercer through the grounds, a man running one of the smaller attractions caught Riley's eye. She realized that she noticed him because of the way he kept glancing at them. Trying to appear that he was looking in some other direction, he was shooting sideways glances at them.

When she turned to look directly at him, he quickly looked away again.

He was running one of the smaller attractions—a game in which patrons shot water guns at a clown face painted on a piece of plywood. The patrons tried to shoot enough water into the clown's open mouth to fill its nose, which was a red balloon. The object of the game was to explode the balloon and get a prize.

Although the man himself wasn't in a costume and his face wasn't made up, he was wearing a red nose and a shaggy red wig. And he couldn't seem to stop himself from watching Riley and Crivaro.

Of course, that didn't necessarily mean anything. It was only natural that Crivaro had provoked some curiosity among onlookers by producing his badge. The man wasn't the only person eyeing them with curiosity, but Riley thought that one had a particularly shifty expression. She decided she'd keep an eye on him.

She turned and followed Crivaro, who kept asking Mercer questions as they wandered among the attractions—all of them standard carnival stuff as far as Riley was concerned. There was a small Ferris wheel, bumper cars, a couple of scary-looking rides that spun patrons high in the air with tremendous centrifugal force, and other more child-appropriate rides, like spinning tea cups. There was a merry-go-round with rather tired-looking animals.

There were also the usual booths and vendors—the water-balloon game, coin toss games, shooting galleries, a whack-a-mole game, and some food stands.

Riley was struck by how small and crowded the place seemed—not at all labyrinth-like, with only a few shacks and portable toilets.

She found it harder and harder to imagine that this place had anything to do with the murders.

As they walked along, Crivaro asked Mercer about his personnel. Mercer said that they were mostly touring carny folks, with a few locally hired temp workers mixed in. When Crivaro pointed out a hobo-like clown who wandered among the patrons making balloon animals, Mercer said he'd been with the carnival for years.

Crivaro watched the clown somewhat warily. But Riley was all but sure he couldn't be the killer. She remembered the lecture Danny Casal had given them the day before yesterday about clown types—the European "Pierrot," the vagabond "Auguste," and also the "tramp" …

"… often personified as a hobo or a vagabond, with a worn-out hat and shoes, sooty sunburned makeup, a sad frown, and a painted stubble of beard."

The clown who was shaping balloon animals fit that

140

description perfectly. The slain women, on the other hand, and been made up as "grotesque whiteface" clowns. Riley felt sure that the killer himself would wear the same sort of costume and makeup as his victims.

Mercer's tour brought them back near to where they had started. Crivaro was jotting down some notes in a pad as he walked along.

But when they approached the water game again, Riley saw that the man who was running it wasn't there.

Then she spotted him hurrying away, still wearing his red nose and wig. He kept looking back, and when he saw her watching him, he broke into a run.

Riley dashed after him.

The man glanced back again, and stumbled.

She was gaining on him.

Looking frantic, the man whirled around and darted up a wooden ramp.

He disappeared into the huge, wide-open, grinning mouth of a scary painted clown.

CHAPTER TWENTY SIX

Riley hesitated for a moment.

Above the huge clown face a sign said "Fun House."

She looked around and saw that Crivaro was still standing next to Mercer. Crivaro was staring toward her, but she could see that he was too far away to catch the fleeing man.

Riley whirled and dashed up the ramp, ignoring the angry shout of a woman in the ticket office.

She pretended she didn't hear Jake yell, "Sweeney! Where the hell are you going?"

She rushed through the clown-mouth entrance, pushing aside hanging pieces of black plastic that draped the opening.

Once she was inside, Riley felt like she was caught in a nightmare.

She was bathed in weird, dim light and strange sounds—cackling and screaming and moaning and creepy organ music. She was surrounded by black walls with glowing images of scary faces—clowns, skulls, and various kinds of monsters—painted on them.

Riley's pulse was pounding now, and a word escaped her lips …

"Labyrinth!"

This was the only structure she'd seen on the carnival grounds that might be large enough to serve as the killer's lair.

Was this really it?

Be careful, she told herself.

The man was in here somewhere, and he was surely dangerous.

But at the moment, she didn't even know where to go.

Suddenly dark winged shapes dropped down and buffeted her on all sides.

Startled and shaken, she tried to wave the creatures off.

Bats! she thought.

But not real ones, she quickly realized. They were rubber bats bouncing from unseen elastic cords.

The bats disappeared upward, and then one of the walls slid away, opening into complete darkness.

Cautiously, Riley stepped forward.

With a burst of light and a chorus of shrieks, a glowing white full-sized human skeleton appeared, dancing right in front of her.

Riley let out a yelp of alarm, but she quickly scolded herself ...

This is all just make-believe.

And yet, she knew that whoever she had followed into this place was all too real.

The skeleton gave a final shriek and whipped out of sight as quickly as it had appeared.

Now pale lights came on, showing her that she was standing in what appeared to be a shadowy hallway. A figure was moving away from her down the hall, staggering and lurching as if drunken.

It's him! she thought.

And he had almost reached another opening at the far end of the hall. which was draped with strips of plastic like the front entrance.

He's about to escape, Riley thought.

Ignoring a roar and two red, gigantic, wolf-like eyes, she started down the hallway after him.

After just a couple of steps, she almost toppled over.

The floor was tilting underneath her feet! Just a little, but enough to throw her off balance.

This was why the man had been staggering.

But of course, he surely knew this place much better than she did. He was better prepared to cope with its tricks and pitfalls.

She tried to run through the hallway, but the floor tilted first one way and then another. She knew she was moving more slowly than her nemesis was.

When she finally pushed the through the plastic strips hanging over the doorway, she found herself in a room bathed in colored light again, and she was facing a wall with ...

Three doors!

A deep, mocking voice echoed through the room ...

"Which door do you choose?"

Riley felt an irrational surge of anger toward the voice.

She wanted to yell out ...

"I don't have time for games!"

But of course, the voice was recorded. Worse, the man she was chasing surely knew which was the right door already and had already gone through.

Letting out a groan of frustration, Riley pulled open the middle door.

She was surrounded by countless images of herself. It was a cluster of mirrors arranged to multiply her reflection seemingly into the infinite distance. The recorded voice let out a cackle and shouted …

"Wrong door!"

Riley stepped backward and the door shut by itself in her face.

Riley let out a groan of despair. She reached for the door on the left and pulled it open. This time she faced three wavy mirrors that grotesquely distorted her image, one making her short and fat, another tall and skinny, and the other wildly misshapen in a variety of ways.

Again the voice laughed and said …

"Wrong door!"

Growing more angry and frustrated by the moment, she backed away and the door flew shut.

There was only one door left. She yanked it open and was almost blinded by the outdoor light.

She breathed a sigh relief.

But as she took a step down an exit ramp, she was startled by a surge of wind that erupted from the floor under her.

It was one last prank—one designed to embarrass girls and women by making their skirts fly up. Fortunately Riley was wearing slacks.

She pushed through the gust of air and looked around.

The man she was chasing was already some distance off, running through the carnival grounds as fast as he could, pushing people out of his way as he went.

Riley felt an unexpected fury rising inside her.

She shouted at the top of her lungs …

"Hey! You! Stop!"

As she took off in a run after him, her whole body felt ready to explode with anger. She wanted to get hold of that man and pummel him as she had the punching bag in the gym.

She, too, pushed people aside as she ran after him.

Suddenly, she saw her prey fall to the ground

Another man had tackled him.

CHAPTER TWENTY SEVEN

Riley felt disappointed. She knew she should be relieved that somebody had taken down the man she'd been chasing. But instead, she felt frustrated at not having been able to take on the guy herself, especially after following him through those bizarre tricky rooms with fake monsters.

When she pushed past the carnival patrons who were already surrounding the pair on the ground, she saw that it was Crivaro who had captured the suspect.

Now Crivaro had turned the man face down so that his red clown's nose squashed against the pavement. His red wig was lying nearby from having been knocked off in the tussle. The gawking onlookers bunched up closer around them.

Crivaro waved his badge at them and yelled, "Stay back, folks. I'm here on FBI business."

The group obediently stepped back a little and continued staring.

Crouching down next to the man, Crivaro looked up at Riley as he got out his handcuffs. Gasping for breath he said to her ...

"After you ran inside there, I realized you'd spotted somebody. So I waited to nab him when he came out."

Crivaro added with a winded chuckle, "But the bastard's fast and nimble, and he wasn't easy to grab. I wound up chasing him myself. Had to resort to tactics I haven't used for a while."

Crivaro snarled at the man as he handcuffed his hands behind him ...

"You gave me quite a chase, buddy. I don't know your name, but you're under arrest on suspicion of murdering two women."

The man twisted his head toward Crivaro with a shocked expression.

"Huh?" he yelped. "I didn't murder nobody!"

The man kept protesting as Crivaro read him his rights.

"Never," he wailed. "I'm no killer. Wouldn't do nothing like that."

Finally Riley asked him, "If you're innocent, why did you run?"

The man stared wild-eyed at Riley as Crivaro hoisted him to his feet.

He looked really panic-stricken now.

Nodding toward Crivaro, the man said to Riley, "I saw him pull out his badge when the two of you came in. And I thought—"

Crivaro interrupted, "That we were going to arrest you? Smart kid."

"Not for murder!" the man said. "I never did nothing like that in my life!"

A couple of local cops had pushed through the crowd. They helped Crivaro keep the man subdued as he started to struggle against the cuffs.

Crivaro said to him, "What's your name, buddy?"

The man shook his head and groaned. "Aw, Jesus."

"You might as well tell me," Crivaro said.

One of the carneys stepped out from the surrounding group and yelled …

"I'll tell you what his name is. It's Orson Trilby. And I'll tell you what he did, too. He's jumping bail. He told me all about it."

Crivaro's mouth dropped open.

He said to the carney, "And you didn't report him to the police?"

The carney blanched, obviously realizing he blurted out something he shouldn't have said.

"He told a lot of us about it," the carney said. "We all just thought it was bullshit. He seemed like that kind of a guy, a regular bullshit artist, trying to impress everybody, especially women."

As the cops broke up the group of people, Crivaro and Riley escorted Orson Trilby back to the ticket booth and seated him inside. Trilby was more than willing to talk now. He admitted that he was jumping bail. He'd been convicted last week on charges of drug delivery and was facing a long prison term. So he'd tried to skip out before sentencing took place.

As Riley listened, she realized the guy wasn't the least bit bright.

For one thing, he ought to have fled the DC area right away instead of trying to blend in as just another carnival worker.

But as Trilby explained to Crivaro, he'd thought he could stay on with the carnival when it left tomorrow and stay clear of DC until he'd been forgotten by the law here.

Crivaro kept firing off questions at Trilby. Watching them, Riley could sense Crivaro's growing discouragement. With every answer, it became more and more apparent that Trilby wasn't the killer they were looking for.

In fact, Riley now felt sure of it in her gut.

She had sensed that the killer was both intelligent and sadistic.

This guy is neither, she thought. *Just a dumb minor criminal.*

Finally, Crivaro seemed sure that Trilby wasn't their killer. He turned the subdued man over to the local cops for arrest. As the cops led Trilby away, Riley and Crivaro started making another tour of the carnival grounds.

The carney who had called out to them earlier followed them a little ways, asking them whether he'd get a reward for identifying Trilby.

"If there was bail posted, a percentage is a reward for catching a jumper, right?" he demanded.

A couple of his friends argued with them that they were the ones who really deserved a reward.

They all struck Riley as perfectly laughable.

Crivaro kept brushing them off, telling them they'd have to talk to the police about it. Eventually the guys gave up.

As Riley and Crivaro walked through the carnival again, they asked workers questions, hoping that maybe someone else might emerge as a suspect.

But their hopes soon faded. Not only did all the people they talked to seem to be innocent, they hadn't noticed anybody else except Trilby behaving suspiciously.

Riley and Crivaro also checked out the carnival's every nook and cranny, trying to find someplace that might be the "labyrinth" mentioned in the poem—a place where the murderer might have held and tormented and killed his victims.

The funhouse was the largest single building in the carnival, and it was built entirely inside a semi-trailer. A security guard told them that it was locked up tight at night, and that the grounds were well patrolled during those hours. Riley and Crivaro examined both the entrance and the exit and saw that nobody could possibly get in there without the keys when it was closed up and locked.

"I don't think it's even big enough," Riley said despondently. "That's not the killer's labyrinth."

Crivaro replied in an irritated growl, "Come on. Let's go get something to eat."

After that, he didn't say a single word to Riley as he drove them to the nearest fast food restaurant. She realized …

He's mad at me again.

But she couldn't blame him. Her theory had been a bust, and the poem probably had nothing to do with the murders after all.

She must be doing absolutely everything wrong.

Crivaro maintained a sullen silence as they sat down at a table to eat.

Riley cautiously said, "I'm sorry, Agent Crivaro."

Crivaro shook his head and took a bite from his hamburger. For a long silent moment, he glared at her as he chewed and swallowed.

Then he snapped, "What the hell were you thinking, Sweeney?"

Riley's heart sank.

This is going to be worse than I thought.

CHAPTER TWENTY EIGHT

Riley braced for the blast of words she was expecting from Crivaro. He looked really upset, but she sensed that was only part of how he felt right now.

He's disappointed, she thought.

That was even worse.

Riley dreaded Crivaro's disappointment a lot more than she did his anger.

Then she realized that he was actually waiting for her to answer his question—*"What the hell were you thinking?"*

She stammered, "I—I know I screwed up. But when I read that poem, I really thought—"

Crivaro interrupted, "To hell with the poem. I'm not talking about the goddamn poem. You were right about the poem, I'm still sure of that. I'm talking about how you took off after that guy. You should have left him to me. You're not an FBI agent, Sweeney. You're not trained and you're not certified. You've got no business putting yourself in that kind of danger."

Riley was startled. It had barely occurred to her that she was doing anything dangerous.

She said, "I was afraid he was going to get away."

"Well, he wasn't," Crivaro said. "All you had to do is tell me you'd spotted him. I mean, I *did* catch him on my own. And the cops got right there to help. What would have happened if you'd caught up with him first?"

Riley swallowed hard.

It was a good question—maybe a better question than Crivaro knew.

His worry was that Riley might have gotten hurt.

But Riley remembered the flood of outrage she'd felt when she spotted the guy fleeing from the funhouse—the same naked anger she'd felt while pounding the punching bag in the gym.

She'd really wanted to beat him to a bloody pulp.

And if she'd caught him, she might very well have done exactly that.

The realization surprised her. She'd never thought of herself as a violent person. A momentary image flashed through her mind—her father's face knotted in anger, as she'd seen it many times.

Crivaro shook his head again and said, "You've got some serious impulse control issues, Sweeney. You've got to get over that if you want to keep working with me. Do you think you can do that?"

Riley hung her head in embarrassment. As she tried to think of what she should say in reply, Crivaro's phone rang.

Crivaro took the call, replying mostly in monosyllables while he listened.

When he ended the call he told Riley …

"That was Agent Flack. He sent some FBI guys to the newspaper office to find out what they could about whoever wrote that poem. It came in the mail, they said. And there was also a drawing in the envelope with the poem—a sketch of a clown's face, which looked a lot like how the two victims were painted. The paper didn't print the drawing with the poem because they didn't think it was worth the space."

Riley's breath quickened a little.

"Did the FBI guys find out his name?" she asked.

Crivaro said, "The picture was signed 'Joseph Grimaldi.'"

Riley gasped.

"The name of the first real circus clown," she said.

Crivaro said, "Yeah, just like you told us a while ago. So it's obviously not the sender's real name. The killer wrote the poem, all right. If we had any doubts, we can be sure of it now. The picture and the name pretty well prove it."

Riley's head was buzzing with confusion.

She said, "So how could we have been wrong about the carnival?"

Crivaro breathed slowly, as if trying to keep his temper under control.

"Sweeney, that's the nature of this work. Some clues lead to dead ends. And some suspects turn out to be the wrong guy. And lots and lots of mistakes get made along the way."

"I understand all that," Riley said.

Crivaro shook his head and drummed his fingers on the table.

"No, you don't understand that, Sweeney. If you did, you wouldn't have run off half-cocked like that. You'd have talked to me first. You've got to learn some patience, damn it. You can't expect to solve a case like this by snapping your fingers."

"I'm sorry," Riley said.

She hated the way the words came out. They sounded whining and pleading. She sure didn't want to sound like that right now.

Crivaro sat and thought for a moment.

Finally said, "Look, there's a lot more to do today. I've got to check in with McCune and find out how his team has been doing, and what everybody else has been up to. And we've got to get the killer's note and sketch into the hands of the forensics people. Maybe they can learn something from the handwriting, or maybe they'll get prints. But …"

Riley dreaded what was going to come after that "but."

"I'm giving you a time-out," Crivaro said.

Riley cringed.

A time-out—like I'm a little kid!

That seemed downright cruel of him.

She almost protested, but managed to keep her mouth shut.

Crivaro continued, "I'll take you back to the Hoover Building. There are other workshops and classes still going on today. Check something out. Learn something. Meanwhile …"

He paused for a moment, then said …

"Think about what happened just now. And take a long, hard look at yourself. You've got to develop some discipline, Sweeney. Nobody can teach you that. It's all up to you."

As they finished eating, Crivaro called McCune and arranged a time to meet with him. Riley and Crivaro barely spoke at all during the ride back to the Hoover Building.

When she got there, she found out that a lecture was already in progress in the auditorium where Agent Flack had spoken yesterday. Assistant Director Marion Connor, the assistant director of the intern program, was giving a long talk about criminal statistics.

It didn't sound like an exciting subject, but Riley reminded herself of what Crivaro had said …

"You've got to learn some patience, damn it."

Of course she knew Crivaro was right. But she felt embarrassed and ashamed that he'd had to tell her that.

She walked into the auditorium, where a lot of interns were listening to the lecture.

Of course they turned around to look at her as she came in.

And of course Connor looked up from his notes in mid-sentence and scowled at her.

Riley fought down a sigh of despair.

It's just that kind of day.

But as she came on inside, she saw the face of at least one person who wasn't unhappy to see her. John Welch turned around and waved at her with a smile. Riley noticed that a seat next to him was empty. She wished she could go sit beside him, but he was in the second row, and she'd attracted too much attention already. She found a seat behind everybody else.

At first, Riley felt daunted by the display of complicated graphs that Connor was pointing to in front of the auditorium. She wondered if she'd come too late to understand what the lecture was all about.

But the understanding of statistics she'd learned as a psych undergrad quickly kicked in, helping her catch up at least somewhat. And some of the facts and figures were actually fascinating.

For example, violent crime in America had been declining since its peak in 1993. Property crime was also following a similar pattern. Of course, as Connor explained, the experts didn't know whether those trends were going to continue into the twenty-first century.

Riley was surprised at this. After all, everybody she knew acted as though violent crime was getting worse all the time. Indeed, the statistics also showed that Americans had trouble believing that the rate of violent crime was going down.

I guess people always assume the worst, she thought.

And in a way, that seemed perfectly natural. After her own horrifying experiences with a ruthless murderer back in Lanton, she found it hard to feel comforted by cold, abstract numbers and graphs. She also thought about her encounters with Janet Davis's distraught husband and Margo Birch's grieving parents. What did they care about facts like these? For victims and their loved ones, there would always be too much violence in the world.

And there would always be work for people in law enforcement.

Riley felt a pang at the thought. She wanted to be one of those people, dedicated to a lifetime of fighting for justice.

But was that really going to happen?

Was she up to the challenges of that kind of life?

Riley learned many more startling facts during the rest of the lecture—for example, that most crimes were never reported to police, and most of the ones that were reported were never solved.

There's so much work to do! she kept thinking

And there was also a killer to stop—right now, right here in DC.

She wondered …

Could anyone stop him before he killed again?

CHAPTER TWENTY NINE

Riley had a hard time focusing on the rest of the lecture.

She kept thinking about the killer, wondering …

What's he doing right now, at this very minute?

What's he thinking?

Had he already chosen another victim?

Had he already taken another captive?

Or was another woman already dead?

Was a painted and costumed body lying somewhere, not yet discovered?

Riley hated being shut out of the case, unable to try to answer such questions herself.

When the lecture ended, she got up from her chair quickly, hoping to slip away before the rest of the interns. But once she got out into the hallway, she came to a stop.

She had no place else to go right now.

She felt stranded as groups of interns came out of the auditorium. As she stood there in indecision, the others made their way past her without comment.

Was she just being paranoid, or were most of them gawking at her and whispering to each other about her?

She was relieved to hear John's voice call out to her …

"Hey, Riley!"

She turned and saw John walking toward her. He had a sheepish, embarrassed look on his face. For a moment, Riley couldn't guess why.

Then he stood in front of her and shrugged and said …

"Uh … about yesterday."

Then she remembered how he'd fled out of the morgue at the sight of the murdered body.

She laughed and said, "Oh, come on. That's nothing to worry about."

John grinned, looking relieved.

Just then an attractive young female intern came toward John, pretty obviously trying to distract him away from Riley.

She said, "Hey, John—are you still planning on joining us at King Tut's over in Georgetown?"

John glanced back and forth between Riley and the young

woman.

He said, "I don't know, Natalie …"

Natalie laughed and tugged him on the arm.

"Well, make up your mind, silly," she said. "Happy hour isn't going to last forever."

John looked at Riley and said, "Want to come too?"

Riley could see a look of annoyance on Natalie's face. Obviously, she was trying to stake her own claim on John and didn't want any competition from Riley. Riley couldn't really blame her. John was definitely an attractive and charming guy. Still, the situation felt rather awkward.

She tugged John aside and whispered to him …

"You do remember I'm engaged, right?"

"Sure, don't worry," John said. "This isn't a date. This is more like a group expedition. Hey, maybe your guy would like to join us."

Riley hesitated.

Should she invite Ryan? Would he feel comfortable with this group?

Will I even be comfortable with this group? she wondered.

But she couldn't see anything wrong with giving it a try.

"Give me just a minute," she said to John.

Taking a few steps away, she got out her cell phone and called Ryan.

"Hi, Riley. What's going on?" Ryan asked.

She said, "I'm heading out to a little get-together with some of the interns. Want to join us? It's in Georgetown, a bar called—"

Ryan sharply interrupted, "Can't. I'm still at work. I have to be here for a while."

Riley felt a chill at his tone of voice. He was obviously still angry after their argument last night.

"That's OK," she said a bit weakly.

"It had better be," Ryan said. "You're not the only one who'll have to work late sometimes, you know."

Riley felt her throat tighten. She didn't know what to say.

Ryan said, "Go on, have a good time."

"I'll do that," Riley said.

They ended the call, and Riley stood staring at the phone.

Ryan's words nagged at her …

"Go on, have a good time."

She knew that tone of voice. Obviously he hadn't meant it.

And how was she going to enjoy herself as long as he felt like that?

She felt a twinge of anger.

He's not being fair, she thought. That made her determined not to let his pettiness spoil her evening.

She glanced back at John, who was standing with several other interns, including Natalie. John was looking toward her expectantly, but the others didn't appear happy that Riley was holding them up.

Riley gathered her courage and said …

"OK, I'll go."

John grinned cheerfully, and Riley followed him and the group into the building's garage. She climbed into a waiting van with the others, and within moments they were on their way to Georgetown.

When they got to King Tut's, Riley saw that it was a high-class, two-story establishment with lots of different rooms. The whole place was flashily decorated with Egyptian motifs and images.

Even on a weeknight, the place was crowded because of happy hour. The clientele was markedly young—mostly well-to-do college students, Riley thought.

And most of them male.

In fact, she and Natalie were the only females in the small group of interns that had just arrived in the van. They all headed over to the bar, where sports events were playing on big television screens.

Shouting over the general noise, John said to Riley, "I'm thinking of ordering some chicken wings. Does that sound good to you?"

Riley nodded.

John asked, "What'll you have to drink?"

Riley reminded herself that she mustn't drink anything alcoholic.

She said to John, "Sparkling water will be fine."

John looked a bit surprised, but he caught the bartender's attention and made the order. When their food and drinks arrived, they followed the rest of the group into a nearby room with tables surrounding a dance floor. A few young people were dancing to a recent up-tempo pop song.

Natalie and the four guys were just getting seated at a table large enough for several more people. But as John and Riley approached the table, Riley was startled by the furious stare she was getting from Natalie. The other intern definitely didn't want Riley there.

Riley hesitated. Were things about to get really ugly?

She was relieved when John gently tugged her arm. "Come on, let's sit over here."

He led her over to a smaller table, away from the rest of the group.

When they sat down, John said …

"Never mind Natalie. She's a first class bitch."

Riley forced a smile.

"Well, she seems to think rather highly of you," she said.

"I guess," John said with a shrug. "Believe me, the feeling's not mutual."

Neither Riley nor John seemed to know what else to say for a few moments. Riley noticed that John kept glancing over at the table where the other interns were talking and laughing.

Would he rather be sitting with them? she wondered. *In spite of Natalie, would he rather be talking with his friends?*

She hated to think that she might be ruining his evening.

Riley found herself struggling against rising tides of self-pity. Maybe she shouldn't even be here. Maybe she should have just said she couldn't come.

She seemed to be at odds with simply everybody in her life—Ryan, Agent Crivaro, and now her fellow interns. Looking at the cheerful group at the other table, Riley remembered happier times back at Lanton.

I used to have friends like that, she thought.

I used to enjoy going out with them.

Those days seemed like a long time ago.

Then she heard John say …

"I'm sorry. This 'group expedition' isn't working out quite like I had in mind."

Riley turned and looked at him and breathed a little easier.

He's concerned about my feelings, she realized.

It felt really wonderful to have a friend right now—even one she didn't know very well.

Riley looked over at the group again.

She shook her head and said, "I don't seem to fit in very well."

John let out a good-natured scoff.

"It's not your fault, believe me," he said. "Natalie doesn't like you because—well, just because *I* like you. As for some of the others …"

He paused for a moment and looked at Riley intently.

Then he said, "Riley don't you realize they're kind of daunted

157

by you? Hell, *I'm* kind of daunted by you. It's like I told you when we first met, none of these interns has done anything like what you've done already. They've never actually worked on a real murder case, let alone pretty much solved one. And they certainly aren't working on a real case right now."

Riley winced a little.

Should she admit to John that she'd gotten a "time-out" from the case, and she might never get back to it?

Then John said, "You can't blame them for being a little ..."

He stopped again.

"A little what?" Riley asked.

"Jealous," John said.

Riley shook her head and said, "Oh, John. Please don't tell me *you* feel that way."

John chuckled.

"Me? Huh-uh. Daunted, sure, but not jealous. I'm not the jealous type."

Riley smiled, feeling a surge of warm and friendly feelings toward him.

John said, "The truth is, I'm sure I could learn a lot from you. Stuff that I'm not getting in any of the classes or workshops. I really wish you'd tell me what it was like—solving that case back in Lanton, I mean."

Riley's smile faded a little.

Did she really want to tell him anything about that?

He probably thought it had been like some kind of Nancy Drew adventure.

How would he react to the real horror of what she'd been through?

Would he get freaked out and wish he hadn't asked?

Would he want nothing more to do with her?

Riley held his gaze for a moment, and then she realized ...

I trust him.

I really trust him.

Maybe she was being naïve, but she felt like she could talk to him about anything. He really was a nice guy. He really didn't have any hidden agenda.

Before she quite knew it, she was telling him the whole story—how she'd found poor Rhea Thorson's body in her dorm room, her throat brutally slashed. She told him about the horrors of the next few days, including how she'd found her own best friend, Trudy, dead and bleeding in the room they'd shared.

She told him about how she'd become mistakenly convinced that one of the professors was the killer. And she told him of her harrowing ordeal when the real killer, another professor, took her captive and would have killed her if Agent Crivaro hadn't come to her rescue.

But perhaps the most disturbing parts of her story had to do with her own discovery of her rare ability to get into the killer's mind.

By the time she was finished, John's eyes had widened and his mouth hung open.

He whispered, "I'm so sorry you had to go through all that."

Riley felt a lump in her throat.

She felt an urge to tell him something else—something she barely ever talked about with anybody.

Slowly and carefully, she said …

"The truth is, I guess I was better prepared for that kind of thing than most people. You see, I …"

She hesitated, then added …

"I saw my own mother shot to death when I was six years old."

John shook his head slowly and said …

"Oh, Riley."

Riley felt a world of kindness and sympathy in those two words.

She realized how desperate she'd been for someone she could talk with openly and freely—especially since she and Ryan had been at odds.

Could she talk to John about all that had happened since she'd joined the program?

Was it OK for her to talk about the case?

She leaned across the table toward him and said …

"John, if I tell you what I've been doing with the Clown Killer case, do you promise … ?"

"I won't say a word to anybody," John said.

Riley wasn't sure why, but she felt as though she knew for a fact that she could trust him.

More than that, she knew that she really *needed* to talk about it.

She started with Crivaro's five o'clock phone call to her three mornings ago, and how he'd driven them to the field where Janet Davis's body had been found. She described how shockingly the victim had been dressed and made up—and how, right then and there, Riley had correctly sensed that the sadistic killer had literally frightened the poor woman to death.

She told him about the darkroom and the costume store, and about her disturbing encounters with Janet Davis's husband and Margo Birch's parents. She described her continuing feelings of connection with the killer in the Birches' back yard, behind the movie theater, and especially during her clandestine trip to Lady Bird Johnson Park

She also told him about her rocky relationship with Special Agent Crivaro, and how he'd scolded her more than once. Finally, she described how her behavior at the carnival had gotten her taken off the case—at least temporarily.

Finally, she took the newspaper with the poem out of her purse and read it to him, explaining all the clues she'd found there.

John took the paper and read the poem to himself, then said ...

"Wow, Crivaro must be crazy giving you a 'time-out' like that. It sounds to me like you're doing a hell of a job. Cracking this poem is a really big deal. And what's wrong with giving chase to somebody as suspicious as that guy at the carnival?"

Riley sighed deeply.

She said, "Crivaro says I've got to learn discipline and patience."

John chuckled a little and said, "Sort of a Yoda, Luke Skywalker kind of relationship, huh?"

Riley laughed. She hadn't thought of it that way.

She said, "Someday I'll tell you about my Darth Vader of a dad."

But John didn't seem to hear her. He was gazing at the newspaper, apparently fascinated by the poem.

Finally he looked up at her and said ...

"Riley, let's solve this case. Just the two of us. Right here. Right now."

CHAPTER THIRTY

Riley's mouth dropped open. For a moment, she wondered if she'd heard John correctly.

She asked, "What do you mean, solve the case?"

John looked at her for a few seconds.

He stammered, "I'm—I'm not quite sure, I guess. Probably not *really* solve it, once and for all. But at least give it a try. Just as an exercise. Come up with a plan, but not something we'd really do."

He shrugged and added, "Look, I'm just really fascinated with how your mind works. I could learn a lot from you. And maybe if we just brainstormed for a little while ..."

His voice faded off.

Riley felt both flattered and intrigued.

Maybe this is a good idea, she thought.

Just as an exercise, anyway.

She asked, "How do you think we should start?"

John scratched his chin and said, "Well, where would *you* start? What would you want to do next if Crivaro let you have your way?"

Riley thought for a moment, then felt the tingling of an idea forming in her head.

She said, "I'd try to draw him out. The killer, I mean."

"How so?" John asked.

Riley took the killer's poem back from him and skimmed over it.

Then she said, "He loves riddles. He likes to make them up—and I'll bet he can't resist them when they come from others. Right now, maybe he even feels disappointed that nobody's trying to match wits with him."

John smiled eagerly.

"Go on," he said. "I'm listening."

Riley sat thinking as she nibbled on a chicken wing. She took a sip of sparkling water.

Finally she said, "Maybe we could tempt him to return to the scene of one of his crimes, and we could be ready to catch him there."

John exhaled sharply.

"Wow, that sounds like a tall order," he said. "He'd have to be willing to take a huge risk."

Riley leaned across the table toward him.

She said, "Yeah, but he's already inclined that way. It takes a serious risk-taker to commit the kinds of murders he does. We just need to trigger that aspect of his behavior, make it work to our advantage."

Riley kept looking at the poem for a moment.

Pulling her ideas together, she said …

"Right now, he can't possibly know that anyone has cracked at least part of his riddle. He doesn't even know if anybody has *noticed* the poem. For all he knows, he wasted his time writing it. So … we could tell him!"

"How?" John asked.

"With another poem!" Riley said, pointing to the poem in the paper. "I'll bet he reads this feature daily—otherwise why would he have submitted his own poem here? We could print our poem right in the same space. We wouldn't tell anybody about what we were doing—not even the newspaper editors. It would just look like another nice little poem, the kind they publish every day."

John nodded and said, "But it would be a riddle like the killer's poem—a riddle that nobody except the killer would notice, much less try to figure out."

"That's right," Riley said.

She took out her notebook and a pen, then added …

"Uh, there's just one problem."

"What's that?" John asked.

"I can't write poetry."

John laughed.

"I might be able to help with that," he said. "I've dabbled in it all my life. I even got a couple of poems published in the university literary magazine while I was an undergrad. Come over, sit closer. We'll write it together."

Riley pulled her chair around next to his and sat down. It felt surprisingly comfortable to be so physically close to him. She offered him her pen and notebook and watched as he set to work playing with both of their ideas.

He said, "First, we need to think of a voice, a point of view."

Riley's brain was clicking away now. It was an exciting feeling.

She said, "What if we wrote it *as if* it were by one of the dead women, reflecting on what had happened to her?"

John squinted at her and asked, "You mean like a ghost? Do you think he'd believe that?"

"No, of course not," Riley said. "He'd know it wasn't really by a dead person, but that wouldn't be the point."

"It would sure get his attention," John said with a nod.

"Right," Riley said.

John's pen sped along, jotting down Riley's thoughts.

Riley said, "Maybe the woman could be thinking about the moment when he'd abducted her."

John said, "Like maybe when Janet Davis got snatched from the marina at Lady Bird Johnson Park?"

"Exactly!" Riley said.

Riley described the photos Janet had taken at the park—especially the last one, with its blurred view of the marina.

She said, "I'm sure she was taking that one at the exact moment when he knocked her out cold and carried her away."

John nodded slowly and said, "So in the poem, she could decide to go back to the marina at sunset to try to recapture that moment, to try to understand what happened. She'd say she was going at sunset that same day. That would give the killer a time and place to expect some sort of rendezvous. Still, I can't help wondering … won't he expect the police to be waiting for him there? I mean, I understand that he's got a risk-taking personality, but …"

Riley said, "That's why we've got to make this so intriguing that he can't resist, despite the risk. We can make the poem read like it wasn't written by the police or the FBI at all—just some mysterious private person who knows more than she should."

As soon as the words were out, Riley realized …

I almost seem to be talking about myself.

After all, she wasn't part of the case now.

What would Crivaro think if she knew what she was doing?

He'd probably hate it, she thought.

Worse, he'd probably tell her why it was a lousy idea.

But what did it matter? After all, like John had said earlier, this was just an exercise …

"Not something we'd really do."

What harm was there in exploring it just as an idea?

Riley and John set to work. First they came up with a title …

My Lost Sunset

Then they worked on the poem itself. Riley supplied the ideas and images, which John shaped into lines and stanzas. Riley was impressed by his turn of phrase and how easily rhymes came to him.

Before Riley quite knew it, they had the whole thing written. John read it aloud …

The last things that I saw that dusk,
The waning of that day,
Were sparkling waters, calm and still,
And blurs of white and gray.

I let my lens fall from my hand
My shaking was to blame,
And then I slipped and lost that view;
To miss it, such a shame!

If I'd looked better, would I know
What shapes escaped from me?
Tonight when sunset comes again
I must go back and see!

"Wow," Riley whispered when he finished. "That's really good."

John nodded and said, "To any ordinary reader, it would just look like maybe some schoolgirl was imitating Emily Dickinson. But it describes exactly what happened to Janet that evening—especially how she dropped her camera."

John pointed to the last two lines and read them aloud again …

Tonight when sunset comes again
I must go back and see!

Then he said, "She's telling him she'll be at the marina that very evening, at the exact time of her abduction. But do you think it would really catch the killer's attention?"

Riley felt a chill—a fleeting sense of the killer's cunning, and also his curiosity.

"I'm sure of it," she said.

Then Riley shook her head and said again …

"Wow."

John continued, "But it's got to be signed by somebody. We need to come up with a name for the poet herself—the person who supposedly sent it to the newspaper."

Riley said, "The killer signed his name 'Joey,' and the picture he sent as 'Joseph Grimaldi.' They weren't his real names. They were clown references. We should use a fake name too."

Riley thought for a moment, then said …

"The victim's name was Janet Davis. Could we maybe turn that into an anagram?"

"Great idea," John said.

Together they started putting the letters together in different ways. Riley quickly realized that coming up with an anagram was going to be harder than writing the poem itself. But eventually they came up with …

Tina D. Vejas

Riley said, "I guess that sounds like a real name. The last name sounds a little odd, though."

"Not so odd," John said. "It sounds like a Spanish name. In fact, it has some extra significance in Spanish."

John sat smiling at her, as if inviting Riley to make a guess.

Riley squinted and said, "Well, I really sucked at Spanish in high school, and—"

John gently interrupted, "It's a second-person singular form of the verb *'vejar.'"*

Riley shrugged. She couldn't remember that word, or if she'd ever learned it at all.

John said, "*Vejar* means to vex or to mistreat—or to humiliate."

Riley's eyes widened.

She said, "So the poet's last name literally means 'you humiliate' in Spanish! Which is exactly what the killer does to his victims by dressing and making them up as clowns!"

John nodded, smiling broadly.

Riley silently read the poem yet again.

She could imagine that killer's fascination and delight at this poem's riddles …

Or …

Maybe he wouldn't notice it at all.

Anyway, she was still sure that Crivaro could give her a dozen reasons why it wouldn't work. And of course, he'd be right.

Besides, she reminded herself, it was just an exercise …

"Not something we'd really do."

She and John kept sitting together, not returning to their

165

original places on opposite sides of the table, even though they'd finished the work they'd started. It felt right somehow to stay close—and it made it easier to hear each other over the talking and the music in the room.

They read the poem to each other over again and talked about how clever it was, really relishing what they'd just done together.

Riley was startled at how good she felt—better, she thought, than she'd felt in days.

After all, even when Crivaro had congratulated her on doing something right, the pressure really didn't let up. She'd still felt the need to keep proving herself to him. His occasional words of praise didn't erase the chronic insecurity she'd been feeling lately …

But this … right now …

Being around John was so different

It was so easy and effortless.

It felt like such a huge relief to be able to talk openly with him about things she seldom ever talked about. And it was so stimulating and energizing to generate ideas with him, come up with a plan together, even if it was only a hypothetical exercise.

As they continued talking about one thing or another, Riley's enjoyment began to fade into melancholy. She wondered …

Why is it so rare in my life … this simple thing I've got right now, this friendship?

Soon John seemed to notice a change in her demeanor.

Finally he said, "You seem sad, Riley. Is something wrong?"

Riley sighed deeply.

"Well, I guess I've already told you about most of it, but …"

She hesitated for a moment, then said …

"Things aren't good between me and Ryan, my fiancé. They ought to be great. He's got this wonderful job as an entry-level attorney at a law firm, and here I am training for the FBI, and …"

She stopped herself short from telling John she was pregnant.

She knew it wasn't because she thought there was anything wrong with telling him, but she hadn't told anyone in the intern program. She hadn't even told Crivaro.

Instead she said, "Ryan and I have been spending more time apart. And whenever we *are* together …"

Riley's voice faded.

John said, "You feel at odds with each other, don't you? Like you're having trouble understanding all the new things that are going on for both of you. You're not connecting like you think you should."

Riley nodded, and she felt a knot of emotion in her throat.

John was so empathetic—and she really needed a little empathy right now.

Then John said, "Well, it sounds perfectly natural to me, with all the changes that are going on in both of your lives. It's just a transition. You'll get through it."

He shrugged and said, "But what do I know? I've never been engaged."

Then he laughed and added, "And besides, *I'm* not the one with a psych degree."

Riley laughed too.

Their laughter faded, and John sat looking at her with a kindly expression.

Then he said, "Just answer one question for me—yes or no."

"OK," Riley said.

John leaned toward her and said ...

"Is Ryan an idiot?"

Riley's eyes widened with surprise.

"What?" she said.

"It's really a simple question. Yes or no?"

Riley laughed nervously and said, "Actually, Ryan's really very intelligent and—"

John interrupted, "That's a 'no,' so stop right there. That's all I needed to hear. He's not an idiot, so he knows a good thing when he's got it. He's not going to let go of you."

John leaned back in his chair and stroked his chin with mock-sagacity.

He continued, "And I know from first-hand experience that you're anything but an idiot. Which means you wouldn't be with Ryan if he weren't right for you. And you're not going to let *him* go."

John snapped his fingers and said, "So ... there you have it. You're both smart enough to know when you've got a good thing going. That means you're going to be all right together. Just give yourself some time."

Riley smiled a smile that felt like it went all the way down to her toes.

When was the last time anyone had said anything so sweet to her?

Maybe he's even right, she thought.

Just then a fast and loud pop song came to an end, and the dancers on the floor shifted gears as a softer, slower song started.

Riley felt a bittersweet pang as she recognized the song: "One More Night" by Phil Collins.

It had been a favorite of hers for a long time now. Of course it was an old song, and she'd taken some teasing about it from her friends at Lanton, who were generally into the latest upbeat pop fare.

She especially remembered how Trudy used to nudge her and call her "grandma" whenever they listened to it together.

Then she and Trudy would both laugh.

She remembered the musical sound of Trudy's laugh, the brightness of her smile ...

I'll never hear that laugh again.

I'll never see that smile again.

It was an almost unbearable thought.

But even so, those were beautiful memories to have.

John touched her on the shoulder and said, "Do you like this song?"

Riley smiled at him and nodded.

John gently took her by the hand and said, "Come on, then."

He led her out onto the dance floor, and within moments they were close together and cozily swaying to the music.

Riley felt so warm and safe and relaxed, she thought she might melt into John's arms.

It was an amazing feeling—all the more so because there was nothing sexual about it.

John was a kindly, sympathetic friend—nothing more, nothing less.

And she was sure that he felt the same way about her.

Then Riley was jarred by the sound of her phone buzzing in her pocket.

"Oh, I'm sorry," she said to John.

"It's OK," he said. "You'd better get that."

Riley took out her phone. As she'd expected, she saw that the caller was Ryan.

She was shocked by the abrupt shift in her feelings.

As she took the call, she wondered ...

Why do I feel so down all of a sudden?

CHAPTER THIRTY ONE

Stepping off the dance floor, Riley moved away to find a quieter spot so she could talk with Ryan on her cell phone.

"I hear voices and music," Ryan said. "Where are you?"

Riley felt yet another pang as the Phil Collins song kept on playing.

She realized …

Ryan doesn't even know how much I like this song.

I've never told him.

For some reason, that seemed to matter a lot right now.

She said, "I'm at a Georgetown bar called King Tut's."

Ryan said nothing in reply.

Feeling a little irritated, Riley said …

"Look, I told you I was going out with some friends. I thought you were OK with it."

"I am," Ryan said.

But he didn't sound to Riley like he was OK with much of anything right now.

And she couldn't help feeling a pang of guilt at having said that word …

Friends.

Was she being dishonest by making it sound like she was out with friends—plural?

She'd had next to nothing to do with the other interns except John. They certainly hadn't seemed to want anything to do with her.

Riley asked, "Where are *you?*"

"I'm still at work, but I'm headed home soon. I just wondered if there's anything to eat at home."

Riley sighed and said, "You ought to know. You made a nice tuna and pasta salad. There's some left over in the refrigerator."

"It's kind of old," Ryan grumbled.

Riley stifled a groan and managed not to say …

"You made it only yesterday."

She knew it wouldn't help. Ryan was in no mood to agree with her about anything.

Finally Ryan said, "It's OK. I'll pick up something on the way."

Then he ended the call.

Riley stood there staring at the phone in her hand. She didn't know whether she felt more furious or hurt.

He wants me to feel guilty, she realized.

What bothered her most was that she *did* feel guilty.

Just why, she wasn't sure.

She heard John say, "Is something wrong?"

She turned and saw him standing next to her with a concerned expression on his face. Riley wondered—what should she tell him? She more than half wanted to say ...

Nothing's wrong. Let's keep right on talking and dancing.

But that wasn't an option now.

It was no longer possible for her to enjoy her evening.

Finally she sighed and said ...

"I guess it's time for me to get home."

John nodded and said nothing. Riley sensed that he'd figured something was off between her and Ryan and that she'd rather not talk about it.

Riley gave him a quick, friendly kiss on the cheek, then turned to leave the bar.

"Wait a minute," John said. "How are you going to get home?"

"Like I always do, the metro," Riley said.

John rolled his eyes and said, "Oh, don't be silly. I'll get you home. I was planning on taking a cab myself. We'll catch one together."

Riley waved her hand in protest.

"Oh, no," she said. "You mustn't cut your evening short. You should go spend your time with your friends over there."

John looked at the table where the other interns were sitting. He laughed.

"With that bunch? That would be kind of a letdown after ..." He broke off whatever he was going to say, then added, "I'm ready to call it quits. Come on, let's go."

Riley left a tip on the table and followed John outside, where he flagged down a cab for them.

Neither of them said much on to the ride to Riley's apartment. It wasn't exactly an awkward silence. Riley was in no mood to talk, and John obviously respected that.

As they neared Riley's apartment building, she noticed John looking out the cab window at the rundown neighborhood where she lived. It looked especially seedy at night, with young men loitering on the sidewalks dressed in what looked like gang attire.

Riley didn't notice any particular change in John's expression, but she could imagine what he might be thinking. Coming as he did from a wealthy family, John surely lived in much more upscale surroundings.

Was he shocked by where she lived?

He's lived such a sheltered and privileged life, she thought, remembering again how John had run out of the morgue at the sight of a teenaged corpse.

Was he really ready to live the life he had chosen—the life of a dedicated law enforcement agent, almost constantly faced with horrors that most people could scarcely imagine?

Riley knew that he was hopeful and idealistic, but …

Does he know what he's in for?

The cab pulled up to Riley's apartment building. Riley reached over and squeezed John's hand.

"Thanks so much for such a lovely time," she said with a smile.

"Thank *you*," he said, smiling back. "Let's do it again soon."

Riley climbed out of the cab and went into the building, then downstairs to their basement apartment. When she went inside, she was relieved to see that the lights were still off. Ryan hadn't gotten home yet.

She turned on the lights and went straight to the refrigerator and took out the glass bowl of tuna and pasta salad that Ryan had made yesterday. She took the aluminum foil off the top and saw that it looked as fresh as it had yesterday.

"Kind of old," my ass, she thought crossly. It smelled good and Riley realized she was hungry.

She got a glass of water, a plate, and some utensils, and sat down at the table. While she ate, she took out her notebook and looked the poem she and John had written together. She noticed two lines in particular …

> *… sparkling waters, calm and still,*
> *And blurs of white and gray.*

It's really quite pretty, she thought.

Of course, she had to give John credit for any qualities it might have as a poem. He really was a sensitive, intelligent, and imaginative guy—and more talented with words than he probably realized.

But as she read the rest of the poem now, that was all it seemed to be …

Pretty.

The idea that anyone could use it to bait the killer now struck her as farfetched and silly. Not that she and John had ever been serious about that. It was only an "exercise," after all. But at least it had been fun to write.

She was still sitting there, nibbling at her dinner and reading through the poem again, when she heard the apartment door open. Ryan came in, carrying a bag from a fast food place. As soon as she saw him, a strange feeling came over Riley.

She felt positively nauseous, and her head hurt.

What's the matter with me? she wondered.

Ryan looked at Riley with surprise as he closed the door behind him.

"You're home sooner than I expected," he said. "But I did bring two burgers."

Riley shrugged, trying to ignore the pain.

"I've already eaten," she said. "I took a cab home."

Ryan squinted with disapproval as he plunked the bag on the table.

"A cab?" he said. "Not the metro? How much did you spend tonight, anyway?"

Riley frowned. She wanted to say …

"Is it any of your business?"

But of course, they were poor, and it was a natural thing for him to worry about.

"I hardly spent anything," she said. "I left a tip on the table of the bar when we left, that was all."

She saw Ryan's expression darken, and she immediately knew why.

I said "we."

And now Ryan wasn't just irritable. He was suspicious and jealous as well.

CHAPTER THIRTY TWO

Abruptly, Ryan sat down at the table with Riley. His eyes were full of suspicion.

He thinks I'm cheating on him, she realized.

And she was feeling too sick to explain to him why he was wrong. She pushed away her plate with the remains of tuna and pasta.

In a tight voice Ryan said slowly, "So you didn't spend anything on food or drinks or even the cab home?"

Riley sighed and said, "Look, a friend paid for my drinks and food this evening. We shared a ride home in the cab, and he paid for that too."

Ryan was glaring at her now. He still hadn't opened his bag of food.

Meanwhile, Riley's stomach was cramping badly, and a splitting headache seemed to be underway.

Was she coming down with the flu all of a sudden?

Had something been wrong with those chicken wings back at King Tut's?

Or was she wrong about the tuna and pasta still being fresh?

Or was she just so upset that it was making her sick?

Feeling plenty irritated herself now, Riley said …

"It was a guy, OK? It wasn't a date, and I'm not involved with him or attracted to him or anything like that. He's another intern in the summer program. We're just friends."

The words jarred as she said them …

Just friends.

The word "just" hardly seemed right.

Tonight a little friendship had seemed like a huge and important thing.

But she didn't want to try to explain that to Ryan now. Things were bad enough already.

Riley pointed to the bag on the table. "Your food is getting cold."

Ryan ignored her and left the bag untouched. He sat staring into space for a long moment. Finally said, "Riley, we've really got to talk. What's going on with us?"

Riley almost had to bite her tongue to keep from saying …

173

"I sure as hell don't know."

Instead she managed to keep silent.

Sounding like he was trying to keep his own anger under control, Ryan said, "A few days ago I asked you to marry me. I gave you a ring. You seemed happy. But ever since then I've felt like you were digging in your heels."

"I'm not digging in my heels," Riley said.

"Then why can't we set a date?" Ryan asked. "Why can't we set any plans?"

Riley was feeling more physically ill with each passing moment.

It wasn't helping her mood.

She could no longer keep her bitterness and resentment out of her voice.

She said, "Look, just yesterday you admitted why you were in such a hurry about the wedding. You're embarrassed. You don't want your parents to see that I was pregnant."

Ryan gasped.

"I didn't say that," he said.

"Yes, you did," Riley snapped. "I remember your exact words when I suggested that you felt that way. 'Can you blame me?' you said. 'Don't you feel the same way?' That's exactly what you said."

Ryan slumped in his chair, obviously stung by her words.

"I just want what's best for both of us," he said.

They both fell silent. Riley's head hurt so much now that it made her dizzy. She stared at the food on her plate with disgust.

Finally Ryan said in a soft, sad voice …

"Maybe what's best for both of us is … that we just give up on the whole thing."

Riley felt her eyes sting with tears. Things were much worse than she'd imagined.

She wished they could just shut up and pretend this argument had never started.

But it was much too late for that.

Then Ryan said, "Do you want me to move out?"

"I don't know," Riley said, struggling to keep her voice from shaking. "Do you want your ring back?"

Ryan's head dropped, and he let out a sound that sounded like a sob.

Oh, God, Riley thought. *We've both said way too much.*

But there was no turning back.

It was coming clear to her—they'd both been holding in their resentment and anger and it was breaking out now.

But it was all happening so fast.

Just a little while ago, things had been so different.

She'd felt so comfortable with John. Was it possible for her to feel so completely at ease with Ryan?

Had she ever felt that way with him, really?

Suddenly, that seemed like the most important question in Riley's life.

And she felt desperate for an answer.

Riley took hold of Ryan's hand. Fighting down both her physical and emotional pain, she said ...

"Ryan ... are we friends?"

Ryan looked at her with an expression of stricken bewilderment.

"What?" he asked.

"Are we friends?" Riley repeated.

Ryan squeezed her hand.

"Of course we're friends," he said. "We're in love. We're engaged to be married. We're going to have a baby. How could we not be friends?"

Riley tried to take comfort in his words, but she couldn't.

He doesn't understand, she thought.

He doesn't even understand the question.

She suddenly buckled over, seized by a fierce stab of pain in her belly.

Ryan put his hand on her shoulder.

He said, "Riley, is something wrong?"

Riley sensed something different in his voice—a deep and sudden concern.

She shook her head.

"I'm really feeling pretty sick," she said. "I think I'd better go to bed."

"Is there anything I can do to help?" Ryan said.

"No," Riley said as another spasm of pain shook her body. "I'm ... so sorry ... about all of this."

"I'm sorry too," Ryan said.

Ryan supported her as she got up from the table and staggered into the bedroom. She found her nightgown and went in the bathroom, where she took some aspirin and got out of her clothes and got ready for bed.

Then she went back into the bedroom. Ryan was still standing there, looking at her with alarm.

She fell into bed, and Ryan pulled the covers around her.

For a few moments, the pain in her head and belly seemed to be getting worse and worse.

But then the pain ebbed away, and all she felt was a terrible sadness. She felt tears running down her cheeks.

The tears were strangely comforting.

*

Riley was crying as she wandered through the vast, empty hallways of the J. Edgar Hoover building, feeling lonelier than she could ever remember feeling. She saw nobody anywhere. She was all alone in this vast, unwelcoming place.

She knew she didn't belong here.

But she had no idea how to find her way out.

Her sobs resounded through the corridors.

"Can somebody please help me?" she called out in a choked voice.

Her words echoed around her, mingled with what sounded like mocking laughter.

Then she heard something behind her—the sound of footsteps.

She turned quickly around but saw nobody. She realized the footsteps must be coming from one of the adjoining hallways.

She almost called out ...

"Is somebody there? Please come and help me!"

But then it occurred to her that maybe someone was stalking her—someone who meant her harm.

Yes, that seemed more likely. She had no reason to imagine that anybody might be approaching with friendly intentions.

She scurried along as quietly as she could until she reached a corner of another hallway. She ducked around the corner and flattened herself against the wall.

Keep quiet, *she told herself.*

But for some reason, she couldn't stop sobbing.

And her sobs kept echoing far and wide.

And the footsteps were still approaching.

She broke into a run. But she soon saw that the hallways were shifting and breaking off in different directions, becoming more mazelike and labyrinthine.

She turned a corner and froze in her tracks as she saw a shadowy figure standing right in front of her. She tried to run again but couldn't move. Then something bright flashed in the figure's hand ...

A knife! *she realized.*

Her pursuer plunged the knife into her belly, and again she felt that sharp, terrible pain ...

Riley awoke to the sound of her own scream.

She heard Ryan's voice ...

"Riley! What the hell!"

She opened her eyes. The bedroom was dark. The pain in her belly was now unbearable, and so was the pain in her head

She thrashed around until she felt something warm and sticky.

She held her hand to her face, but couldn't see it in the dark.

The lamp on Ryan's side of the bed clicked on, blinding her for a split second.

Then she saw that her hand was covered with blood.

Ryan said ...

"Riley! Oh, my God!"

Riley sat bolt upright and saw that the sheets underneath her were splotched with blood.

Ryan turned her face toward Ryan's. His expression was alarmed, but also somehow comforting.

He said, "Riley, it's going to be OK. I'll take care of everything."

He helped her move over to his side of the bed, where the sheets were still dry, and he stretched her out on her back.

Then he grabbed his cell phone from his nightstand.

Riley lay there staring at the ceiling while Ryan called 911 to say that his girlfriend had a medical emergency.

When he finished, he peered down at her face and gently stroked her hair.

Riley gasped and stuttered ...

"Ryan, wh—what's happening? Am I dying?"

Ryan smiled a deeply reassuring smile.

"Of course not, darling," he said. "Just lie still and try to relax. You're going to be fine. I promise."

Riley shivered, feeling cold all over.

I'm in shock, she realized.

Then, before she knew it, she heard sirens, and the room was quickly flooded with men dressed in white who lifted her onto a gurney.

As the men rolled and carried the gurney up the stairs and into the ambulance, Ryan never left her side.

He kept saying over and over again …

"It's going to be all right, Riley. I'm here. I'll stay right with you."

Riley believed him.

How could I ever doubt him? she wondered.

But she also wondered …

What's happening to me?

CHAPTER THIRTY THREE

Riley lay in a narrow bed with partitions on either side. At the foot of the bed, a white curtain was drawn across the opening. Even though the ER was brightly lit, she felt as though she were in some kind of a mysterious fog.

In fact, she really was in a fog—a mental and emotional fog. The sharp pains in her head and abdomen were gone, and her thoughts were vague and uncertain.

She'd been sedated as soon as she'd been put into the ambulance, and she'd been aware of its powerful effects well before she was brought in here. She'd felt numb and indifferent during the physical examination a doctor had done a little while ago.

Still, she was aware of the bustling activity all around her little secluded space. Through the gaps on either side of the curtain, she could see white-clad hospital personnel hurrying about, and gurneys carrying patients rattling back and forth. She heard voices chattering, and bells, and urgent PA announcements summoning physicians to different stations.

She'd been alone for a little while now.

But she felt oddly unworried about that.

The male physician who had checked her in had told her with a sincere and comforting smile ...

"Don't worry, you're going to be fine."

She'd had no reason not to believe him—at least as far as her physical health was concerned.

She was also sure that the same was not true for many of the people in that melee outside her curtain. Out there, people were suffering from dire illnesses, injuries, and wounds that demanded the sort of immediate attention that she didn't need.

And yet she wondered ...

Where's Ryan?

Then she remembered—she'd been told that Ryan couldn't see her just yet.

But he'd be here soon, the physician had said.

Nobody had told her yet what had happened to her, but she knew perfectly well without being told.

At least she knew it intellectually.

The emotional repercussions hadn't yet kicked in. Riley

179

wondered how bad they were going to be.

Soon the curtain parted and a white-clad woman with large eyes and a friendly, birdlike face came into her area. Ryan was right there beside her.

The woman smiled and said, "I'm Melissa Pascal, and I'm the on-duty OB/GYN. How are you feeling right now?"

"Weird," Riley said.

Dr. Pascal patted her on the shoulder.

"I don't doubt it."

She held Riley's gaze for a moment and said with a sympathetic smile …

"I'm afraid you've had a miscarriage."

Riley gulped hard.

Of course that was exactly what she had expected.

But despite the sedation, hearing the word spoken aloud came as a shock.

Dr. Pascal looked over some papers on her metal clipboard.

She said, "Your fiancé put me in touch with your physician back in Lanton, and I've talked with her. It seems that your pregnancy was just fine during your last checkup. I also see that you've been on a healthy regimen of supplements. You've been taking good care of yourself."

"So what happened?" Riley asked.

Dr. Pascal shook her head and said in a gentle voice …

"You have no idea how common this is. Believe it or not, about fifty percent of all pregnancies end in miscarriage. Most of the time those happen before the woman even knows she is pregnant. Between fifteen and twenty-five percent of *known* pregnancies end in miscarriages, most of those just the way yours did."

Questions started to pour into Riley's mind.

Had she done anything to bring this on?

Was this her fault somehow?

Ryan said to the doctor, "Riley has been under a lot of stress lately."

Stress, Riley thought.

Yes, that was definitely the right word.

But she wondered—what was Ryan thinking when he said that word?

Was he feeling guilty for how hard things had been between them lately?

Or was he angry with her for putting herself in stressful situations?

He doesn't even know, she reminded herself.

Ryan had no idea of what she'd been doing lately. He knew nothing about her wrenching anxieties about success or failure, the dead body she'd seen that wasn't in a morgue, the distraught family members she'd encountered, and especially not her unsettling and sometimes terrifying feelings of connection with a killer.

He'd just thought she'd taken on too much by getting into the intern program.

And he'd found that annoying enough.

If only he really knew, she thought.

Dr. Pascal spoke to both Ryan and Riley. "Don't worry about stress. Stress is a fact of life for all of us, some of us more so than others. I'm sure it didn't cause this miscarriage."

"But what did?" Riley asked.

Looking through the papers again, Pascal said, "Well, we can eliminate most of the common causes. You don't have diabetes or thyroid problems or blood clotting disorders. According to your earlier examinations, you don't have uterine or cervical abnormalities. You don't smoke, and I don't suppose you've been abusing drugs or alcohol."

"No," Riley said.

Pascal tucked the clipboard under her arm.

"That leaves the most common cause of all—chromosomal abnormalities. Something was wrong with the fetus—something truly incompatible with life. Your body sensed this and ended the pregnancy. I know this is hard to accept right now, but in a way, what happened was a good thing, the right thing. And it wasn't in any way your fault."

Riley wanted to feel reassured, but somehow she couldn't.

And she could tell by Ryan's expression that he wasn't reassured either.

He stammered, "But—but Doctor, could you tell us … ?"

Seeming to guess Ryan's question, Dr. Pascal said to him …

"Mr. Paige, your fiancée is a perfectly healthy young woman. There's no reason to believe she can't have children in the future."

Turning to Riley, she added …

"Someone will come by soon to check you over again. Then you'll be able to leave. I promise that the worst of this is over. You might have a few symptoms, possibly some slight continued bleeding. If things get really bad, contact me right away. But you really needn't worry."

Ryan and Ryan thanked Dr. Pascal, who left them alone. Ryan

sat next to the bed holding Riley's hand, looking at her steadily. She found it hard to return his gaze. She wasn't sure why.

Soon another doctor came and gave her a quick examination, then said it was OK for her to leave. Ryan had followed the ambulance here, so he went outside to get the car.

The effects of the sedative had faded almost entirely, but Riley still felt wobbly and weak as she got to her feet. An orderly helped her into a wheelchair and took her outside, where Riley saw that the sun was just coming up. Ryan pulled up to the curb in his car, and the orderly helped her into the passenger seat.

Neither Riley nor Ryan spoke a word during the ride home.

Ryan's expression was pained and sad.

This is hard on him too, Riley thought.

When they got back to the apartment building, Ryan helped her out of the car and into the apartment, then put her directly to bed. Soon Ryan got into his pajamas and climbed into bed beside her.

He held her close, with her head on his shoulder.

His strength and warmth felt comforting. Even so, troubling thoughts tugged at Riley.

She realized how little thought she'd given to being pregnant lately.

Sometimes she'd almost forgotten about it altogether.

Much of the time it hadn't seemed quite real.

But now that she wasn't pregnant anymore …

It seems more real than ever.

And a deep sense of loss was coming over her.

She remembered what Dr. Pascal had said …

"I promise that the worst of this is over."

The doctor had also said …

"There's no reason to believe she can't have children in the future."

Riley wanted to believe that, and she knew that Ryan did as well.

But she knew that she was going to feel this sense of loss for quite some time, and Ryan was going to feel it too in his own way.

She also wondered …

How is this going to affect things between us?

Was it going to bring them closer together?

Or was it going to drive them farther apart?

She found herself thinking about all the things she'd been keeping secret from him lately.

Was he keeping secrets from her as well?

And was there any hope at all for their relationship?
Riley started to cry, and Ryan pulled her closer.
Soon she was fast asleep.

CHAPTER THIRTY FOUR

Riley felt as though she'd scarcely gotten to sleep before Ryan gently disentangled his arms from around her and climbed out of bed. Sunlight was pouring into the window now. Ryan walked around to Riley's side of the bed and crouched down and whispered …

"Are you awake?"

Riley nodded.

"It's time for me to go to work," he said. "But I could stay home today."

"No," Riley murmured tiredly. "Please don't."

"But what about you?" Ryan asked.

Riley rubbed her eyes, remembering the trauma she'd just been through.

That's a good question, she thought. *What* about *me?*

Ryan squeezed her hand a little.

He said, "Please don't go to the Hoover Building today. You're allowed one day of leave per month from the program. Take this one off. You need it. You deserve it."

Riley thought for a moment.

The pain in her belly was gone, but her head hurt badly, and she was so limp and exhausted she could barely imagine getting out of bed.

"That's a good idea," she muttered.

Ryan smiled at her and kissed her on the forehead. She lay there listening as he bustled around the apartment. Finally, when he was fully dressed and ready to go, he came back to the bed and kissed Riley again.

"Take it easy," he said, stroking her hair.

"I will," Riley said.

Ryan left the apartment, and she heard his car pulling away.

She almost went to sleep again, but realized …

I've got to call in, say I'm not coming today.

She sat up on the bed reached for her cell phone and called the number of Hoke Gilmer, the training supervisor for the intern program. When a secretary answered, Riley hesitated for a moment.

What should I say? she wondered.

Should I tell the truth about what happened?

It just seemed too personal. Instead she said she was sick, probably from eating something bad yesterday, and that she couldn't stop throwing up. The secretary expressed her sympathy and said that she hoped Riley got better.

The call ended, and Riley sat staring at the cell phone wondering …

What about Agent Crivaro?

She hadn't talked to him at all since he'd scolded her yesterday afternoon for chasing the suspect at the carnival.

What if he decided he wanted her to come and work on the case today?

I can't, she thought. *I can't do it.*

It wasn't just that she felt so sad and exhausted. She doubted that she could get away without Ryan finding out about it. And that might be the last straw for their whole relationship, which had been rocky enough lately. She definitely didn't want to spoil the caring mood that he was in now.

She punched in Crivaro's number and got his voice mail.

At the sound of the beep she said …

"Agent Crivaro, this is Riley Sweeney …"

Her voice faded. For some reason, she couldn't bring herself to tell Crivaro an outright lie. But that didn't mean she had to tell him the whole truth.

Finally she said, "I'm taking a sick day today. I'm really not well. So if you want me to work with you today … I'm sorry, I'm not going to be available."

Riley was surprised at how hard it was to say those words.

They sounded lazy and irresponsible somehow. But it was the best she could do.

She hesitated again, then said …

"I hope … I hope you're making good progress on the case."

She ended the call, climbed out of bed, and went to the bathroom and looked in the mirror.

She was shocked by what she saw.

Her face was pale and puffy, and her eyes were swollen and red from crying.

The very sight of her face made her headache worse.

I made the right decision, she thought.

She had no business being around other people today, much less trying to get anything done.

She washed up a bit and brushed her teeth, then went right back to bed. Her whole body went limp again, and she realized how truly and deeply exhausted she was.

She found herself remembering Dr. Pascal's words of reassurance last night …

"In a way, what happened was a good thing, the right thing.

"And it wasn't in any way your fault."

Riley wanted very much to believe that.

But so soon after her ordeal, she didn't know what she really believed.

In a matter of seconds, she was fast asleep again.

*

She awoke to the sounds of footsteps in the hallway and the apartment door opening.

She was seized with a rush of alarm …

An intruder! she thought.

Then she heard Ryan's voice call out …

"Riley, I'm home."

She breathed easier, but wondered …

Why is he home so early?

Then she looked at the clock on her bed stand. It was evening already.

She had slept all day.

Ryan peeked into the bedroom from the doorway.

"So what have you been doing all day?" he asked.

Riley chuckled and stretched her arms.

"Sleeping, I guess," she said. "Nothing else at all. Just sleeping."

Ryan grinned and said, "That's great. That's just what I want to hear. I brought home a pizza. Do you want me to bring it in here, or …"

"Oh, no," Riley said, interrupting. "It's time I got out of bed. I'll come out and we can eat in the kitchen."

She and Ryan ate pizza together while Ryan talked about his busy, exciting day at the law firm. Riley could tell by his voice how happy he was with his job, and she felt glad for him.

He'd also brought home a newspaper—the same publication the killer's poem had appeared in just yesterday. She opened the paper to the daily featured poem. This one was signed by someone named Toni Anderson, and it was a little ode to the writer's beloved wiener dog, Tipsy.

Riley read it over several times, looking for clues or riddles.

But no, it was a joyful, playful, sentimental little piece, without a trace of darkness in it. It also struck Riley as pretty bad, but she figured it was written by some girl in middle school, and it probably pleased many of the newspaper's readers.

Riley thumbed through the rest of the paper, but didn't find any news at all about the so-called Clown Killer.

When she and Ryan settled down to watch television, there was nothing on the evening news about the killer either.

She told herself …

No news is good news, I guess.

Still, she was a bit unsettled by how quickly the media seemed to have lost interest in the sensational case. No dead bodies dressed like clowns had been found for four days now—too long, it seemed, to hold the public's gnat-like attention span. Now the news was all about a sordid political scandal.

Meanwhile, Riley wondered what Crivaro had been doing and thinking.

She was sure he was still putting his energy into capturing the killer.

But was he making progress, or just feeling discouraged?

While it was surely a good thing that there had been no more murders, would that make it harder to find the killer?

Might the Clown Killer simply disappear now without a trace?

Riley remembered something Crivaro said to her a few days ago …

"Damn, but I hate cold cases."

Riley shuddered a little. She understood how Crivaro felt. It was horrible to think that the man was still out there—a twisted killer who dressed his victims as clowns and then scared them to death.

Where was he right now?

What was he doing?

Did anyone he knew have any idea what a monster he really was?

Was he shunned and alone, or did he live an ordinary-seeming life?

Riley wanted to find out. She wanted to do anything she could to help bring him to justice.

*

The next day was a Saturday. Ryan had work to do, but he

decided to do it at home instead of going in to the law office, so he set up his computer on the kitchen table.

As Ryan worked, Riley puttered around doing one thing and another. At first she felt a little shaky, but the activity helped to keep her mind occupied. She cleaned the apartment, did a couple of loads of clothes in the building's laundry room, and prepared dinner. She had a nice casserole ready by the time Ryan had finished his work.

Ryan was appreciative of her efforts, and Riley told herself that she could learn to enjoy living a normal life like this rather than chasing down a killer.

She got another good night's sleep and awoke later than usual on Sunday morning. This time, when she got out of bed and looked in the bathroom mirror, she saw that she looked almost her normal self.

Ryan's smiling face appeared behind her in the mirror, and he put his arms around her.

"Looking good this morning, eh?"

Riley chuckled a little.

"Better," she said. "Still some dark circles under the eyes …"

"I don't see any circles," he said, kissing her on the neck.

Riley pointed to her eyes and said, "They're up here, silly."

Ryan looked up and said, "I still don't see any circles."

"That's because you're not me," Riley said.

"Well, if you're the only one who can see 'em, they don't matter, do they?"

Riley laughed as he tickled her neck with more kisses.

Then Ryan said, "Hey, let's get out of here. Let's go somewhere."

"Where?" Riley asked.

"Anywhere. It's a beautiful day. We've got nothing else to do. Let's enjoy it."

It sounded like a great idea to Riley.

Ryan fixed a nice breakfast of bacon and scrambled eggs and when they finished eating they got dressed and ready to go out. They didn't bother to make any plans, just got on the metro rail and headed downtown.

When they came out of the station near the National Mall, they saw the Washington Monument in the distance, all covered with scaffolding for renovations. It was just a short walk from there to the National Air and Space Museum, and Ryan tugged her in that direction.

"You should see this," he declared. "I've been here before. It's wonderful."

Riley got a kick out of his enthusiasm, and she quickly fell in love with the museum. Its exhibits offered a dizzying excursion through the history of flight. On display was the Wright Brothers' rickety 1903 Flyer, the first airplane to ever take flight. So was the Spirit of St. Louis, in which Charles Lindbergh made the first solo, nonstop flight across the Atlantic in 1927.

The exhibit that held Riley's attention was a red Lockheed Vega once flown by Amelia Earhart, the pioneering female aviator who had mysteriously disappeared in the Pacific Ocean while trying to fly around the world.

She felt an odd sense of kinship with Earhart—perhaps because she, too, was venturing into a career not common for women.

She shivered a little as she considered Earhart's fate …

Things didn't always end well for pioneering women.

Also on display were the Bell X-1 rocket plane, the first aircraft to break the sound barrier; the tiny space capsule in which John Glenn orbited the earth in 1962; and the Apollo 11 Command Module, which had taken American astronauts to the moon and back in 1969.

Ryan was looking like a kid as they continued among the exhibits,

"Imagine!" he said. "It hasn't even been a hundred years since the Wright brothers first flew! Think of all that's been accomplished in that time! What kinds of amazing things are still going to happen in our own lifetimes?"

Riley, found that to be a breathtaking thought.

They'd done quite a lot of walking by the time they'd left the museum, and they were ready to find a place where they could sit down and have some lunch. As they wandered along a nearby street checking out restaurants and cafés, an old brick building caught Riley's eye. The sign on it read …

FORGOTTEN D.C.

Riley stared at the sign for a few moments, shaping the words silently with her lips …

"Forgotten D.C."

She wondered—why did those words intrigue her so?

CHAPTER THIRTY FIVE

The words on the building, "Forgotten D.C.," cast a sort of lonely spell, which somehow hit a chord with Riley.

I guess I've been feeling pretty lonely myself lately.

Pointing to the sign, she said to Ryan, "That's an odd name. What do you think that place is?"

Ryan glanced at it and shrugged.

"Whatever it is, it doesn't look like a place to eat," he said. "I thought you were hungry."

Riley tugged on his arm playfully.

"Oh, come on, let's go have a look," she said.

Ryan replied with a laugh, "Wow, you really *are* feeling better, aren't you?"

Riley grinned and took hold of his hand.

She said, "Let's see if you can keep up with me."

When they went inside the building, they found that it was another museum, although a much, much smaller one than they'd just visited. It was obviously not part of the Smithsonian or any national exhibition.

A woman with unruly puffs of graying hair was sitting at a table, where a sign said that admission was five dollars.

Ryan grumbled in a whisper, "We didn't have to pay anything to get into the Air and Space Museum."

But Riley was curious. She took two five-dollar bills out of her purse and gave them to the woman, who handed them a couple of tickets.

The woman smiled and remarked in a raspy but pleasant voice, "You two are our first visitors today. It's nice to know that *somebody* is interested in our local ghosts. It's an awful thing, to be left behind, to be forgotten—to be utterly lost. Our ghosts deserve better, I think."

Riley and Ryan looked at each other. She could see that he, too, was a bit startled by the woman's statement.

Riley went on inside, and Ryan followed her.

The place was dimly lit—and oddly spooky, Riley thought. It looked like it had probably been a small office building many, many years ago. Walls had been torn down and iron braces put up to support the ceiling, creating a lot of space for displays and exhibits.

Lying in glass display cases in the center of the floor, a series of enormous maps showed stages of the city's grown and development—from the swampy, tentative settlement the nation's founders had started during the 1790s, through the city's wild burst of growth after the Civil War, continuing on to the sprawling metropolis that Washington was today.

Display cases, exhibits, and photographs told stories of a truly forgotten past—the ornate facade and interior of burlesque Gayety Theater; the enormous building where the Center Market had once been housed; the Washington Penitentiary where the conspirators who planned Lincoln's assassination had been executed; the eccentric, castle-like mansion known as "Stewart's Folly"; and a host of other long-lost wonders.

Riley took particular notice of a series of pictures of an old amusement park called Whopping Escapades. The place looked like it must have been truly vast, with enormous roller coasters, gigantic Ferris wheels, and a wildly decorated merry-go-round …

A true "labyrinth," Riley thought, thinking of the poem the killer had put in the newspaper.

But of course, that place was long gone now.

Finally they came to an open doorway leading into a gift shop. Riley glanced inside. The shop was full of small trinkets and items that looked like they had been salvaged from ruins of long-lost places.

Riley was fascinated.

She took a step inside, but before she knew it, her legs went out from under her and she found herself sitting on the floor.

She heard Ryan cry out after she hit the floor …

"Riley! What happened?"

For a moment, Riley wasn't sure herself. Since when had she gotten so clumsy? But then she felt the floor and realized …

It's wet.

In an instant, Ryan and the woman were both helping her to her feet.

The woman was saying, "I'm so, so sorry. I hope you're OK."

"I'm fine," Riley said.

As he was helping Ryan out of the gift shop, Ryan said, "Riley, you've got to watch your step. You're still on the mend."

"I'm not hurt, just embarrassed," she replied.

Following behind Riley anxiously, the woman called back to somebody in the shop, "How many times have I told you to put out the sign when you're mopping?"

A male voice called back …

"Sorry."

Ryan glanced back in time to see a lanky man put a yellow plastic sign in the entry way …

WET FLOOR

Riley assured both Ryan and the woman that she was fine.

The woman said, "It's a nice little shop. You could wait just a few minutes until he finishes mopping and the floor is dry."

But then Ryan whispered to her, "Come on, Riley. I'm not crazy about this place. It kind of gives me the creeps. I don't want to waste any more money here. And I'm definitely hungry."

Riley nodded silently and followed Ryan toward the front entrance.

The woman called out as they left …

"Thanks for coming in! Do come back soon!"

*

A little while later, Ryan and Riley were eating sandwiches in a nearby outdoor café. It was still a lovely, sunny day, but Riley sensed that Ryan's mood had changed. He was saying very little now.

They ate in silence for a little while until Ryan spoke up …

"Riley, I've been thinking …"

His voice faded, and Riley waited for him to go on.

Uh-oh, she thought. *This doesn't sound good.*

Finally Ryan said, "I think you were right."

Riley was a bit puzzled. It wasn't the sort of thing Ryan had been saying to her a lot lately.

"Right about what?" she asked.

"Right about not getting married right away," Ryan said. "We really shouldn't rush things."

Riley was really taken aback now.

"Really?" she said. "What made you change your mind?"

Ryan shrugged and said, "Well, you gave me some pretty good reasons when we talked about it before. This job of mine—I love it, but it's an even bigger challenge than I'd expected. And you—well, I'll respect whatever you decide to do this summer. But whatever you decide, you'll be going through lots of changes. How can we even begin to make plans for a wedding right now? That's really a huge deal."

Riley felt her mouth drop open a little.

She tried to tell herself ...

This is what I wanted.

She knew she ought to feel relieved that Ryan was seeing her side of things at long last.

But why this sudden change of heart? After all, he'd even told his parents they were engaged.

Riley said, "But your parents—"

Ryan interrupted with a smile, "They can wait. They won't mind."

Right then it dawned on Riley.

Ryan didn't have to worry anymore about Riley's pregnancy showing.

His parents didn't need to know it had ever happened.

Was that why he wasn't in a hurry anymore?

Ryan looked a little troubled by Riley's silence. He said, "I thought you'd be happy that ... you know ... I agree with you."

"Oh, I am," Riley said. "Thanks. This will ... help a lot, I think."

But as they ate on in silence, Riley knew she was lying.

Her mind started filling up with strange, ill-formed suspicions.

Was Ryan maybe having second thoughts about their getting married after all?

Had the miscarriage affected how he felt about her?

Maybe he's worried that I'll never be able to have children, she thought.

It seemed like a strange, paranoid idea, but Riley couldn't shake it off.

Maybe he'd only proposed to her in the first place because she'd been pregnant.

Maybe he'd only been trying to do the right thing by her. And now, maybe he felt as though the pressure was off.

It was a terrible thought—that Ryan might have felt one way about her when she'd been carrying his baby, another way now that she wasn't.

Maybe we should talk about this, she thought.

But what kind of answer would he give her?

If she mentioned her suspicion, surely he'd deny it, whether it was true or not. There was nothing to be gained by that. Worse still, it would probably lead to an argument, right here in a public place.

And Riley was tired of arguments, and she was sure Ryan was as well.

After they finished eating, Riley and Ryan wandered around town for much of the rest of the day. They window-shopped and joked about all the things they couldn't afford to buy right now. They also joked about how extravagant they would be in the future when Ryan made them rich.

Things seemed relaxed and easy between them now, but Riley couldn't help feeling that it was mostly an illusion.

For one thing, there were so many things she hadn't told Ryan—especially how she'd been involved in an actual murder case.

Maybe now was a good time to come clean about all that.

Maybe Ryan wouldn't be so upset about it now that she wasn't pregnant anymore.

But she quickly thought better of it ...

He might still blame me.

True, he'd been right there when Dr. Pascal had assured her that stress hadn't been a factor in Riley's miscarriage.

But did he really believe that?

Did *she* really believe it?

She felt as though she were holding a whole world of unspoken guilt inside.

Some of that guilt still had to do with the pleasant, funny, stimulating time she'd spent with John Welch at King Tut's on Thursday night.

She wasn't in love with John, she was sure of it.

And she was just as sure that John wasn't in love with her.

But one thing was hard to deny right now ...

She'd felt more comfortable, more truly *herself* around John, than she did with her own fiancé.

What did that say about her relationship with Ryan?

It can't be good, she admitted to herself.

Riley realized that now, even while they seemed to be having a good time together, she had no idea where this relationship was going.

CHAPTER THIRTY SIX

When they got back to their apartment later that afternoon, Riley was still troubled by doubts about her future with Ryan. But she felt sure that they were both tired from all the walking they'd done.

It's best to just leave things alone, she thought. *At least for now.*

She realized she was letting herself off the hook, too. She wasn't any more eager to discuss future plans than she thought Ryan would be.

Anyhow, she was right about his being tired. Ryan headed straight to the bedroom and dropped onto the bed. When she looked in on him a few moments later, he was sound asleep.

A nap sounded like a good idea to Riley as well. But just as she was getting ready to lie down beside him, she heard her cell phone rang. It was in the living room where she had put her purse down when they came in, and she hurried back there to answer it.

Her heart jumped when she saw who the call was from.

"Agent Crivaro—what's going on?" she asked, sitting down on the sofa to talk with him.

She heard a familiar growl.

"I wish I had news," Crivaro said. "The team has been following up on everything clown-related throughout the whole DC area. We must have been to a hundred different places during the last two or three days. We've checked costume shops, magic and novelty shops, services that hire out clowns, even a couple of clown schools. I've learned more about clowns than I ever wanted to know, but we've turned up nothing. And the forensic results on the killer's note and drawing were a bust. He's too smart to leave fingerprints or anything like that."

Crivaro fell quiet for a moment.

Then he said, "Riley, I'm afraid we're going to lose him. I'm afraid this is the Matchbook Killer all over again."

His words gave Riley a sudden warm feeling.

He called me Riley, she thought.

He doesn't often do that.

He was even opening up to her about his frustrations.

She said, "This case won't wind up like that. It won't go cold.

I'm sure of it."

Another silence fell.

Riley wished Crivaro would tell her more about how he was feeling.

Then he said, "Riley, I'm afraid I was pretty hard on you Thursday, after that thing at the carnival. You probably didn't deserve that. It's just … well, I'm responsible for your safety, and you gave me a good scare."

"I understand," Riley said. "It's OK."

"But I almost forgot—you called in sick on Friday. I was sorry to hear that. Are you feeling better?"

"Much better," Riley said. "I'm ready to get back to work."

She heard Crivaro heave a deep sigh.

"Naw, that's not such a good idea. I've been keeping you away from away from the intern program with this case. You've been a big help, especially figuring out that poem, but I'm not being fair to you. I'm taking up too much of your time, so you're not learning the stuff you're supposed to be learning, not the regular nuts and bolts stuff. You might as well stick to the program for now. I promise to stay in touch."

Crivaro ended the call, and Riley just sat there, feeling flabbergasted.

Crivaro had just talked to her in an unusually open, vulnerable way.

He seemed to be genuinely concerned about her.

And for that very reason, he didn't want her on the case.

What can I do? she wondered.

How can I convince him that I can still be of help?

She got up and peeked into the bedroom. Ryan was still fast asleep. A few moments ago, she'd felt ready to take a nap herself, but now …

I couldn't sleep if my life depended on it.

She dug around in her purse and found her little notebook—the one she and John had used to write the poem. She read it over a few times and realized again what a shrewd, clever idea it was.

Maybe this is more than an exercise after all.

Maybe it's just the thing to draw out the killer.

Should she call John and talk it over with him?

No, the first person she should talk to was Crivaro.

She started to punch in Crivaro's number on the phone, but stopped to ask herself …

What do I think I'm doing?

Hadn't she heard what Crivaro had just said—that he felt that he'd been unfair to her for taking up her time, that he'd felt responsible for safety, that he wanted her away from the case for her own good?

He'd been perfectly sincere about every word.

There was no way on earth that Crivaro was going to agree to this idea, no matter how Riley tried to present it to him.

And of course Riley had to consider …

He might well be right.

I probably should just steer clear of all this.

But as she tried to mentally talk herself out of it, she felt frustration rising inside her.

So much had gone wrong in her life during the last few days.

The worst thing by far had been the miscarriage, which had left her feeling frail, vulnerable, and helpless.

I won't take this anymore, she thought.

I won't keep on feeling helpless.

She found a copy of today's newspaper and opened it to the page with the poetry feature. She saw two addresses for submissions—one a physical mailing address, the other an email address. Without stopping to think about what she was doing, she flipped open Ryan's computer and opened up his email program.

Looking at her notebook, she typed the entire poem into the body of an email, ending with the name of the "poet" …

Tina D. Vejas

Then, with a single swift stroke of her finger, she hit "Send."

And the poem was gone.

Riley gulped hard as a wave of panic started to rise inside of her.

Oh my God, she thought.

What did I just do?

She had no doubt that the poem would catch the killer's attention—that is, if the newspaper actually published it.

Should she write to the editor right now, explaining that she'd submitted it by mistake and she wanted to withdraw it?

She got up from the kitchen table and paced, trying to deal with her agitated uncertainty.

What should I do now? she wondered.

What should I do?

Long minutes passed, and she couldn't make up her mind.

She was still pacing when she heard Ryan's computer make a ringing sound.

She knew that the sound meant that he'd just received an email.

Breathless, she sat down at the computer and read the email.

Dear Tina—

Thank you so much for submitting your poem. We like it very much. We didn't yet have a poem for tomorrow, so we received yours just in time for tonight's deadline! You'll be seeing it in the paper in the morning!

Sincerely,

Caitlin Gilbert, Features Editor

Riley was almost hyperventilating now.

Should she write to the editor and explain that this was just a mistake?

No, she couldn't bring herself to do that. She just couldn't.

If she backed out of this now, she'd never forgive herself.

But then another problem dawned on her ...

I used Ryan's email!

There was no way he wouldn't see both emails—the one she'd sent and the one she'd received.

Without a moment's pause, Riley deleted both of them.

Then she sat staring at the computer screen, gasping for breath ...

What have I done?

But she knew the answer to that question.

She'd just requested a rendezvous with a killer.

And she felt sure that he'd be more than eager to oblige.

CHAPTER THIRTY SEVEN

Michelle Yeaton's field of vision was filled with shining objects that were flashing and flitting and darting everywhere.

Stars, she thought.

But since when did stars fly around like that, appearing and disappearing in and out of the darkness?

Was she gazing into a dark sky full of meteors in flight?

And why did her head hurt so badly?

Nothing made sense.

Where was she right now?

How had she gotten here?

Why could she see nothing except this dark field riddled with shiny things?

Then she heard a man's voice speaking out of the darkness …

"This changes things. This changes everything."

Realizing that her eyes were closed, Michele opened them. She was lying on a concrete floor in a dimly lit place.

How did I get here? she asked herself again.

Then she started to remember …

She had just gotten out of her car in the parking garage. It was morning, and she was on her way to job at the Maxim and Abel department store, where she worked selling women's clothes. She'd heard the padding of soft-soled footsteps running up behind her, but before she could turn to look …

A sharp pain in the back of my head.

The pain I feel in my head right now.

She must have been knocked out cold and brought to this place. The blow must have caused her to see all these stars, which were visible even now that her eyes were open.

Again, she heard the man's voice …

"Oh, yes. Everything's different now. So unexpected."

She pulled herself up to a crouching position and looked around.

She saw that she was in a small area surrounded by chain-link fencing in what looked like a large dark room.

There was one spot of light, though.

It fell on a round wooden table. Sitting on the table were a roll of duct tape, a medical syringe, a small round mirror, and what looked like a fishing tackle box. Someone was sitting at the table, a newspaper lifted to his face so that she couldn't see him. In the dim light, his clothes looked strange and puffy.

Her own clothes felt strange, loose, and ill-fitting, but she couldn't focus her eyes well enough to see them.

She moaned aloud, trying to gather her senses.

Seeming to hear her, the man spoke from behind the newspaper …

"Are you awake now? Good. Listen to this …"

Then, sounding as though he was reading from the paper, he said …

The last things that I saw that dusk,
The waning of that day,
Were sparkling waters, calm and still,
And blurs of white and gray.

It was a poem, Michelle realized.

But why was he reading it to her?

The man said in a cheerful voice …

"Somebody knows! Somebody understood my riddle! Isn't it marvelous? Such a challenge! Such a thrill!"

He lowered the newspaper from his face and Michelle's breath froze in her chest at what she saw.

It was the bizarre painted face of clown.

And he was dressed entirely in a clown costume.

She glanced at her sleeve and saw that she was dressed in the same way.

Her heart pounded as she remembered the news stories and rumors …

The Clown Killer!

It's him!

He's going to kill me!

She tried to scream, but she couldn't even breathe.

The clown opened the box, which was filled with what appeared to be tubes of stage makeup.

"Well," he said, "I was just getting ready to do your face, make it *real,* like mine. But …"

He walked over to the cage and crouched down, pointing to the newspaper again.

"I'm sure you understand … this changes everything! I mustn't hurry now. I must be patient, take things slow. And so must you."

At long last, Michelle's breath came unfrozen, and she let out a piercing shriek that exploded through her skull.

The clown peered calmly at her through the fencing, the whites of his eyes looking weirdly yellow in contrast to the white paint on his face.

When her shriek faded, he said ...

"You've got an excellent voice. Could you do that again?"

As if to oblige his wish, Michelle screamed yet again.

When she finished, she was panting desperately.

Like a dog, she thought.

"Yes, excellent," the man said. "Again, please."

But Michelle was out of breath now. And besides, why was she doing exactly what he asked her to do? Wherever they were, it must be far away from other people. Surely no one could hear her scream. And of course he knew that. She was only adding to his enjoyment.

The man chuckled a little.

"Oh, well, maybe later. Yes, later, surely. But meanwhile ..."

He lifted the newspaper, which was folded to the page he'd found, and he read aloud again ...

> *"I let my lens slip from my hand*
> *My shaking was to blame ..."*

He chuckled with admiration. "Isn't it marvelous? So very clever. I'm terribly pleased."

Michelle started sobbing and whimpering and she felt tears scald her cheeks.

The clown tilted his head in what almost appeared to be genuine sympathy.

"Yes, I understand how you feel. They're going to leave you behind, aren't they? They're going to forget you. I know just how that feels, believe me. It's a terrible feeling, being lost ... forgotten."

Looking at the paper again, he added ...

"And whoever wrote this—apparently a young lady like yourself, says that her name is Tina—she knows that feeling, just like we do. I've got to meet her. So do you. Then... then we can get on with things. She's strong, I sense it, and I think maybe you are too, not like the others. Maybe this time ... things will be different."

He rose to his feet and walked back to the table and took out a canister and a packet of tissues and looked in the mirror.

"Meanwhile," he said, "I must put on my costume, my disguise. I must make myself look like all those others out there in the world. After all, I do have an appointment later on …"

He sat down and put cold cream on his face and began to wipe the makeup off with a tissue and murmured …

Tonight when sunset comes again
I must go back and see!

Michelle gathered up her breath and let out another long shriek.

The man was humming now as he continued to take off his makeup.

He didn't seem to mind her screaming at all.

CHAPTER THIRTY EIGHT

As Riley walked across the footbridge that led over to Columbia Island, she muttered those words that she and John had written back at King Tut's bar …

Tonight when sunset comes again
I must go back and see!

Looking over the water, Riley could see that dusk was setting in.

I'm really doing it, she thought with a shudder.

And for the umpteenth time that day, she wondered if she had lost her mind.

She almost jumped out of her skin when her cell phone buzzed in her pocket.

She took it out and saw that it was a call from John. She sighed and shook her head and whispered …

"Not now, John. Not a good time, I'm afraid."

She turned her cell phone off without taking the call, put it back in her pocket, and continued on her way. She felt a bit annoyed by the call. She hadn't seen or heard from John all day long. Why did he have to pick right now to get in touch with her?

This morning Riley had heard that John had already left the building. He and his group were attending in a special technician training class, learning to identify components of exploded bombs. They were actually spending the whole day out in the countryside watching bombs blow up, then examining whatever was left of them.

It had sounded like fun to Riley, and she'd been sorry to miss it. Instead, she'd put in a slog of a day, listening to a lecture about analyzing crime data and attending a couple of long workshops, one of them dealing with warrants and other legal issues.

Or as Crivaro had called it …

Regular nuts and bolts stuff.

It had been hard concentrating on such mundane matters, all the while contemplating whether she was really going through with her self-assigned task at the end of the day.

But what choice did she have?

The poem had appeared in the paper, just as the editor had promised.

The killer was either going to notice it or not notice it.

Wasn't it up to her to find out one way or the other?

Ryan had unintentionally helped Riley make up her mind to do this. When her classes ended, he'd called to say he'd be working again at the office well into the evening. Riley had told him she'd be going out later herself. Ryan had assumed she meant she'd be socializing again, and Riley hadn't said anything to correct that assumption.

If he knew, he'd kill me, Riley thought as she passed by the familiar statue of the metal birds flying over an ocean wave.

Crivaro would kill me too, she thought.

But as she continued on her way toward the LBJ Memorial Grove Monolith, she assured herself that she'd thought things through quite thoroughly.

All she wanted was to get a good look at the killer so she could identify him. And she would call the police right away.

She wasn't going to put herself in danger, much less try to apprehend him …

If he shows up at all.

And of course, there were no guarantees of that happening.

As she continued on through the grove of pine and dogwood trees, she noticed that people were walking the other way, heading out of the park. Soon the park would be fairly deserted for the evening, just as it had been when she'd come here before …

… and just like it was when Janet Davis was abducted.

At last she approached the marina, where the waning daylight was glittering on the water's surface. When she'd been here before, she'd noticed a nook in the side of one of the wooden boathouses. She found the place she was looking for and stepped inside.

Sure enough, the nook gave her a clear view of the marina, even though she herself was pretty well hidden from view.

And now …

All I have to do is wait.

The trick would be to stay out of sight when he showed up.

Or maybe she'd be *really* lucky and …

He won't show at all.

She found herself more than half-hoping things would work out that way.

Then she could go home satisfied with her modest effort and never have to explain anything to Crivaro or anybody else.

204

Clever girl, Joey thought as he peeked through the leaves of a bush. He'd watched the girl approach the nearby boathouse. Now she was hiding in a little nook there, some fifty feet away from where he was crouching.

It had to be the one who had signed the name Tina D. Vejas. He'd quickly figured out that the name was an anagram for Janet Davis.

Now he could see that she hadn't meant to meet him after all.

She was just trying to check him out.

All she wanted was a good look at him.

Joey wasn't the least bit disappointed. The girl was a trickster, just like himself. She was going to suit him well, once he had her in his thrall.

Of course, she was about to learn an important lesson …

Never try to trick a trickster.

He'd spent the whole day wavering about whether to come here, whether to answer the invitation in the newspaper.

He couldn't ignore the possibility that it might be a police trap.

But as he read and reread the poem, he became convinced otherwise.

He felt sure that she wasn't working with the police. The message seemed too intimate, too personal. This was a private affair for her. She rightly sensed her kinship with him.

He thought about those lines …

I let my lens slip from my hand
My shaking was to blame …

He wondered—how had she known that had happened here on the marina well over a week ago?

How did she know about Janet, the girl he'd snatched up while she'd been taking pictures here?

She's quite the little detective, he thought.

In a little while, he'd have a chance to ask her about all that.

Meanwhile, he felt a pang of sadness at the sight of that remarkable young creature in those jeans and that blouse, her face so plain and dry and ghostlike. The same as he was at this very moment, she was wearing a costume, trying to fit into a world where she didn't really belong.

And she didn't even know it.

Oh, when I'm able to teach her who she really is!

How wonderful that was going to be!

He was sure that this one would be strong enough to come through his test.

This one definitely belonged in his own world of wild color and merriment—a world of garish paint and red noses and billowy clothes, of horns and bells and fake flowers that squirted water in people's faces.

Maybe the other girl belonged with him too—the one he had spared for a time and left alive back in that cage.

If things had gone as planned, he'd have subjected her to his test by now.

If she'd failed to survive, he'd have left her body in a chosen place.

All that was on hold now. But he would test them both, and maybe both would pass this time. He always hoped his captives would survive.

He almost laughed aloud as he thought …

Two of them! Imagine that!

He'd never in his life dared to dream of such companionship.

Meanwhile, dusk was deepening. The girl in the nook was looking at her watch. She must be beginning to think he was going to miss their appointment.

He fingered the short piece of steel pipe he'd used to knock out the other girls. He fought down a powerful urge to take advantage of this girl's unwariness, spring out of his crouched concealment right now, charge toward her like a beast of prey, and render her unconscious with a single swift blow.

Patience, he told himself.

The trick was to have just a little more patience than she did.

*

Riley sighed deeply as the sky grew darker and the water surrounding the docks sparkled less in the waning light.

Wait just a few more minutes, she told herself.

But with every passing moment, she became surer that the killer wasn't going to appear.

Had he even noticed the poem in the newspaper?

How could he have helped but notice it?

So why isn't he here?

206

She remembered something John had said when they'd started writing the poem …

"Won't he expect the police to be waiting for him there?"

Riley had wanted to believe they'd come up with such a tantalizing riddle that the killer would feel compelled to take that risk.

Apparently they had failed.

If the killer had noticed the poem, he was no fool. He'd known better than to come anywhere near here this evening.

Meanwhile, Riley's head started to flood with new worries …

If he saw the poem but didn't respond …

Might she have caused further problems without meaning to?

Now the killer must realize that *someone* else knew how and where he had abducted Janet in the first place—presumably the police.

And of course, he'd be right.

She knew that Crivaro had been doing his best to keep any details about the killings away from the public. Surely the last thing he'd want would be to tip his hand to the killer himself.

What have I done? Riley wondered miserably.

Maybe she needed to tell Crivaro the truth about her poem.

If so, she knew he'd be beyond furious. She murmured aloud to herself …

"He's got every right to be."

Anyway, she was sure she was wasting time hanging around here. She stepped out of the nook and was starting to walk away from the marina when she heard a flurry of footsteps and caught a flash of movement in her peripheral vision.

She whirled around in time to see a man taking a swing at her with a length of pipe. She tried to duck, but the blow glanced across her head, stunning her and throwing her off balance.

Her assailant was fast and strong.

In another instant, he had pinned her on her back on the ground.

CHAPTER THIRTY NINE

Riley lay pinned on her back, feeling helpless. She wanted to strike the man with her fists or lift her knee into his groin, but she was immobilized.

He was tall and wiry and strong, and he seemed to be made out of arms and legs. He had both of her legs pinned under his knees, and with one large hand he was holding both of her wrists onto the ground above her head. In his free hand, he still held the length of pipe.

Riley cringed for fear of another blow to her head.

But instead of striking, he shoved the pipe in a pocket and waved something else in front of her face.

With a snapping sound, a blade flashed out, gleaming bright and sharp even in the dusky light.

"I could do it right now," he said breathlessly. "I could make you look like your true self. You've never seen what you really look like, but I swear, I'm not going to let you go until I can show you."

Riley lay there absolutely petrified.

Her captor tilted his head curiously and said, "It doesn't have to be painful like this. I don't have to do it with a knife. I can do it back in the labyrinth—paint your face without cutting it, give you your true face at last. Just stop fighting. Come with me."

The labyrinth! Riley thought.

She still had no idea where or what the labyrinth was, but she wasn't going to let him take her there.

She spit in his face.

He drew sharply back, and his face reddened with rage. As he swung his knife she wrenched her body to one side, but she felt the sting of the blade grazing her shoulder.

Then she heard a different voice yell out …

"Riley!"

Suddenly she was free from her assailant. Riley looked up and saw two men tangled in each other's arms. One, of course, was the killer.

The other was John Welch. He had pulled the killer away from her.

Riley called out …

"John, be careful! Don't try to—"

Just then the killer gave John a mighty shove to his chest, sending him toppling awkwardly backward. As John fell, the killer started to run away, but then he turned back and yelled at Riley …

"You're making a mistake. You think he's your friend, but he's not. You have no friends. Everybody hates you. They'll forget you. They'll abandon you. Everyone in your world. You'll be lost. I know."

He inhaled sharply and shouted …

"I'm the only one in the world who knows … who you really are."

He took off running again toward the parking lot. Through the trees, Riley could glimpse him climbing into an old car and driving away.

Meanwhile, John had climbed to his feet and was helping Riley get up.

He said, "Jesus, Riley. It looks like he clipped you on the head. And he cut your shoulder."

Riley's shoulder stung, but when she touched it she felt only a little blood.

"I'll be fine," Riley said.

But as she tried to stand, she toppled against John.

John helped her over to a nearby bench and got her seated.

"Relax," he said. "Put your head down. It'll help with the dizziness."

Riley obeyed and felt the blood flowing back into her head. She heard John jabbering on the phone a short distance away. Riley guessed that he was calling either the police or the FBI.

"I need help," she heard him saying. "A friend of mine has been attacked—by the Clown Killer, I think. Her name is Riley Sweeney. She's hurt but not badly. We're at the marina in Lady Bird Johnson Park."

Then he came back and sat down beside her.

She lifted her head, feeling less dizzy now. She stammered …

"How did you … know … ?"

John put his arm around her shoulder and said, "Damn it, Riley, I'd like to throttle you. I bought a newspaper when my group got back from the explosives class. When I saw the poem I knew what you were up to, and I drove right here. What the hell's the matter with you? I thought we both agreed it was just an exercise. Just something we were doing for fun."

"I'm sorry," Riley murmured pitifully. "I was wrong."

"You sure as hell were," John said.

They sat together in silence for a moment. Then John got up and walked out onto a dock, where he paced up and down with agitation.

Riley's mind boggled at how bad things suddenly were. And there was no question about it—it was all her fault and no one else's.

It was going to take a long time to undo the damage she'd done, but she needed to get started right now.

And before she did anything else, she needed start putting things right with Ryan.

No more secrets, she told herself.

She took out her cell phone and punched in his number.

When he answered, she couldn't keep her voice from breaking with emotion.

"Ryan, I … something bad has happened, and I …"

A sob broke through her throat.

Ryan shouted, "Riley! Are you okay?"

"I'm fine, Ryan, but … I need for you to come and pick me up. Right now."

She gave him directions to the marina parking lot and ended the call without further explanation.

How can I begin explaining? she wondered.

It wasn't going to be easy.

Meanwhile, she heard the sound of approaching sirens, and several vehicles pulled into the parking lot. Soon a group of men came striding from their parked vehicles toward the marina. One of them was carrying a first aid kit.

In front of them all was Jake Crivaro.

Riley gulped hard, dreading Crivaro's wrath.

But she knew she shouldn't be surprised that he was here. On the phone, John had mentioned the Clown Killer and had also given Riley's name. It was no wonder that Crivaro had been alerted right away.

As the cop with the first aid kit started tending to Riley's two small injuries, Crivaro walked up to the bench and stood in front of Riley, staring at her with a fierce expression.

"What happened?" he asked her.

Riley shook her head miserably.

"He was here just now," she said. "The Clown Killer. He attacked me, but John pulled him off. Then he drove away—I didn't get a good look at his car, but it looked pretty old, like maybe from the seventies."

Crivaro crossed his arms and asked …

"And just how did you and the killer happen to wind up being here at the same time?"

Riley stifled a moan of despair. As she started to tell the whole story, she saw that John was now standing nearby listening. Her first impulse was to try not to mention John's involvement in the incident. She didn't want to get the poor guy in trouble.

But she quickly realized …

John didn't do anything wrong.

Not the slightest thing.

She was the one who had told John too much about the case. Nobody had forced her to do that, least of all John himself. And she'd led him to believe that writing the poem wasn't going to lead to any trouble.

None of this was John's fault. She could tell the whole truth without getting him in trouble.

As Riley explained everything as well as she could, Crivaro's face tightened with rage.

He seemed to be struggling for control as he asked, "Can you even give me a description of the man?"

Riley thought back. She'd been so shocked by his attack, so focused on fighting her way free of him …

Then she said weakly, "Not a very good one."

Crivaro just stared at her for a long moment.

Finally he said …

"You're through, Sweeney."

"I'm off the case?" she asked.

"You're off the case. You're out of the intern program. I don't want to see you around the Hoover Building ever again. I don't want to see *you* ever again."

Crivaro turned to John.

"What about you?" he snapped.

They walked away together, and Riley could tell that John must be giving Crivaro a description of the killer, something she hadn't had wits enough to do. She was glad that someone had sense enough to do that, but her own failure overwhelmed her.

Crivaro gave John a pat on the arm and then started giving orders to the other cops and agents about examining the area.

Riley fell apart completely, collapsing into uncontrollable sobs. John sat down next to her again and held her hand as Riley hung her head and wept.

After a while she heard Ryan's voice call out …

"Riley! What happened? Are you all right?"

Riley looked up and saw Ryan coming toward her. Then she noticed how his expression seemed to darken with anger.

She quickly realized …

John's holding my hand.

Riley carefully removed her hand from John's.

Ryan glared at John and said, "Who the hell are you? What did you have to do with this? And what is this anyhow?"

Trying to pull herself together, Riley said in shaky voice …

"This is John, Ryan. He's my friend. He came here to help."

Ryan squinted at John angrily and silently. Looking shocked by his hostility, John simply turned and walked quietly away.

"Come on," Ryan said to Riley, helping her up from the bench. "Let's go home."

As he helped her walk to the car, Riley could feel that his whole body was tight with anger.

She knew that an already awful evening was about to get much, much worse.

CHAPTER FORTY

Riley climbed into the car with Ryan. He was silent as he pulled out of the parking lot and started driving them out of the park.

Riley said timidly, "Ryan—"

Ryan interrupted in a tight voice. "Not now. When we get home."

Riley wished she could tell him everything right now and get it over with. But if Ryan wasn't ready to listen, there was nothing she could do about it.

The ride home seemed endless to Riley, and the night rapidly grew darker around them. She felt as though some terrible darkness was falling over her life as well.

After Ryan parked in front of their building, he got out of the car and headed on inside as if she weren't even there. Riley followed him into the apartment, feeling an awful, anxious numbness all through her body.

Ryan headed straight toward a kitchen cabinet and pulled down a bottle of bourbon. She knew he kept it there, but he hadn't touched it since they'd moved to this place. She'd guessed that he was trying to be sensitive to the fact that she couldn't drink hard liquor as long as she was pregnant.

But now, of course, it didn't matter—to either of them.

Ryan took down a couple of glasses and set them on the kitchen table. They both sat down, and Ryan poured himself a large drink and silently offered to do the same for Riley. She shook her head no.

Ryan took a large gulp of whiskey and grimaced as he swallowed it.

In a small, frightened voice, Riley said …

"Ryan, I know I've got a lot to explain and—"

Ryan interrupted again.

"Who was that guy, Riley?"

Riley was startled. For a moment she wondered …

What guy?

Did he mean Jake Crivaro? Surely Ryan remembered Crivaro from back at Lanton.

Then she realized who he meant.

213

"I told you, his name is John," she said. "He's a friend."

Ryan sneered and said, "A friend. Just a friend. I saw you together, holding hands. Do you expect me to believe that?"

Riley was dumbstruck. She'd been preparing herself to explain all sorts of things to Ryan, but she hadn't really considered that she was going to have to explain about John.

Ryan said, "How long have you been involved with him? Ever since the program started?"

Riley said, "I'm not involved with him. I'm really not. He's a friend. He's ..."

She paused and added, "He's a really good friend."

It was the truth, of course. So why did Riley feel as though she were lying?

The answer came to her quickly. She'd been more open and honest and communicative with John lately than she'd been with Ryan.

Maybe he's got a right to be jealous, she thought.

Still, she couldn't allow Ryan to think her involvement with John was romantic or sexual.

"Ryan, I promise you. There's nothing between John and me—nothing like you're thinking, anyway. I've done a lot of stupid things during the last few days, but not that."

Ryan held his glass tightly, then took another swallow.

Riley sensed that he was at least making an effort to believe her.

Riley said, "At least let me try to explain to you what happened at the park. You see, I ..."

But her voice faded.

How could she explain what had happened this evening without explaining about a thousand other things first?

She needed to start from the beginning, so that was what she tried to do.

She began with her first day in the intern program, telling how she'd been assigned to shadow Agent Crivaro, and how she'd gone with him and his partner to a drug house, where she'd helped find a stash of money.

Ryan glared at her in disbelief and interrupted again ...

"You were *working* on an actual *case?*" he said. "Riley, this is just supposed to be an intern program. You're just supposed to be taking classes and going to lectures and stuff. But you were working on a *case*?"

Riley was startled by the fierceness in his voice.

She couldn't talk around the truth anymore.

I've really got to tell him flat-out.

She said, "Have you heard of the Clown Killer case?"

Ryan said, "The serial killer who dresses his victims up like clowns? Yeah, what about it?"

Riley swallowed hard and said ...

"I've been working with Crivaro on that case too."

Ryan set his glass down so hard that bourbon splashed out of it onto the table.

"You've been *working* on a *murder* case?" he said.

Riley nodded. "That's what I was doing at the park this evening. I went hoping to get a good look at the killer. But then he attacked me and that's how I got these injuries, and if John hadn't shown up ..."

Ryan was starting to look hurt as well as angry.

He said, "Riley this is insane. I don't guess it's a secret that I've been against your doing this summer program from a start. But I respected your wishes and I decided to let you do it."

Riley felt a tiny flash of anger herself now.

He let me do it?

Had Ryan's permission been necessary?

Ryan said, "Why didn't you tell me any of this?"

Surprised by the bitter tone in her own voice, Riley said ...

"When did you ever ask me?"

Ryan shook his head and squinted a few times, as if he were trying to hold back tears.

He said in a choked voice ...

"Riley I can't do this anymore. It's all too much. How can I possibly start a career with all this going on? How can I make a good life for both of us? I thought losing our baby was the worst of it, but now ..."

He paused for a moment, then said ...

"I can't trust you anymore, and I can't ... I can't *stay* here if I can't trust you."

Riley almost fell out of her chair at the enormity of what he was saying.

Without another word, Ryan got up and rushed into the bedroom. Riley went to the bedroom door and watched helplessly as he got out a suitcase and started packing some necessary things. He didn't say another word while he was doing that. Finally he closed the suitcase, picked it up, stormed right past her, and headed out the front door.

Calling his name weakly, Riley followed him into the hall and up the stairs toward the building entrance. She stood watching helplessly as he went out to his car and slammed the suitcase in the trunk. The tires skidded as Ryan drove angrily away.

Riley stood in the apartment doorway in a complete state of shock, shaking from head to foot. Then she made her way numbly back into the apartment and sat down at the kitchen table.

There was still some bourbon in Ryan's glass. Riley filled it up some more and took a long swallow. The burning in her throat felt comforting. Then she went over to the sofa and lay down with her head propped up on a pillow.

Noticing the engagement ring on her finger, she took it off and looked at it sadly.

I guess I'll have to give this back, she thought, setting it on the coffee table.

As she continued to drink, she turned things over in her mind.

I barely told him anything at all, she thought.

She'd said nothing about the murdered girl's body, or about her encounters with the grieving parents and husband, or about writing the poem to draw out the killer, and certainly nothing at all about her terrifying feelings of connection with the killer.

How would Ryan have reacted if he'd known everything?

He already hates me, she thought. *If he knew, he'd hate me worse than either one of us can imagine.*

She got up and added more whiskey to the glass, then returned to the couch.

It had been quite some time since she'd had anything to drink at all, so her resistance to alcohol was low. She quickly started to feel the welcome effects of the whiskey. The muscles throughout her body went slack, like rubber bands that had been suddenly untightened, and she breathed more slowly and easily.

Soon she was fast asleep.

It was morning, and Riley was standing in a litter-strewn field where a carnival had left the night before.

Riley was all alone in the field except for one other person.

That was Janet Davis, and she was dead.

The murdered woman lay at Riley's feet, grotesquely costumed and made up, her dull, lusterless eyes wide open and staring at the morning sky.

Riley knelt down beside the corpse and whispered ...

"I wish you could talk. I wish you could tell me."

To Riley's horrified astonishment, the corpse's lips began to move, as if trying to shape words.

A hideous groaning sound came out of her lungs.

Then came four croaking, ghastly words ...

"It's an awful thing ..."

The mouth grew still again, and Riley was afraid she'd say nothing else.

Riley said to her ...

"What's an awful thing? Please tell me. I need to know."

The mouth moved again and the woman said ...

"It's an awful thing ... to be left behind ... to be forgotten ... to be utterly lost."

Riley was about to beg the woman to tell her more.

But suddenly, the corpse collapsed and turned to into a dusty skeleton before Riley's very eyes.

The morning light suddenly began to fade, and soon Riley was surrounded by impenetrable darkness.

Riley's eyes snapped open. She was still lying on the couch, and morning light was streaming in through a window.

I slept here all night, she realized.

She tried to remember how much she'd had to drink last night.

It hadn't been a whole lot—the glass on the coffee table still had a fair amount of bourbon in it.

She felt physical aches throughout her body, but she was sure that was mostly because of yesterday's struggle with the killer. It wasn't exactly a hangover. But she'd had more than enough whiskey to put her fast asleep for a long time.

Thank God for small mercies, she thought.

Much worse was the emotional pain of remembering how Ryan had left last night.

She tried to put thoughts of their ugly scene aside as she went to the kitchen area. She started the coffeemaker, put some bread in the toaster, and poured herself a glass of orange juice.

She sat down and the table and thought ...

I had a nightmare.

For a few moments, she had trouble remembering what it had been about.

But then the images came back to her—the murdered woman lying in the field in the morning light, her mouth moving as she'd said ...

"It's an awful thing ... to be left behind ... to be forgotten ... to

be utterly lost."

Riley shivered deeply.

How familiar those words seemed!

Where had she heard them? She was sure it had been even before that dream.

Just then some other words rattled through her mind …

"Our ghosts deserve better."

Had those words even been spoken in last night's dream?

No, she'd heard them somewhere else.

Someone had said them to her just yesterday.

She felt a tingle all over as she remembered who had said them and where.

She also remembered Crivaro saying yesterday …

"You're off the case. You're out of the intern program. I don't want to see you around the Hoover Building ever again. I don't want to see you ever again."

Riley suddenly felt wide awake.

It doesn't matter if I'm off the case, she thought.

There's something I've got to do.

CHAPTER FORTY ONE

As Riley got off the metro at the same stop where she and Ryan had gotten off on Sunday, she wondered ...

What do I think I'm doing?

Her life was a shambles, and here she was following up on some vague hunch she'd gotten from a nightmare. Riley sighed as she began walking along the route she and Ryan had taken on that happier day.

Well, at least this isn't a waste of time, she thought.

After all, she had nothing else to do right now.

For that matter, she could think of nothing meaningful she had to do for the rest of her life. Everything important had come to an end yesterday.

Riley continued on past the National Air and Space Museum until she arrived at her destination—the little brick building with the sign that said ...

FORGOTTEN D.C.

She again remembered what the woman who worked there had said to her on Sunday ...

"It's an awful thing, to be left behind, to be forgotten—to be utterly lost."

And of course, Riley had heard the same words spoken by the dead woman in the dream. Maybe those words meant nothing at all. But Riley couldn't help remembering what the killer had shouted at her yesterday ...

"They'll forget you. They'll abandon you. Everyone in your world. You'll be lost."

Her every instinct was telling her ...

It has to mean something.

Riley walked on inside, where the same woman with gray, unruly puffs of hair was sitting at a table ready to sell tickets.

The woman smiled when she saw Riley. "Oh, how nice to see you again! We seldom get return visitors—especially not young ones. People today live purely for the moment. I know that's supposed to be a good way to live, everybody says so, but ..."

She shrugged and chuckled.

"But I can't help but believe that the past deserves our attention too—and our respect, and our consideration, and maybe even a little love. So I'm very glad you're here."

"I'm glad too," Riley said.

But instead of going on inside, Riley just stood there, wondering how to begin.

The woman squinted at her curiously and said ...

"But it seems to me that you're not here solely for nostalgia's sake. What can I do for you today?"

Riley hesitated, then showed the woman her internship ID.

"I'm Riley Sweeney," she said, "I'm studying in the FBI's Honors Internship Summer Program ..."

The words were out before Riley realized they weren't true—at least not anymore.

She didn't like lying to this kindly woman, but she continued ...

"I'm hoping to pursue a career in law enforcement. I want to become an FBI agent someday. And I'm here as part of ... well, a project."

"How exciting for you!" the woman said. "My name is Anita Lockwood, and I've been working here since this place opened."

"Ms. Lockwood—"

"Please, call me Anita."

Riley fell silent. Just what did she want to ask this woman, anyway?

Riley simply couldn't imagine saying that she was investigating a murder. For one thing, she knew it would sound unlikely coming from a summer intern. But more importantly, this woman seemed too sensitive and delicate for any conversation about murder.

She glanced around the exhibit room and saw that the adjoining gift shop was open today. She said, "I'd love to see your shop. Maybe something there would fit into my project."

"Oh, good," Anita said.

Riley walked on inside the shop. As she'd expected, the merchandise was made up of all kinds of items from abandoned places and bygone days—badges and belt buckles once worn by fire fighters, hats and canes and stage props from the demolished Gayety Theater, and chains and shackles from the Washington Penitentiary.

The prices on these and other objects were a lot higher than one might expect in a typical gift shop. But after all, Riley thought, these were no ordinary trinkets. They were rare and unique antique keepsakes.

A group of little toys caught her attention—plastic fish, a couple of swans, and a bright yellow rubber duck.

Riley asked herself …

Where have I seen a duck like this before?

An image came back to her—a collection of toys that included plush bunnies, sheep, giraffes, tigers, and teddy bears, and …

A duck exactly like this one.

Riley had seen it in Margo Birch's cozy bedroom.

Riley pointed to the group of aquatic toys and asked …

"Where did these come from?"

Anita said, "From Whopping Escapades, the old amusement park."

Riley remembered seeing photos of the place during her last visit.

Fingering the toys, Anita explained, "These were part of a carnival-style game where children try to pick up floating toys out of a running stream."

Anita picked up the duck and turned it upside down. On its bottom was written the number 251.

Anita explained, "You see, each of these toys has a number on the bottom. Contestants got prizes that corresponded to those numbers."

As Riley's breath quickened with excitement, Anita added in a wistful voice …

"Whopping Escapades was a wonderful place, just outside of town in Virginia. It closed down more than a decade ago. Oh, I know that doesn't sound like a long time, but these days people forget so quickly. So when I started working here, I insisted that it get an exhibit. The grounds have been in limbo for years, while owners and politicians fight over what can be done with the property. All the rides are gone. The whole park is locked up."

Riley said, "You sound very familiar with the place."

"Yes, I was actually working there when it closed. Just a clerk, keeping records."

Patting a plastic swan, Anita added, "After it shut down, I managed to keep a few of these things in boxes. Then I got this job and brought them here to sell."

Riley asked, "Anita, did you ever have more ducks like this for sale?"

Anita squinted. "Oh, just a very few. A young woman came in

here maybe a couple of weeks ago and bought the last one except for this."

Riley asked Anita to describe the woman as well as she could. Anita's description was vague, but Riley knew that it might well fit Margo Birch.

Riley felt sure in her gut that this was no coincidence.

But what did it mean, exactly?

She started asking questions clumsily, almost babbling, about who else might have bought some of these items recently.

Anita couldn't seem to remember, and she began to look a bit uneasy.

She asked, "What kind of project did you say you were here about?"

Riley stammered …

"It's just … some kind of … crime case I'm supposed to be helping on."

"Oh," Anita said. "Well, is there anything else you'd like to know?"

Riley's head clicked away, desperately trying to grasp what she was she was starting to learn.

Margo bought one of the ducks, she thought.

But what about Janet?

She remembered her encounter with Gary Davis in the Hoover Building, and how distraught, angry, and frustrated he had been. Riley dreaded the thought of talking to him again …

But I've got to try.

She said to Anita, "Do you have a phone book I could use?"

Anita led Riley to the museum's office, showed her the phone book on the desk, and left her alone there. Riley opened the phone book and looked up Gary Davis. She was discouraged but not surprised to see that there was a long list of people by that name in the DC area.

But she remembered the file she'd read about Janet's death. It had included the name of the street where Janet had lived.

Then Riley read down the list until she found that street name.

This must be it, she thought.

She took out her cell phone and punched in the number. A familiar voice answered, and Riley said …

"Mr. Davis, my name is Riley Sweeney, and …"

She hesitated, then added …

"I'm the FBI intern you talked to a few days ago."

She heard the man let out a deep, unhappy sigh.

"What do you want?" he asked. "If you haven't found Janet's killer, I don't want to talk to you."

Riley summoned up some raw nerve and said …

"I'm working on it. I'm—*we're* doing everything we can. We just need some help from you. Did you and Janet ever visit a museum called Forgotten D.C.?"

"Not that I remember."

"Did she mention going there herself?"

"I don't think so."

Riley took a long, slow breath.

He must know something, she thought. *I just have to ask the right question.*

Finally she said, "Mr. Davis, did your wife ever buy an odd sort of keepsake—the kind of rubber or plastic ducks or fish or swans that might be part of a carnival game? You know, the kind of game where you try to pick up toys like that out of a stream of water?"

"No, I don't think …"

His voice trailed off.

Then he said, "Wait a minute. Let me go look."

Riley waited for a moment, then heard his voice again.

"Yes, she bought an odd-looking plastic fish not long ago. She didn't tell me where it came from, but she was amused by it. You see, it has a number on the bottom. The number happens to be the date of our anniversary."

It was all Riley could do to keep from gasping aloud.

She said, "Thank you, Mr. Davis. You've been a great help."

"Wait a minute. What's this all about?"

Riley stammered, "I … we … can't say just yet. But I promise, we'll be in touch."

She hung up. She was having trouble keeping her breathing under control.

I've got to stay calm, she told herself.

But calmness was in short supply. She felt all but sure that, at long last, she'd found a connection between the two victims. They'd both bought items at the gift shop right here at the Forgotten D.C. museum.

Did that mean the killer had first noticed and targeted them here?

She couldn't believe for a moment that the kindly Anita Lockwood was a killer, but …

She left the office and found Anita back at her post at the ticket table.

She asked, "Could you tell me who else works here—aside from yourself?"

Anita squinted at her and said, "Well, hardly anyone. We're very short staffed. This place is owned by a nonprofit historical society. Once in a while I get a college girl in for a day or two. Mostly there's nobody but me. I'm the manager, clerk, and just about everything else."

Riley racked her memory of her last visit here.

She said, "Someone else was here the last time I came. He was mopping the floor in the gift shop."

Anita's eyebrows rose.

"Oh, you mean Joey," she said.

Riley tingled all over ...

Joey!

The signer of the poem!

"Is that his real name?" Riley asked.

"No, but for some reason it's what he likes to be called. His real name is Gordon—Gordon Shearer. He's a little ... off, I guess you might say. He actually grew up out in Whopping Escapades, back when it was open. He never had a proper family, was just raised by different people who worked there. He had a terrible childhood, as you can well imagine. I've known him since my own days at Whopping Escapades. I guess he's in his late twenties now."

She shrugged and added, "When he came around here looking for a job, I gave him something to do."

Riley swallowed hard and said ...

"I've got to contact him. How can I do that? What's his phone number?"

Anita looked surprised by the barrage of questions.

"The truth is, I really don't know. I never really contact him, he just shows up several times a week, whenever he seems to feel like it, and I pay him in cash."

She laughed a little nervously and said, "Oh dear. Maybe that's something I shouldn't admit to someone in law enforcement. Paying him in cash, I mean."

Anita scratched her chin and added, "But I do have his address, I believe. I'm not sure I should share it with you, though ..."

Riley struggled to keep from sounding as desperate as she felt.

"Please, Anita. It's really, really important. I can't tell you how important this is"

Anita gazed at Riley for a moment, then shrugged.

"Well, you seem like a nice enough girl," she said. "I'll take your word for it."

Anita went to her office and came back out with a slip of paper with the address written on it.

Riley thanked Anita—maybe a little too extravagantly, she was afraid—and left the building. She stood on the sidewalk staring at the address in her hand.

What do I do now? she wondered.

It only took a moment before she realized …

Like it or not, I've got to get in touch with Crivaro.

CHAPTER FORTY TWO

Riley's fingers shook as she punched Agent Crivaro's number into her cell phone.

She knew this wasn't going to be an easy call to make.

After hearing his outgoing message and the beep, Riley stammered …

"Agent Crivaro, this is Riley Sweeney and … look, I know I'm probably the last person in the world you want to hear from right now but …"

She took a deep breath and continued.

"If you're listening, pick up, OK? This is really important. I think I'm really on to something. I think I know who the killer is. His name is Gordon Shearer, but he calls himself Joey, and I've even got an address for him."

She read the address aloud, then said, "Please call me. As soon as you can. Call me right now."

When she ended the call, she thought …

Fat chance of Crivaro getting back to me at all.

After what had happened last night, he'd probably never take anything she said seriously again.

He probably wouldn't even bother listening to her message.

Anyway, she still could be wrong about Gordon Shearer.

After all, she wasn't even so much as a bona fide rookie agent, just some raw, stupid intern who had repeatedly made a fool of herself and had no idea what she was doing.

So she asked herself …

What would Agent Crivaro do?

She figured he would go straight to the address she'd gotten for Gordon Shearer and pay him a visit, probably with at least one partner in tow.

Of course, going there for an interview wasn't an option for Riley, but …

I can still go there.

I can check the place from outside.

She wouldn't approach him directly or knock on his door, but if she could only get a glimpse of him, she'd know whether he really was the same man who had attacked her last night.

She didn't need to put herself in any danger.

Just a little reconnaissance, she told herself.

But then she sighed bitterly.

Just a little reconnaissance.

Yeah, right.

That been her exact strategy at Lady Bird Johnson Park last night.

And how had that worked out for her?

Not good, she thought.

Not good at all.

She promised herself that she'd be a lot more careful this time. She'd make sure not to be spotted.

She took a metro schedule out of her purse and figured out how to get to the address she'd been given. It was on the southwestern edge of the city, and she could get a direct ride there by bus.

But Riley's hopes were dashed when she got off the bus, walked around the corner, and stood facing the place where the address should be.

There was nothing there at all.

The entire block had been razed, and a building was under construction there.

Riley felt her heart sink.

But at the same time she was relieved that Crivaro seemed to have ignored her message. She could imagine his reaction if he'd come here with one or more colleagues only to find that the address no longer existed.

Riley felt exhausted and demoralized, and she leaned against a lamppost for support.

That's all I can do, she thought.

Surely this was the end of any effort she could make.

Whether Gordon Shearer was really the killer or not, he had gone to a lot of trouble not to be found. Of course he had to live somewhere, but where might that be? Riley certainly had no way of finding out.

Maybe no one can, she thought. *Not even the FBI.*

Maybe it doesn't even matter.

She'd been wrong way too many times now, about too many things. She remembered the day when she'd first noticed the poem, and she'd wrongly convinced Crivaro that they should try to find the killer in a carnival. They'd gone to the only carnival playing in DC, and it brought them no nearer to the catching the killer.

She still wasn't sure how she'd been so wrong about the carnival.

She'd based that theory on a stanza in the killer's poem …

Let's dance and play amid
The palpable public crush
Of revelers who bid
A wild farewell to flesh.

Riley mulled it over yet again.
A "wild farewell to flesh" …
A "palpable public crush" …
Riley still wondered—what could those images possibly suggest except a carnival where lots of people were gathered?

But as she thought it over now, a single word stuck out in her mind …
Palpable.
At last it started to dawn on her—the word *palpable* had led to her mistake.

The word meant tangible and real, but at the same time …
… it means something completely different!
One described something as "palpable" when it only *seemed* real and tangible.

Feelings were palpable.

A sense of loss was palpable.

A crowd of real, living people—the kind of crowd one would find at a carnival—wasn't the kind of thing you could call palpable.

So when the killer had written about a "palpable public crush," he'd really meant something quite different—an abandoned place haunted by people who were no longer there.

And what kind of place might that be?

Riley felt a growing sense of realization.

She remembered her visit to the museum on Sunday, when she'd looked at all those photographs of the Whopping Escapades amusement park with its huge roller coasters, Ferris wheels, and merry-go-rounds.

She remembered the words that had gone through her mind …
A true "labyrinth."
Riley gasped aloud.

Everything suddenly seemed starkly clear—almost too clear.
Am I right? she wondered.
Or am I just losing my mind?
All she knew for certain was that she simply had to talk to Agent Crivaro—right now.

She punched his number into her cell phone again and gathered up her nerve to leave a much more emphatic message than she had before, possibly using some colorful language this time. Instead, she was startled when Crivaro himself answered.

"What the hell do you want, Sweeney?"

Riley stammered, "Uh, Agent Crivaro—did you get my last message?"

"Yeah, I got it. And I called the city government to check on that address you gave me. Guess what? It doesn't exist. It's a goddamn construction site."

Riley stifled a moan of despair.

She said, "I know that, and I'm sorry. I'm there right now. But I've figured out where the killer really lives. I'm sure of it."

"And I'm sure you're full of crap, Sweeney. The only reason I took this call was to tell you to never get in touch with me again. Ever. I mean it, Sweeney. I'm through with you once and for all. Go get yourself a life of some sort, marry that boyfriend of yours, have lots of kids, and stop with all this craziness. Goodbye."

Riley almost shouted …

"Agent Crivaro, please! Don't hang up! Listen to me just this once last time! If I turn out to be wrong, I promise, I'll never get in touch with you again. I won't bother you. Never, for the rest of my life. It'll be like you've never even heard of me."

A silence fell.

Riley wondered if Crivaro had ended the call already.

Finally he said, "I'm listening."

Managing to sound a lot calmer than she felt, Riley talked him through what she'd found out at the museum—that the two murder victims had bought trinkets there, that a young man who went by the name of Joey sometimes worked there, and that he had been raised by employees at Whopping Escapades until it had closed down about a decade ago.

When she finished, another silence fell.

Again, Riley wondered if he'd hung up on her.

Then she heard him say slowly …

"So you're thinking this Joey guy *lives* on the abandoned site, where Whopping Escapades used to be?"

Riley could barely breathe now.

"Don't you think so too?" she managed to say.

An even longer silence fell.

Finally Crivaro said, "I don't know, Sweeney. I really don't know. This still sounds kind of nuts to me. But this is what we're going to do. McCune and I are on the opposite side of town from the site of the old amusement park. But we'll head over there right away. Stay put where you are, and we'll pick you up along the way."

"You won't need to," Riley said. "I'm just a few bus stops away from the site myself. I can probably get there ahead of you."

Crivaro said, "OK, we'll meet you there. Wait for us outside the front gate."

Riley ended the call. She was really hyperventilating now, and it took a few moments to calm herself. Then she headed back to the metro stop to catch the bus that would take her to the abandoned site.

I'd better be right this time, she thought.

CHAPTER FORTY THREE

When Riley got off the bus and walked the short distance to the park, she saw that it was a vast, desolate-looking expanse surrounded by high chain-link fences with barbed wire along the top. The main gate was chained and padlocked.

A large wind-battered sign said …

PRIVATE PROPERTY
KEEP OUT
TRESPASSERS WILL BE PROSECUTED

Riley looked through the fencing. All she could see beyond the gate were trees, masses of overgrown bushes and weeds, and the badly weathered roofs of buildings that had not been completely torn down.

From the looks of the place, Riley guessed that not many people had disobeyed that warning. At least not for a very long time.

In fact, Riley was starting to wonder …

Was I wrong?

It seemed crazy to imagine that anybody could actually live in there.

She paced back and forth in front of the gate, wondering when Crivaro and McCune would arrive. Crivaro had told her that they were on the opposite side of town, so it might still be quite a while.

Meanwhile, she felt restless.

She wandered around a corner of the fence and saw that a narrow unpaved road ran along the outside of it. The road was weedy and overgrown, but tire tracks revealed that was used, at least occasionally.

She walked along the road until she arrived at another wide gate that stood in the shade of overhanging trees. This gate was pushed closed, but it wasn't chained or padlocked. The tire tracks passed on through it, clearly indicating that someone had driven through there recently.

Riley's pulse quickened and a deep chill came over her.

This is it, she thought.

This is the place.

Joey has been here.

He might even be somewhere beyond that gate right now.

She had to let Crivaro know.

She pulled out her cell phone and typed out a text message to Crivaro—the first text message she'd ever tried to send …

Come to gate on unpaved road to the right of the park.

… and she hit "Send," hoping she'd done it correctly.

Then she pushed open the gate and left it standing open as she walked on into the desolate grounds, following along the car tracks.

The tracks took her past grim, skeletal structures of what must have once been amusement park rides. An eerie feeling came over her—a ghostly sense of what this place must have been like in its heyday, packed with happy people. She could almost hear music and shouting and clanging and other festive sounds. Just like the poem suggested, Riley felt surrounded by a "palpable public crush of revelers."

Finally, the tracks led into a large roofed area held up by columns and fragments of walls. The day was still warm and sunny, which made this place seem particularly dark and dank. As she wandered in among the shadows, her eyes had to adjust to the dimness.

Riley guessed that this area must have once been some kind of arcade for games and amusements. A sort of metal trough passed through the space—possibly where the stream had once run for the game involving the ducks, fish, and swans.

Deeper inside the roofed area, the tracks led her to an old, beat-up vehicle. Was it the same car she had seen the killer drive away from the marina? Riley thought probably so. In any case, somebody was definitely here somewhere right now.

It was a terrifying thought.

Riley decided she'd better explore no further, but instead go back to the gate and wait for Crivaro and McCune to arrive.

But just as she turned around, a high-pitched sound caught her ear.

She stopped dead still to listen.

Soon she heard it again—and she was knew right away what it was.

It was a woman's scream.

The scream was followed by softer sounds that she thought must be whimpering.

She followed the sound through to the far end of the building, where she found herself in the midst of dark hallways that must once have been some kind of vast network of hallways connecting several buildings.

The labyrinth!

Growing more frightened by the second, Riley turned again to go back.

But she heard the voice again—louder, more piercing and urgent.

She forced herself to continue on her way, following a concrete ditch where lay a couple of broken hulls of two-seated boats. She realized she was in what must have once been a "tunnel of love."

For a while, the only light she could see was coming in through broken places in the ceiling. But finally, some distance off, she saw a partially open door that shed some light into the labyrinth.

Shivering all over now with fear, Riley approached the door and cautiously pushed it the rest of the way open. The door led into a large room that was lit by a single glaring white light hanging over a long table.

At the far end of the room was a wire mesh storage cage.

Inside the cage, Riley saw someone in a clown suit crouching on the floor.

Is it him? she wondered.

But then the clown let out a whimper of despair, and Riley realized …

No, it's her. It's his next victim.

The woman's face remained hidden against her knees—she didn't seem to be aware of Riley's arrival.

Without stopping to think, Riley rushed toward the cage to let the woman out.

Suddenly, a wildly colored figure leaped right in front of her.

It was a man in a clown suit wearing the full makeup of a grotesque whiteface clown.

He danced wildly about, waving a short length of steel pipe.

"Oh, you've come, you've come!" he cackled wildly. "I knew you would! I knew last night at the marina wasn't the end! I knew we'd meet again! You couldn't stay away! You couldn't resist!"

Riley was horribly disoriented now.

She felt as though she'd been dropped into the middle of a nightmare.

Seizing the element of surprise, the clown lunged at Riley. She ducked away and he narrowly missed her head with the pipe.

233

Barely able to keep her balance, Riley kept trying to duck and dodge away from the man and his weapon, all the while looking for some hard object she could use in her own defense.

Her eyes lighted upon another length of steel pipe lying on the floor.

But as she reached for it, she felt a sharp crack on the back of her head, and the world went black.

*

When Riley tried to open her eyes again, she was blinded by blazing, hot white light. She tried to move, but realized she was lying prone and bound fast by strong restraints.

She felt fingers touching her all over her face, smearing something cold and wet all over it.

Makeup, she thought.

He's making me up as a clown.

She guessed that he'd already dressed her in a clown costume while she was unconscious.

She managed to open her eyes a little.

She could see his face now—all white with garish colors.

"There," he said, lifting his fingers away from her face. "All done now. Have a look!"

He held up a mirror and Riley saw her own face, horribly painted.

He said, "I'm so glad you came. I kept the other girl alive in hopes you'd come. I want to see which of you is strong enough to stay with me. I have a feeling you'll be the one!"

To Riley's horror, she saw that he was now holding a syringe in front of her.

She remembered what the medical examiner had said about the other two victims—how a fatal dose of amphetamines had brought on horrible deaths from sheer terror.

"No!" Riley cried out. "No! No!"

"Hold still," the clown said. "Who knows? You might even like this!"

She felt the sharp needle against the crook of her arm and braced for it to pierce her skin.

Suddenly, a loud crack resounded through the room.

A spurt of blood exploded from the clown's forehead, and she heard him crash to the floor.

In another instant, she saw the faces Crivaro and McCune

hovering over her.

They were busy severing her bonds.

In a flustered voice McCune said to Crivaro …

"I had to take the shot. He was going to inject her. There wasn't time."

"It's OK," Crivaro told him. "It was a clean kill."

Crivaro paused for a moment to stroke Riley's hair.

"I swear to God, Sweeney," Crivaro said with a smile and a wink. "I've never known a human being who could screw up so many things in so little time as you."

Soon Riley was freed from her bonds.

"Don't get up," Crivaro ordered. "I want you to sit right there until I get this mess sorted out."

Riley obediently stayed where she was.

CHAPTER FORTY FOUR

Riley woke up and opened her eyes.

For a moment, she had a slight feeling of déjà vu.

She was in a hospital bed again.

But it was a different bed this time, and in a different room.

This bed was walled off from the rest of the room with moveable partitions and a closed curtains.

The weird spell of familiarity quickly passed as Riley remembered where she was and how she'd gotten here …

No, I didn't have another miscarriage.

This bed was in the medical clinic of the J. Edgar Hoover Building. She'd been brought here after her desperate struggle against a psychotic killer dressed up as a clown.

She'd survived all that—and she was going to be just fine.

For the moment, though, it felt good to be lying down and not exerting herself. And she smiled as she remembered Agent Crivaro's crazed efficiency when he'd gone into action after McCune had shot the killer.

Crivaro had quickly gotten Riley loose from her restraints. After making sure she wasn't drugged, he'd called an FBI emergency line to get people going on a lot of other problems. He ordered an ambulance to pick up the woman who'd been caged, and he demanded an investigative team to hurry over and examine the site.

Soon the labyrinthine ruins had been swarming with people following Crivaro's orders. Then Crivaro had put McCune in charge of the chaos and taken Riley to his FBI vehicle. He'd rushed here with the siren screaming, phoning ahead to make sure a medic would be ready to meet them in the garage with a wheelchair.

Riley's smile widened as she remembered how Crivaro had almost driven the clinic staff crazy with his frantic demands that Riley be well tended to.

"Check every inch of this girl. She's not been drugged, but she got hit bad on the back of the head and was maybe unconscious for a little while. Make damn sure there's nothing seriously wrong with her, especially not a concussion. And get that awful goo off her face. I'll be back soon."

An anxious nurse had done just that. She'd checked Riley out

236

thoroughly and determined that she wasn't suffering from concussion. She took care of the bump on the back of Riley's head, cleaned and freshly bandaged the older cut on her shoulder, and tended to a few other minor scrapes and bruises. Riley was especially relieved to have the clown makeup washed off her face.

Finally, the nurse had given Riley a sedative and told her to sleep.

And now here she was, awake and feeling remarkably refreshed.

Soon Crivaro came into the room and sat down beside her bed, anxiously asking her how she was doing.

"I'm fine," she said. "Don't worry."

Crivaro growled and said, "Who said I was worried?"

Riley managed not to laugh.

Then she asked, "What about the woman in the cage? Is she going to be all right?"

"Yeah," Crivaro said. "He hadn't drugged her yet, but of course she was traumatized. We sent her to the ER and got in touch with her family. Social services will be working with them. She didn't know exactly how long she'd been locked up there, but it seems to have been a long time, maybe two or three days. She'd barely had anything to eat or drink during that whole time, and she sure as hell didn't get much sleep."

Crivaro paused and squinted.

"It's odd—how the killer kept her alive like that, going against his own MO. He acted so fast with the other two women—abducted them, took them to his lair, drugged them to death, and disposed of their bodies. I wonder why he treated this one differently. I wonder why he took his time."

Crivaro scratched his chin and added, "Anyway, you probably saved her life—first by figuring out where the killer was, then by rushing in there like some damn fool idiot."

Riley knew Crivaro was right—she had saved the woman's life.

But Crivaro didn't know exactly how true that was, or why.

Riley remembered something Joey had said when he had her bound and helpless …

"I kept the other girl alive in hopes you'd come."

He'd been fascinated by Riley—the way she'd cracked his riddle and answered with a riddle of her own, the way she'd escaped his clutches at the marina, and finally the way she'd found her way into his labyrinth.

Riley shuddered a little at the thought …

His obsession with me saved the other woman's life.

Riley figured she should tell Crivaro about all that …

Some other time. Not now.

Crivaro looked at her in silence for a moment, as if trying to evaluate just how well she was really doing.

Then he said, "We've been getting more information about the killer. You deserve to be brought up to speed about it. Do you feel like joining us for a conference?"

Riley was taken a bit aback.

Us? she wondered.

Who is us?

But she sensed that this was something she'd better not miss. She nodded to Crivaro. He waited in the hall outside while she got out of bed and back into her clothes. Then she followed Crivaro to a conference room on another floor of the building.

When they walked into the room, Riley saw three men sitting at the conference table. Crivaro's old partner Elliot Flack was here, and so was Riley's intern training supervisor Hoke Gilmer. And of course, Agent McCune was also present.

She was startled that they all stood when she came in, almost as if she were an important person. She was even more startled that they took turns shaking hands with her, congratulating her on solving the case.

She was flattered, of course. At the same time she couldn't help thinking …

The FBI really could use more women.

When they all got seated, McCune began the briefing, directing his remarks to Riley.

"Of course, the process of our investigation is just getting underway, but we're putting together some preliminary information about the killer, Gordon Shearer—AKA 'Joey.' I personally talked to the woman you met at the museum, Anita Lockwood. She was able to shed some light on things."

McCune glanced over his notes for a moment, then continued.

"According to Ms. Lockwood, Gordon spent most of his life under the radar. Apparently his parents worked at Whopping Escapades for a brief time. They were carney types who never stayed in any one place very long. When they left Whopping Escapades, they abandoned their five-year-old son—just took off and left him there. Nobody ever saw the couple again. Our people are trying to track them down, but so far we've turned up no trace of them. We possibly never will."

McCune drummed his pencil eraser on his notepad and continued.

"Ms. Lockwood gave us the names of some other people to talk to—people who'd worked at Whopping Escapades when it was open. Over the years, a lot of employees seem to have taken turns raising him. For a while, a group of clowns were responsible for him. Something bad seemed to have happened during that time. He became terrified of the clowns, wouldn't go near them anymore. So other staffers took him over."

Riley gasped a little and said …

"So at least one of the clowns must have abused him."

McCune nodded and said, "That's what it sounds like. Maybe even sexually. So it's not surprising that he developed some sort of sick fixation about clowns. But from what people have told us, he was a rather disturbed kid to begin with, even when his parents were still around. His oddness may have had something to do with their abandoning him."

"What kind of oddness?" Riley asked.

"Wild swings in mood and behavior," McCune explained. "Sweet, affectionate, and polite one minute, hostile, angry, and even vicious the next. As he grew up he was in and out of school, and in and out of trouble. Folks breathed easier when he seemed to settle down and work at various jobs at the park. But eventually the park closed down—and apparently nobody realized he had slipped back in there and stayed."

That word ran through Riley's mind again …

Abandoned.

It was the story of the miserable boy's life.

McCune continued, "After the park closed, nobody from his old life had been in contact with him except Anita Lockwood."

Riley added, "And even she didn't know about his real living circumstances."

"That's right," McCune said, looking again at his notes. "That pretty well covers what we've been able to learn so far. Do you have any questions, Sweeney?"

Riley thought for a moment, then said …

"Maybe not so much a question, but I got the distinct feeling that he was very intelligent."

McCune nodded, looking impressed by this insight.

"He was indeed," he said. "We found a hoard of books stashed away in his lair—most of them stolen from public libraries. He seemed to have read incessantly, especially about the history of clowns dating all the way back to the sixteenth century."

Crivaro shook his head. "Smart, twisted, and isolated from the world—a deadly combination. It's small wonder he eventually became a killer."

"A real ticking bomb," Elliot Flack added.

There was a murmur of agreement, and the meeting came to an end.

When they went out into the hallway, Crivaro touched Riley on the shoulder.

"I know I've been pretty hard on you," he said.

"It's OK," Riley said. "I deserved it."

Crivaro chuckled and said, "You sure as hell did."

Then he paused and added, "But I didn't misjudge you when I pushed you into the program. You've got instincts like I've never seen. And ... I hope you don't give up."

Crivaro walked away, and Riley found herself standing alone in the hallway, realizing that she had a decision to make. But at the moment, she had no idea what to decide.

"What next?" she murmured aloud.

As if on cue, her phone rang. Her heart leapt when she saw that the call was from Ryan. When she answered, he sounded nearly hysterical.

"Riley! Are you OK? What the hell's going on? I heard on the news that the Clown Killer's dead—and your name is mixed up in it somehow. Talk to me. Are you safe? Are you hurt?"

Riley said, "I'm fine, Ryan. Don't worry."

"I want to see you. Where are you? Where can we meet?"

Riley was startled by how different he sounded from when he'd stormed out of their apartment just last night.

She said, "I'm at the J. Edgar Hoover Building."

"How soon can you get to the National Mall?"

"I can walk over there right now."

"Great. Let's meet in front of the Lincoln Memorial."

*

As Riley approached the Lincoln Memorial, she saw Ryan sitting on its majestic stairway. She called out to him, and he ran to her and took her into his arms. He seemed to be frantic with relief.

As they sat together on the steps looking out over the vast Reflecting Pool, Riley thought ...

240

No more evasions.

She wasted no time telling Ryan everything that had happened since he'd left, sparing no ugly details. She even told him how the killer had been only seconds away from injecting her with a fatal dose of amphetamines before Crivaro and McCune rushed in to her rescue.

When she finished, Ryan just sat there for a few moments with his mouth hanging open.

Finally Ryan said, "You're a hero, Riley."

Riley laughed nervously.

"No, I'm really not a hero," she said.

Ryan shook his head and said, "You saved at least one woman's life. By solving the case, you may have saved other lives as well. It's crazy. I think maybe you're crazy. But you're also a hero."

Riley sighed. She didn't much like that word—hero.

If people in her life started expecting her to live up to it, they'd surely wind up bitterly disappointed.

A silence fell between them.

Then Ryan laughed nervously and said …

"So what do you want to do with the rest of your life, Riley Sweeney?"

"I've got some ideas," she said.

"I'm hoping they're pretty much the same as mine," Ryan said. He took her left hand in his and added, "We can start by going home and putting your engagement ring back on. And my ideas go on from there."

They looked into each other's eyes, then shared a long kiss. Then they held hands and talked together idly for a while. But before long, Riley found herself distracted by thoughts of Gordon Shearer—the sick young man who called himself "Joey."

Her feeling of connection with him had been terrible and terrifying.

Was that connection severed now that he was dead?

Riley hoped so, but she couldn't help remembering what he'd yelled to her at the marina …

"I'm the only one in the world who knows … who you really are."

Of course those words had been the ravings of a madman. But she wondered—was there maybe just the slightest trace of truth in what he'd said? She felt as though she'd been inside his mind.

Had he felt the same about her?

She remembered something Elliot Flack had said in his lecture
…

"The trick is to understand monsters without becoming a monster yourself. It isn't always easy."

Riley's throat tightened and she squeezed Ryan's hand more tightly.

She stammered …

"Ryan … let's … the two of us … let's just …"

It took a moment for her to think of the words she seemed to be looking for.

"Let's just love each other," she finally said.

She fell into Ryan's embrace, and they kissed again.

LURING
(The Making of Riley Paige—Book 3)

"A masterpiece of thriller and mystery! The author did a magnificent job developing characters with a psychological side that is so well described that we feel inside their minds, follow their fears and cheer for their success. The plot is very intelligent and will keep you entertained throughout the book. Full of twists, this book will keep you awake until the turn of the last page."
--Books and Movie Reviews, Roberto Mattos (re Once Gone)

LURING (The Making of Riley Paige—Book Three) is book #3 in a new psychological thriller series by #1 bestselling author Blake Pierce, whose free bestseller Once Gone (Book #1) has received over 1,000 five star reviews.

As a serial killer, suspected to be using an RV camper, lures and kills women across the country, the FBI, at a loss, must break protocol and turn to its brilliant 22 year old academy recruit—Riley Paige.

Riley Paige is accepted into the grueling FBI academy, and is determined to finally keep a low profile and work hard with her peers. But that is not meant to be, as she is hand-picked to help her mentors to profile and hunt down a serial killer that has terrified the nation. What sort of diabolical killer, Riley wonders, would use an RV to catch his victims?

And where is he heading next?

There is no time for Riley to make a mistake in this deadly game of cat and mouse, with her own future on the line, and with a killer out there that may just be smarter than her.

An action-packed thriller with heart-pounding suspense, LURING is book #3 in a riveting new series that will leave you turning pages late into the night. It takes readers back 20 plus years—to how

Riley's career began—and is the perfect complement to the ONCE GONE series (A Riley Paige Mystery), which includes 14 books and counting.

Book #4 in THE MAKING OF RILEY PAIGE series will be available soon.

Blake Pierce

Blake Pierce is author of the bestselling RILEY PAGE mystery series, which includes thirteen books (and counting). Blake Pierce is also the author of the MACKENZIE WHITE mystery series, comprising nine books (and counting); of the AVERY BLACK mystery series, comprising six books; of the KERI LOCKE mystery series, comprising five books; of the MAKING OF RILEY PAIGE mystery series, comprising three books (and counting); of the KATE WISE mystery series, comprising two books (and counting); and of the CHLOE FINE psychological suspense mystery, comprising two books (and counting).

An avid reader and lifelong fan of the mystery and thriller genres, Blake loves to hear from you, so please feel free to visit www.blakepierceauthor.com to learn more and stay in touch.

BOOKS BY BLAKE PIERCE

CHLOE FINE PSYCHOLOGICAL SUSPENSE MYSTERY
NEXT DOOR (Book #1)
A NEIGHBOR'S LIE (Book #2)

KATE WISE MYSTERY SERIES
IF SHE KNEW (Book #1)
IF SHE SAW (Book #2)
LURING (Book #3)

THE MAKING OF RILEY PAIGE SERIES
WATCHING (Book #1)
WAITING (Book #2)

RILEY PAIGE MYSTERY SERIES
ONCE GONE (Book #1)
ONCE TAKEN (Book #2)
ONCE CRAVED (Book #3)
ONCE LURED (Book #4)
ONCE HUNTED (Book #5)
ONCE PINED (Book #6)
ONCE FORSAKEN (Book #7)
ONCE COLD (Book #8)
ONCE STALKED (Book #9)
ONCE LOST (Book #10)
ONCE BURIED (Book #11)
ONCE BOUND (Book #12)
ONCE TRAPPED (Book #13)
ONCE DORMANT (book #14)

MACKENZIE WHITE MYSTERY SERIES
BEFORE HE KILLS (Book #1)
BEFORE HE SEES (Book #2)
BEFORE HE COVETS (Book #3)
BEFORE HE TAKES (Book #4)
BEFORE HE NEEDS (Book #5)
BEFORE HE FEELS (Book #6)
BEFORE HE SINS (Book #7)
BEFORE HE HUNTS (Book #8)

Made in United States
Orlando, FL
12 October 2023

37810909R00139